MISSING

MISSING

A HARRY STONER NOVEL

Jonathan Valin

Delacorte Press

Published by
Delacorte Press
Bantam Doubleday Dell Publishing Group, Inc.
1540 Broadway
New York, New York 10036

Library of Congress Cataloging in Publication Data

Valin, Jonathan.
Missing : a Harry Stoner novel / Jonathan Valin.
p.   cm.
ISBN 0-385-29966-4
1. Stoner, Harry (Fictitious character)—Fiction.   2. Private investigators—
Ohio—Cincinnati—Fiction.   3. Cincinnati (Ohio)—Fiction.   I. Title.
PS3572.A4125M57   1995
813'.54—dc20   94-9532   CIP

Manufactured in the United States of America
Published simultaneously in Canada

February 1995

10   9   8   7   6   5   4   3   2   1

BVG

280316

To my mother, Marcella Valin,
and my wife, Katherine

"How can we hang a murderer who doesn't exist?"

Our answer could be put in this form: "I can't hang him when he doesn't exist; but I can look for him when he doesn't exist."

—Ludwig Wittgenstein, *The Blue Book*

MISSING

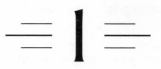

THE woman on the phone, Cindy Dorn, had given me elaborate directions to her house in Finneytown, but I got lost anyway in a maze of twisty side streets named after birds and lined with identical yellow-brick, two-bedroom, split-level houses that began to look, to my jaundiced eye, like yellow-brick birdhouses on yellowing patches of lawn. It was a Saturday afternoon in July, so the householders were out in their swimsuits, the kids six inches deep in the round plastic pools with the hoses in them. I kept driving by in the rusty Pinto—a big sweaty stranger staring sullenly out a car window. It was just a matter of time before the cops were called.

I was kind of wondering what I'd say to them, when I got lucky and turned left at the end of Oriole Lane. And there it was, Blue Jay Drive. The same damn street I'd been driving down for thirty minutes—only this one was called Blue Jay Drive. The Dorn house was third from the corner on the left. Two-bedroom split-level with the bedrooms over the garage, the picture window looking out on a tiny lawn, the dead hawthorn tree in a bed of mulch, like a spade in a freshly turned grave.

I parked on the street and walked up the cement path to the house. A tall, athletic-looking woman in a sweat shirt and jeans came out on the stoop. She was about forty. Attractive, weather-beaten face, curly black hair, green eyes, big smile. I liked the smile so much, I smiled back at her.

"You got lost, didn't you?" she said.

"Yep."

The woman laughed cheerfully, showing a lot of teeth. "It's always tough the first time. The houses look the same."

"The streets, too. Those names."

"The developer liked birds, I guess." She laughed again. "He didn't like people very much, that's for sure. See for yourself."

She waved me through the front door into the living room. It was oblong and incredibly narrow, with a spackled ceiling that dropped so low, I found myself stooping.

"It's like incoming fog," the woman said, pointing up. "The whole subdivision was built for a different race."

She flopped down on a brown tufted sofa, dug a loose red sock from under her butt, and draped it over her knee. I sat on an armchair across the room from her—about eight feet away. It was like sitting in a Pullman car. There were a couple of framed movie posters on the walls—*Chinatown* and *Last Tango*. No other furnishing or decorations—no room for any.

"I'm not much on housekeeping," Cindy Dorn said, toying with the sock as if it were the pet cat.

"There doesn't seem to be much house to keep."

She stretched one arm lazily above her head. "It seemed like heaven when Randy and I first moved in, fourteen years ago."

"Randy is . . . ?"

"My ex. He lives in Denver now with a stewardess. Good old Randy." She made a fist with her right hand and popped it into her left palm. "The son of a bitch broke up with me two weeks before our tenth wedding anniversary. We were in Scotland on vacation. Scotland, for chrissake! I said, 'Randy, we're Jewish. Why Scotland?' Well, it's different, he says. Besides, he wants to see Nessie. So I take a leave of absence from grad school and off we go to the Highlands. We're there about a week, hopping from pub to pub, when he says to me, 'Cindy, I had an amazing experience last night. After you fell asleep, I went back to the little pub we were in and started talking with this old fisherman. We had a few drinks, and he begins telling me about his life. It turns out he's been all over the world. Done things you wouldn't believe. And he's still going strong at ninety. So at last call I ask him, ''What's the secret?'' You know what he says? He says ''The secret is doing what you want to do, because you only pass through here once.'' '

''Now Randy just can't get over this—that you can actually do what you want with your life. Of course, for a Jewish kid from Roselawn, maybe it was a revelation. Anyway, it's all he talks about for the next week. And a week after that, as we're driving to Edinburgh, he tells me he's made up his mind. From now on he's going to do exactly what he wants to do with his life. And he's going to begin by divorcing me!''

Cindy Dorn stared at me incredulously. ''I mean, there are epiphanies and epiphanies. But when a ninety-year-old alcoholic from Aberdeen and a schmuck accountant from Cincinnati start playing darts with *my* life . . . a sense of unreality doesn't cover it. It didn't start to come clear to me until a year later, when I found out about his stew honey-bunny, who just happened to fly the transatlantic route to Scotland. My guess is that most of those long lunches weren't spent with his aged guru. In fact, I don't even think the old man existed.''

Cindy Dorn stopped talking just long enough to catch her breath. She had a low flip voice, and she spoke the way youngest children eat—urgently, with both hands, as if she'd never gotten her fair share of the words in.

''That's how I inherited this house,'' she said when she'd gotten her second wind. ''And the car payments and the student loans. They apparently weren't covered by the 'doing what you want to do' philosophy.''

I glanced at the *Tango* poster and said, ''I hope you're not hiring me to kill Randy.''

She laughed. ''It's a thought, but no. I got over him years ago. It's Mason.''

''Who's Mason?''

''Mason Greenleaf is my lover,'' she said blithely.

"And?"

"And he's disappeared. He's been missing for three days."

We retired to the kitchen—another box within a box—where Cindy Dorn made coffee and told me about Mason Greenleaf. "He's probably the sweetest man I've ever known," she said as she set a teakettle on the range. "And I've known a few guys. After Randy split, I kind of overdid it with men. You know, drowning my sorrows in flesh—trying to prove something. Anyway, it got so that I really didn't like my new life much at all. And then I met Mason." She glanced at the teakettle and adjusted the flame. "You're not supposed to use boiling water for coffee. Did you know that?"

"I've been boiling mine for years."

"Well, you're not supposed to." She came over to the little Formica breakfast table and sat down across from me. "It's tough for me to tell you about Mason. I mean, how do you explain why you love someone?"

"I could take your word for it," I said with a smile.

She smiled back at me. "But I want you to understand what a good man he is."

"Why?"

"Maybe I think you'll do a better job."

"I always try to do the best I can."

"I'm sure you do. I can tell that about you. You're steadfast."

I didn't say anything.

"That's a terrific quality," she said. "Take it from someone who knows. That's part of why I love Mason. He's always there when I need a friend. Not just someone to sleep with. If you're moderately good-looking and have a taste for it, you can always find someone to sleep with. But you can't always find a friend." She shook her head. "See what I mean. That's so trite it makes me shudder."

"I can handle it."

The teakettle began to shriek. Cindy Dorn said, "Crap!" and leaped to her feet. She went over to the range and flipped the burner off. Then turned back to me.

"I'm sorry. I screwed up. I'll start a fresh pot."

"I'm used to boiled coffee."

She sighed. "All right. But I can do better."

She poured two cups of her second-rate brew and brought them back to the table.

"I met Mason in 1990," she said, sitting down again. "At a teachers' conference in Louisville. I teach preschool up here. He teaches at Nine Mile. I'd gone to that conference to get away from a man. He was . . . he'd hurt me. So I went away for a few days to get my head straight—not in the best shape of my life—and I met Mason.

"Right away he started looking after me. The way I felt, I could've been had for a kind word. But he didn't take advantage. He just stayed with me in my room, where I bitched and moaned and shed a few tears. When we got back to town, Mason let me stay at his place in Mount Adams for a week. The week became two and three. And then I lost track of the time, and the other man. Mason and I have been together ever since."

Cindy Dorn cocked her head to one side and stared at me searchingly, as if she'd just then noticed that I was sitting in the room with her. It was a funny time to start wondering who I was, considering how open she'd already been about her life. But then, she was the kind of person who sat down to candor the way older generations used to sit down to the piano in the parlor. It was a peculiarly sixties kind of social grace.

Whatever it was about me that had been hanging her up, she got over it. She stopped staring and smiled at me with her big, engaging smile. "What I am going to tell you . . . well, it's just between you and me. Because I promised Mason I wouldn't tell anyone else. Ever."

"It'll stay between us," I promised her.

Cindy Dorn took a deep breath. "Mason is bisexual. And I'm worried that . . ." She waved her hand as if she couldn't summon the right words. "I'm just worried."

I'm not sure what I was expecting the woman to say, but that wasn't it.

"That bothers you, doesn't it?" Cindy Dorn said nervously. "About him being bisexual."

"I would think it would bother you more."

"You mean because of AIDS?"

"Yes."

"We practice safe sex, and I have my blood tested every six months. Mason is even more fanatic. So far, we're both HIV-negative." She put her fist to her chin and chewed on her knuckles. "That doesn't help though, does it?"

"Generally I don't like taking cases that involve homosexuals."

"What you really mean is that you don't like homosexuals, right?"

I told her the truth. "Queer-bashing's not a religion with me, but no, I'm not crazy about them. I had a case a few years back that left a bad memory."

"Would it help if I told you that Mason is a great lay?"

"Not a whole lot."

The woman dropped her hand to the table and opened it in a frank appeal for help. "Well, do we go on with this? Or do I get out the phone book again and start over with someone else?"

"Let me think about it, Ms. Dorn."

"I'd say you know me well enough to call me Cindy."

I'd been there less than a half hour, but she was right.

Cindy Dorn brewed another pot of coffee—unboiled, this time. While we sat at the table drinking, she picked up the story of her love affair with Mason Greenleaf.

"The funny thing about Louisville was that Mason was on the rebound, too. He'd just broken up with this guy—Del somebody. Del was the one part of his past that Mason would never really open up about. It was not, as they say, a healthy relationship."

"Meaning?"

"I think it had gotten a little rough," she said softly.

Great, I said to myself. "Do you have any reason to believe that Mason might be back with this guy Del?"

"As far as I know, they haven't seen each other in four years."

"Then why are you worried?"

"I don't know why, for sure," she said. "I do know that for the last week Mason hasn't been himself."

"In what way hasn't he been himself?"

She shrugged. "I can't put my finger on it. But when you know someone as well as I know Mason, you sense when something's wrong. And something was wrong. I finally asked him about it on Wednesday night—if anything had happened at summer session to upset him. But he said that it wasn't a school thing, he was just feeling a little low and it would pass. In fact he made an effort to be cheerful for the rest of the evening. We had supper, made great love, watched a little tube until Mason fell asleep, then I came back here."

"You don't spend the nights together?"

"Some nights we do. Some nights we don't. Neither one of us wants the relationship to feel too much like a marriage."

"Have you been sleeping together less often lately?"

She shook her head. "Sex has been great, better than ever. If it was a sexual problem, Harry, I think I would have known it. It was —it felt more important than that."

"When did you realize he was missing?"

"On Thursday afternoon. I called him after school like I usually do, but he didn't answer the phone. We were supposed to have dinner that night, so I went over to his place around six and let myself in with my key. I have a key. I waited there until almost midnight—*potchkying* around the house—and when he didn't show up, I went home. The next morning, Friday, I tried calling him at work. The principal said he hadn't come in and that he hadn't been there on Thursday, either. I called his house all day Friday and got no answer. This morning I finally got the nerve up to get out the phone book and call a private detective. You just happened to be the lucky party."

I laughed. "Has Mason ever disappeared like this before? Without telling you or notifying the school?"

"Once. Last August. He dropped out of sight for a week. He said he'd gone home."

"Did you believe him?"

"Of course I believed him," she said. "Mason never lies to me. Jeez, we've been through so much together and apart, there's no reason to lie to each other. There's nothing left to lie about."

"What makes you think he hasn't gone home again?"

"Because I made him promise never to leave me again without telling me first," Cindy Dorn said, staring straight into my eyes. "He knows how important that promise is to me."

"When you went to his place on Thursday, did you find anything missing? Like clothes or a suitcase?"

She shook her head. "The house looked the way it had on Wednesday night."

"Had his bed been slept in?"

"It was made up. But Mason's always neat, so that doesn't mean much. Anyway, I'm no detective."

I got up from the table. "All right, Cindy, let's go look at the apartment."

"Then you're 'taking the case'?"

"I guess I am."

Cindy Dorn smiled. "Thank you, Harry. Really. Thank you."

"Have you contacted the police yet?" I asked as we walked, single file, from the kitchen to the living-room door.

"No police!" she said so sharply that I turned to look at her. "I don't want the cops involved."

"If Mason's a genuine missing person, I may have to involve them, Cindy. Without police cooperation there may be no other way to find him."

She shook her head. "Then he won't be found. The cops in this city treat homosexuals like dirt. I will not subject Mason to that kind of humiliation and abuse. It's that simple."

I didn't say it to Cindy Dorn, but it wasn't that simple. Not if she wanted her lover back.

I T was twilight by the time Cindy Dorn and I arrived at Mason Greenleaf's condo on Celestial Street in Mount Adams. It was a beautiful, three-story town house perched on the southmost lip of the hill, with a Chinese-red door and black louvered windows on the street side. On the hill side, it was mostly plate glass and railed redwood decks.

As Cindy and I got out of the car, two fox-faced Appalachian boys trotted past us, heading down the slanting street toward the Parkway. One of them was dragging a worn leather dog leash with a chain choker behind him. No dog, just the leash. The chain rattled on the concrete pavement all the way down the hill. The noise made Cindy Dorn laugh nervously.

"Marley's ghost," she said. "I don't know where those kids come from, but there's a flock of them around here all the time."

"It used to be their hill," I said, "before people like your friend Mason bought it out from under them. They still own bits and pieces of it. In fact, a few shrewd hillbillies have made a fortune in Mount Adams real estate."

"It does have the best views of the city," Cindy said, digging through a pocket for the key to the house.

She opened the door, and we went in.

The first floor was walled on the far side with sliding-glass panels that opened onto a railed deck. Through the glass panels I could see the view that Cindy had spoken of, the view that had made the hill a trendy reserve for the rich and arty. The entire city stretched out in the near distance, glowing softly in the twilight. Beyond it, the river coursed past the stadium and the coliseum, picking up different-colored waterlights at each stop. Toward the dark Kentucky side, a July moon bobbed restlessly in the current.

"How can Mason afford a place like this on a teacher's salary?" I asked.

"Mason is from a wealthy family," Cindy said. "He moved here from Nashville to get away from them, but he's got a trust fund or something that he can draw on whenever he likes." She came up beside me. "You want to go out on the deck?"

"Sure."

She took my hand and guided me through the dark room to the sliding-glass door. Throwing a latch, she opened it, and the room, which had been as quiet as it was dark, filled with the night sounds of crickets and distant traffic.

A warm breeze was rushing up the hillside, rustling through the tops of the trees. Cindy Dorn went over to the railing and leaned into the wind, letting it tug at the edges of her curly black hair. She stood that way for some time.

There were two wrought-iron chairs and a wrought-iron umbrella table with a glass top on the right side of the porch. Something sitting on the deck beside one of the chairs caught my eye. A glass tumbler with a saucer on top of it.

"Were you and Mason sitting out here on Wednesday night?"

"Yes," Cindy said, turning back to me. "Why?"

"There's a glass and a plate by that chair."

She glanced over her shoulder. "It's funny I didn't notice that before. They must be mine." She wrinkled her brow. "It's not like Mason to leave them out, though. He's a real pain in the ass about cleaning up."

"When did you leave here on Wednesday?"

"Around one A.M."

"Did you drive yourself home?"

She nodded. "Mason was asleep. But his car is gone, too, if that's what you're getting at. He always parks on Celestial, as close as he can to the house. I checked the whole street and a couple of adjoining streets, but the car's not there."

"What kind of car does he drive?"

"A Saab 900 Turbo. He's got the license plate number written down upstairs in his desk."

"Maybe we should get it."

Cindy walked briskly back into the living room, flipping on a dimmer switch by the door. Overhead spots lit the room up, giving me my first look at Mason Greenleaf's digs. The place was sparely but expensively furnished in svelte Italian furniture and creamy enameled Parsons tables. A Kilim rug covered the pegged hardwood floors. The walls were hung with watercolors—street scenes mostly, some of them by local artists. There was one in a small, ornate gold frame that turned out to be a Utrillo. I paused a minute to look at it before following Cindy up a circular staircase to the second floor.

Cindy flipped on another dimmer at the top of the stairs, lighting up track lights that ran the length of the ceiling. The second story was one large bedroom, with another sliding-glass window on the far wall and another deck looking out on the city and the river. The walls of the bedroom were hung with modern art—huge canvases streaked with black and red and framed in gleaming stainless steel. A made-up bed sat on the street side of the room, elevated on a wooden pedestal and lit by its own soft yellow spot. A white enamel desk sat across from it on the east wall.

Cindy walked over to the desk. "Mason loves beautiful things," she said, bending over the desk.

"With this kind of money, why does he bother to teach?"

"You have to do something with your life, if you're going to call it a life. Mason picked teaching because he liked working with children. His own childhood was miserable."

"You've met his family?"

"His mother and father are dead. I met his brother once." She pulled a folder from the desk drawer and walked over to where I was standing near the bed. "Here it is. This has all the vital information in it. His Social Security number, his credit cards, bank accounts, driver's license, health insurance, will . . ."

Frowning, she sank down onto a corner of the bed. "Christ, I hope nothing's happened to him. He's endured so many rotten things in his life, and he's still so damn cheerful. So good to people, so generous, so willing to—forgive."

Cindy Dorn put a hand to her face. "I'm sorry."

I walked over to the bed and touched her shoulder. She patted my hand with one of her own. "He's really all I've got."

"We'll find him, Cindy," I told her.

I spent the next half hour searching the bedroom and didn't come up with anything that would lead me to Mason Greenleaf. As Cindy Dorn had said, he was a fastidious man. His clothes were tucked away in built-in closets and drawers that slid right out of the walls —the shirts smelling of naphtha and wrapped in plastic bags; the socks joined with plastic clips as if they'd just been purchased; the suits, slacks, and ties all pressed and dry-cleaned and carefully arrayed on hangers.

"Amazing, isn't it?" Cindy Dorn said. "I'm such a slob, and he's so orderly. Do you know that he even changes the sheets on the bed after we make love? He's got a thing about cleanliness. I used to kid him by telling him he was born to be a housewife."

"You joke like that?"

"Sure," she said, smiling. "What did you think? We spend all day avoiding the subject? Mason's perfectly open about his past. In fact, he kids himself all the time."

Cindy walked back over to the desk and picked up a framed photograph. She stared at it fondly, then brought it over to me. "You haven't even seen him yet."

She handed the photograph to me. It was a picture of Cindy and a short, thin, dark-haired man in his mid-to-late thirties. He had fair skin and blue eyes. His face was lean and angular, hollowed out dramatically at the cheeks and beneath the eyes. The dark hollows gave him a look of romantic suffering and made the smile on his lips seem ironic.

"Three years ago Mason bought a camera with a self-timer," Cindy said. "This was the first time we tried it out. As you can see, neither one of us was sure when the flash was going to go off. Mason kept the picture because he said it was just the way he usually felt about life."

"And how is that?"

"Never sure when to smile," she said.

She took the photograph back to the desk and set it down gently, brushing the frame with her fingertips as if she were caressing Mason Greenleaf's face. Her lips began to tremble, and she bit into the lower one lightly.

"Go downstairs," I told her. "Have a drink and a few minutes to yourself. This kind of work is no fun."

Cindy Dorn nodded. "I'll look around down there. See if I can do us any good."

There was a john built into the west wall of the bedroom. I went through it and found nothing but a few bottles of over-the-counter remedies in the medicine cabinet. The bathtub was as shiny as a polished apple; the toilet bowl had azure blue water in it; you could have eaten off the tiled floor. I didn't even see a loose hair in the drains or the soapdishes.

I walked back into the bedroom, went through the desk, and struck out again. Aside from a few bank books, some school papers, and a teak box filled with pencils, there was nothing in it. The house was like a model showroom for the rich and rootless: it had the look but not the feel of being lived in. Only the abstract artwork, its black ground slashed with red, had the idiosyncratic pull of personality. But I wouldn't have wanted to speculate on what the canvases meant.

I found Cindy downstairs on the blue couch. An uncorked bottle of Chivas and a glass with a little whiskey in it stood on an enameled Parsons table to her right.

"Feeling better?" I said, sitting beside her.

"No," she said heavily.

"Have that drink." I nodded toward the glass.

"That's the one from outside. I brought it in." She stared at the glass for a moment and shook her head. "It's not mine. I mean, it's not the one from Wednesday night like I thought it was."

"Are you sure?"

"I don't like Scotch. And that's Scotch." She picked up the Chivas bottle. "I found this, too, in the wastebasket in the kitchen. I didn't notice it on Thursday." She turned the bottle upside-down, and a single drop of Scotch rolled out of the spout and dropped to the pegged-wood floor. "This bottle was almost full on Wednesday night. I know because I had to move it to get to the bourbon."

"Maybe Mason decided to tie one on."

She shook her head. "Mason doesn't usually drink Scotch."

We stared at each other.

"Looks like there was somebody here after I left," Cindy said, trying to sound indifferent and not succeeding. "Somebody who really liked Scotch."

"Who does Mason know who drinks Scotch by the fifth?"

Cindy righted the bottle and set it down hard on the Parsons table. "Del, the guy that Mason used to live with, the guy I told you about . . . he drank a lot of Scotch." She smiled forlornly. "That's one of the few things Mason told me about him—that Del drank Chivas like soda pop and did a lot of drugs."

She folded her arms across her chest and turned her head away from me, staring out the picture window at the winking lights of the city. In spite of the emotional openness that was her chief article of faith, Cindy Dorn wasn't prepared to handle the reality of a rival.

"We don't know what happened yet," I said.

"Except that he wasn't alone," she said in a hollow voice.

"Del could have paid a chance visit. Or it might have been someone else—a stranger."

She shook her head. "I've been through this before, Harry. I know the signs. Mason wouldn't have gone off with a stranger. But he might have gone off with a friend. If he was in a hurry, he might have left that goddamn glass out on the deck. He might even have forgotten the promise he made to me."

She put a hand over her eyes and drew her knees to her chin.

"How do we find Mason's friend?" I asked after a time.

"Sully would know where Del lives," she said, still huddling on the couch. "Ira Sullivan. He's been a friend of Mason's for years."

I glanced at my watch. "It's ten-thirty. You think Sullivan would mind a visit?"

"He's a night owl and he loves company."

"Where does he live?"

"On Telford in Clifton."

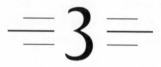

I T took us about ten minutes to reach the Clifton hillside and
another five to find Ira Sullivan's brownstone apartment building
on Telford. I parked beside a gas lamp and sat there for a time,
waiting for Cindy to decide whether she still wanted to press the
question of where Mason Greenleaf had disappeared to.

"I guess I gotta do this, huh?" she finally said.

"No, you don't. It's my bet that Mason will show up in a couple
of days. You could wait and let *him* explain it to you."

"Half of me is so pissed off, I could care less about explanations. But the other half—" She turned on the car seat and stared at
me with that frank look of hers. "I gotta find out, Harry. I'd worry
too much if I didn't."

"All right."

I opened the car door, and the hot night air came pouring in, full
of the smell of magnolia and the rasping of crickets. Cindy got out
and started for the brownstone apartment building. I fell in behind
her.

The apartment house was old and well-tended—the kind of neat,
bundled-up Clifton address that caters to elderly couples and well-
to-do singles. No children, no pets, no nonsense. Ira Sullivan's
place was on the second floor, up a wide staircase trimmed in brass

and floored in marble. The wide landings were cool like marble and shot with the soft glow of burnished wood and polished brass.

When we got to Sullivan's door, Cindy gave me a cautionary look. "Sully's a little odd."

"Meaning?"

"Meaning I should do the talking."

"Fine."

She stared at the polished door with foreboding. "He's going to eat this up," she said under her breath.

Raising a hand, she knocked.

A moment passed, and then an extremely tall, ungainly-looking man answered the door. At first glance he looked like a wildly overgrown Tweedledum. He had that same petulant, downturned mouth and barrel belly. His red hair stood straight up about three inches high, mowed level on top like a fade. His blue eyes were so lively, they looked electrified, as if he'd just pulled his hand from a socket.

"Cin," he said in a booming bass voice. "What brings you to my neck of the woods? And where the hell is Mason?" He craned his neck and stared at me so intently, I thought his eyes would pop. "You're not Mason."

"Harry Stoner," I said, holding out a hand.

The man shook with me. "Well, come the hell in, Harry Stoner. And Miss Cindy."

He waved us through the doorway.

The living room was papered in stripes and furnished in dark blue chintz. A gilt Japanese screen, picturing geese flying over a temple pagoda, blocked off the view of the street. A red Persian rug covered the floors. We sat down on the chintz couch. Sullivan sat across from us in a fanback chair the size of a stuffed bear.

"Can I offer you a drink?" Sullivan said. "Or is this a social visit?"

I could feel Cindy squirm beside me. "We're looking for Mason, Sully."

"You won't find him here," the big man said amiably. "In fact, I haven't seen him in ages. Not since the last time we all got together at the Cincinnati Club. You remember that evening, don't you, Cin?''

Cindy shuddered. "I remember."

Sullivan laughed a booming laugh. "I never did apologize for my behavior, did I? Well, I was a little drunk and you both forgave me. Right?

"People always forgive Sully," he said merrily. "It's written in the social contract. 'Sully is to be forgiven his excesses.' "

"About Greenleaf?" I said.

Sullivan arched an eyebrow at me. "Yes?"

"He's disappeared, Sully," Cindy said, getting it over with.

For a split second Ira Sullivan looked shocked. Then he smiled cynically. "When you say 'disappeared,' Cin, honey, exactly what do you mean?"

"He hasn't been at home or work for three days. His car is gone, too."

"Is he out of town, perhaps?"

"I don't think so."

Sullivan put on his thinking cap. "Could he be staying with a friend?"

"It's possible."

"Uh-huh." Sullivan gave Cindy a wry look. "Did you two have a little tiff, maybe?"

"Sully, this is serious. Mason vanished three days ago without a word. We need to talk to him. *I* need to talk to him."

Sullivan took this in dispassionately, then shifted his gaze to me. "And who are you, sir?"

"I'm a detective Ms. Dorn hired to find Greenleaf."

Sullivan paled. "Detective? You say you are a detective?"

I pointed a finger at him. "Right the first time."

Sullivan turned back to Cindy—his expression completely changed. "This is rather melodramatic, Cin, even for you. You hired a detective?"

"I'm worried, Sully."

"You must be crazed with anxiety," he said caustically. "What is it you want from me?"

"She wants the address of Greenleaf's friend Del," I said.

Sullivan bit his lower lip. "You think he's with Del again?"

Cindy nodded. "I think it's possible."

"Well, I don't." Sullivan leaned back in the huge chair, folding his arms across his Tweedledum belly. "That's over with. Anyway, Mason wouldn't do that to you, sweetie. For better or worse, he loves you."

"I didn't think he would, either," she said sadly. "But somebody was with him in the apartment. We found an empty bottle of Scotch and a glass. Mason once told me that Del drank a lot of Scotch."

"A lot of people drink a lot of Scotch, for heaven's sake. That's no reason to call a cop. I myself have been known to drink a lot of Scotch."

"*I* don't," Cindy said. "Neither does Mason. Please, Sully. Help us find Del."

Sullivan shifted uncomfortably in the chair. "The man you're talking about has problems of his own right now, hon. Serious problems. The last things in the world he needs in his life are burly detectives and hysterical women."

"Why don't you just give us the address," I said, "and let Del decide what he does or doesn't need?"

"Don't try to intimidate me," Sullivan snapped. "I'm a lawyer. So don't you try to intimidate me, Mr. Stoner."

"I'm not trying to intimidate you. Just give us the address, and we'll leave."

"Please, Sully," Cindy said.

Sullivan sighed dramatically. "Del Cavanaugh lives on Rose Hill in Avondale. 52 Rose Hill Place. But for chrissake, don't *you* go upsetting him." He shot me an angry glance, then said to Cindy, "He's a sick man, Cin. A dying man."

"AIDS?" Cindy said, looking horrified.

Sullivan nodded. "If Mason did have a drink with him, if he did go to visit him for a few days . . . well, it was just to comfort an old friend. Keep that in mind, okay?"

Cindy Dorn whispered, "Okay."

Out in the car again, in the hot, too-sweet-smelling night, Cindy stared through the windshield at Sullivan's apartment house.

As I started up the engine, she turned on the seat and said, "I think you'd better take me back to Finneytown."

"What about Del Cavanaugh?"

She shook her head. "I can't do it."

"Then why don't you let me do it? That's what you hired me for."

"No, Harry. If Mason is with Del . . . well, he's got a good reason to be there. And I should have known that. I shouldn't have doubted him."

"If you're satisfied, I'm satisfied."

Cindy frowned. "I won't be satisfied until Mason is back, until I can touch him and hold him again. But I'm not going to barge in on a dying man. That would be unforgivable. Mason will come home when he's ready. And he'll explain it or not explain it. That's just the way it'll have to be."

"All right, Cindy."

I pulled onto Telford and circled around to Ludlow, then down the hill to the expressway. It took me about twenty minutes to get her home, back to the yellow-brick birdhouse on Blue Jay Drive.

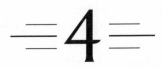

A COUPLE of days went by, days and nights of fierce mid-July heat. I thought about phoning Cindy Dorn to see if Greenleaf had checked back in but thought better of it. She'd settled on a scenario she could live with until he returned, and there was no point in reminding her that that scenario was founded on speculation and an empty bottle of Scotch.

So I didn't call her. And then on a blistering Tuesday morning she called me. I knew at once that something had gone badly wrong. I could hear it in her voice—a trill of terror.

"Harry," she said, "could you come over to Mason's house? Right away?"

"What's the trouble, Cindy?"

"Some police are here. They found—" Her voice broke, and she began to sob.

There was a confusion of noises on the other end of the line, then a man came on, speaking in the mechanical accent of a beat cop.

"Are you a relative of Ms. Dorn's?"

"I'm a friend. What's the problem, officer?"

The cop didn't say anything for a second. "We found a body. A guy . . ." I could hear him leafing through papers on a clipboard. "Mason Greenleaf."

"Where?" I said, feeling bad for poor Cindy Dorn.

"The Washington Hotel, down there on Main."

The Washington Hotel was a run-down, by-the-day residential hotel, one step above a flophouse. I couldn't imagine how Mason Greenleaf had ended up dead in such a godforsaken spot.

"Put the lady on the line," I said to the cop.

Cindy came back on, crying. "Harry, he's dead. Mason is dead. They want me to—" Gagging, she swallowed hard. "They want me to identify the body."

"I'm on my way," I told her. "It'll take me about ten minutes. Just hang on until I get there."

"I'll try," she said.

It took me closer to fifteen minutes to get the car out of the Parkade, climb Gilbert Avenue, and curl around the Park Road to Celestial Street. On the way I kept thinking about the Lessing case. Ira Lessing was a homosexual who had been beaten to death by two teenage male prostitutes. His case was the reason why I'd avoided homosexual clients. His case was also the reason why I no longer routinely carried a gun. What I'd done to Lessing's killer one rainy summer morning five years past—done in cold blood and then covered up like a common criminal—had left an indelible mark.

By the time I pulled up in front of Mason Greenleaf's condo, the TV people had arrived for a midday sound bite. A WLW camera crew was setting up on the sunlit sidewalk to the right of the Greenleaf house. Several cops watched them work from the shade of the condo's front stoop. A group of street kids—like the ones Cindy and I had seen on Saturday evening—sailed noisily up and down the pavement, flitting and darting around the TV truck like jays.

I walked up to the front door, and one of the cops lounging in the shade held up a meaty hand.

"Hold on, fella. Nobody's allowed inside."

"My name is Stoner," I told him. "I'm a friend of Ms. Dorn's."

"Just a minute."

The cop went through the doorway into the house and came out again a few moments later, grinning.

"Fucking unbelievable," he said, as if he were responding to something outrageous inside the house. "You can go in," he said to me.

A couple of other patrolmen were standing inside the door, laughing. One of them elbowed the other as I walked past them, and the second one stopped laughing immediately.

Cindy Dorn was sitting on the blue couch. A CPD homicide detective sat across from her. I knew him to say hello. His name was McCain.

"Oh, God, I'm glad to see you," Cindy said.

Reaching up, she clutched my hand tightly in hers. Her eyes were red from crying, her voice hoarse from it.

"Hello, Stoner," McCain said, nodding at me.

"Jack."

It was hot in the living room with the morning sun pouring through the huge glass windows. McCain's flaccid, brick-red face was coated with sweat. I could feel sweat popping out on my forehead, too.

"You think you can make the identification now, Ms. Dorn?" McCain said.

Cindy nodded weakly.

Looking relieved, McCain stood up and wiped his brow with his coat sleeve. Cindy stood up, too, using my arm as a brace. Outside one of the beat cops guided her over to a squad car parked at the curb. I hung back to ask McCain a few questions.

"Who found the body?"

"The hotel desk clerk. About an hour ago. He got complaints about the smell from other roomers on the floor."

"Greenleaf's still in the hotel?"

McCain nodded.

"Have any idea how long he'd been dead?"

"From the look of him, I'd guess ten, twelve hours. He isn't a pretty sight, Harry. Not after half a day in this heat."

I glanced over at Cindy, who was staring at us, pasty-faced, through the back window of the cruiser. "Does she have to see it?"

McCain shrugged. "Somebody does. Did you know him?"

I shook my head.

"Then I guess it's gotta be the girl." McCain wiped his brow with his coat again and squinted up into the blazing noonday sky. "Sometimes I hate this job."

We started across the sidewalk to the cruiser.

"Do you have any idea what the cause of death was?"

"There was a tin of pills on the dresser. A bottle of booze on the nightstand. My guess is suicide."

I got in the backseat of the cruiser beside Cindy. McCain got in front.

"Let's go," he said to the patrolman behind the wheel.

The cop took off down Celestial, then jogged right onto a walled stretch of Columbia Parkway. Cindy Dorn stared wide-eyed at the cagelike interior of the cruiser. It was her first time in the back of a cop car, and the first time is always a shock. Everything about it smacks of punishment and the raw work of detention. I'd made the trip she was taking more times than I cared to remember. But the one that stuck with me was Len Trumaine on the Lessing case. Cindy had the same blasted look on her face that Trumaine had had on his—the look of someone who has stepped right through the crust of the world.

Cindy didn't say a word as the cruiser blew down an exit ramp and headed straight into the lower east side. She was going to see a terrible thing, and she knew it. She was girding herself for it. There was very little I could do to make it any less terrible, except to be there with her.

The cruiser bucked as we rounded Fourth Street, throwing Cindy against my shoulder. The jolt seemed to rock her out of her trance.

"He's going to look awful, isn't he?" she said in a sick voice.

I said, "What he looks like doesn't matter to him. It happens *after* someone dies."

"I've seen this in movies. It feels like we're in a movie. Only I can't get up and leave."

"That's a pretty fair description."

Cindy bent toward me, lowering her voice until it was just a bitter, heartbroken whisper. "They were laughing at him, Harry."

"Who was?"

"Those cops. They were laughing at him because he was a homosexual."

"How did they know that?"

She shook her head. "They knew." She started to weep. "It's like he didn't matter because he was gay."

We were on Main Street by then. A block later, the cruiser jerked to a stop beneath the wrought-iron arcade of the Washington Hotel. There was an ambulance parked just ahead of us. The cops had set up sawhorses on either side of the hotel door to block off the pedestrian flow. A few lunchtime bystanders were stacked up on either side of the obstacles, wondering what all the fuss was about. Jack McCain turned in the seat.

"Can you do this now, Ms. Dorn?" he asked gently.

Cindy raised her head from my chest. "I guess I have to, right?"

"It may help us find out what happened."

Drawing herself up on the bench seat, Cindy nodded sharply. "Then I'm ready."

McCain opened the back doors of the cruiser, and we stepped out into the brilliant midday sun. Side by side we walked out of the sunlight into the darkness of the old hotel.

A narrow wainscoted hallway led to the clerk's desk—a booth on the left-hand wall. Beyond it the hall opened into the lobby proper, which in the Washington Hotel was little more than a dingy common room lined with secondhand chairs and benches. An old man in a stained shirt and yellow rayon slacks sat on one of the benches, resting his dazed-looking head in his hands. He had a red, heavily weathered face, with a band of paper white around his forehead, where a cap had shielded his head from the sun. In front of him a small portable TV, propped on an old mahogany table, flashed silent pictures. The place smelled of dust and mildew and old, tired men.

A stout, genial-looking man in his midfifties came out from behind the reception desk. He was wearing a T-shirt and khaki trousers and had a Reds cap on his head.

"Are you going to want to be going back up there?" he said to McCain.

"Yeah. One more trip."

"C'mon, then."

The clerk led us over to the open door of an elevator to the left of the reception desk.

"Keep an eye on things, will ya, Pat?" he called back to the man on the bench. Without taking his eyes off the TV, the guy raised one hand to acknowledge that he'd gotten the message.

"Christ, I don't know about Pat," the clerk said with a nervous laugh. "It's like he's wired to that damn box."

McCain and I stepped into the elevator. The fat clerk helped Cindy Dorn through the doors.

"Are you a relative of the deceased, ma'am?" he said with surprising gentleness.

"I was his friend."

"I'm very sorry," the man said.

He tipped his cap, smoothing down the thin gray hair underneath it before reseating it on his head.

The clerk threw a switch, and the elevator lurched up with a sound of rattling chains.

"What floor is he on?" Cindy said in a distant voice.

"He's on five, ma'am. All the way to the top. When he checked in last night, he asked if he could have a room on the top floor. I guess he wanted to look out at the view."

The fat man cleared his throat nervously.

"He seemed like a nice man. Leastwise he was polite to me."

When we got to five, the clerk held the elevator door open with his right hand as we got off. "You wanta come back down, you press the bell." He pointed to a painted-over buzzer on the jamb. "I'll come up quick as I can."

He tipped his hat again to Cindy and released the door, disappearing behind it with a rattle of pulley chains.

"It's down here on the front right," McCain said.

Diffuse daylight was coming from a bank of windows at the end of the hall. Through the grimy glass you could see the east side of the city, crumbling away in a rubble of faded brick to the green base of Mount Adams. Atop the hill the brilliant white steeple of St. Gregory's Church blazed in the sun.

"You can see Mason's house," Cindy Dorn said heavily. "There on the hillside."

I squinted into the glare and could just make it out, a tiny drop of red on the green hillside.

A CID man with a pair of magnifying goggles perched on his forehead came out the door of Greenleaf's room.

"We're set," he said to McCain. He glanced at Cindy. "You'll want to wear a mask, ma'am."

He handed her a blue hospital mask. Cindy stared at it with a sick look of terror.

"Let's just do it," I said.

The CID guy stepped out of the doorway. "He's on the bed at the back of the room. Take a look at his face, ma'am. Just a look."

The blue mask dangling loosely in her hand, Cindy stepped through the hotel room door. I went in behind her. The smell of death rose up like an animal and ran toward us in a blind rush that made the girl's knees buckle. I grabbed her arms to steady her. He was lying on the mattress at the back of the grim little hotel room—something the color of a roach wing, swathed in white sheets. Somehow the girl made herself stare at it before collapsing against me with a sob.

"It's him," she said, gagging.

I lifted her to her feet and maneuvered her out of the room into the hall. McCain ducked his head with embarrassment.

"Sorry, Ms. Dorn," he said heavily. "Very sorry."

By the time we got back out to the car, the girl had gone into shock. I told the driver to take her to the emergency room at Jewish. McCain rode with us to the hospital. No one said a word on the ride.

The emergency room was triaged, but McCain flashed his badge and they took the girl immediately, wheeling her in a chair into one of the curtained-off examination carrels. I didn't know McCain particularly well, but the concern he was showing for Cindy Dorn was enough to make me like him.

We sat in a waiting area, drinking vending machine coffee. All around us weary, sad-eyed people sprawled on hospital chairs and benches. Above them, on wall consoles, television sets murmured late-afternoon fare.

"Do they let you smoke anymore?" McCain said, pulling a pack of Luckies from his shirt pocket.

"You have to go outside."

"Smokers are the new niggers, you know that?" He rammed the cigarettes back in his pocket as if he were stabbing himself in the heart. "The nineties are starting to depress me. The whole world depresses me." McCain got to his feet. "I gotta have a nail."

I followed him through the exit door, out onto a cement concourse. The afternoon sun lit the pavement like sheet ice.

"Christ, it's hot," McCain said, squinting into the glare as he screwed a cigarette into his mouth and touched its tip with a lighter. "When's this weather gonna break, huh? It's been like a hundred for a solid week."

"That was a nice thing you did back there for the girl."

McCain shook his head. "She showed a lot of guts, considering."

"When do you figure you'll get criminalistics on Greenleaf?"

"Day or two. There wasn't much for them to do. Hell, you saw the hotel room. Now why would a guy like him end up in a place like that?"

I remembered what Cindy Dorn had said about being able to see Greenleaf's house from the top floor. "It's close to the hill. You can see his condo from the window."

"If he was homesick, why didn't he just go home? I mean, it's just a mile or two away."

"Maybe he didn't want to leave a mess."

"Fags," McCain said listlessly. "They're a different breed."

"How'd you guys know he was homosexual?"

"How'd you think?"

"He's got a record?"

McCain nodded. "Indecent carriage, soliciting. The usual."

"When was this?"

"Six, seven years ago."

"Nothing more recent?"

"No. He got probated to some shrink. Judging by the girl, maybe it helped. She seems like a nice kid." He took a couple of drags, then stubbed the butt out on a concrete pillar. "I gotta get back downtown. Tell the girl I'll be in touch soon as I know the details. If he's got other family in the area, steer 'em to me."

McCain started to walk away, then turned back. "How'd you get involved in this, anyway? You a friend of the woman's?"

I shook my head. "She called me last week when Greenleaf went missing."

"Yeah, she said he'd dropped out of sight for several days. Wonder where the hell he went?"

McCain turned away and walked off toward the parking lot, leaving the unanswered question frying in the July sun.

THE examining intern decided to keep Cindy Dorn in the hospital overnight. They'd already moved her to a fourth-floor room by the time I got back to the emergency room. I took an elevator up to four and followed a series of signs to the west wing. I found the girl propped up in bed with a bottle of saline plugged into her right arm. She had some color again and a sharper focus in her eyes, but she still didn't look fully there. Part of her was still standing in that run-down hotel room staring in terror at the raw remains of Mason Greenleaf's life and death.

"I'm sorry," she said as I came in. "I freaked out."

I could tell from the slur in her voice that they'd given her a tranquilizer of some kind.

"You've got nothing to apologize for." I sat down on a plastic chair by the hospital bed. Cindy Dorn held out her hand, and I took it in mine.

"Is there anybody you want me to call? A friend? Your ex?"

The woman smiled weakly. "No. I'll be all right. Later tonight, I'll talk to Mason's family. Everything'll get taken care of. It always does when somebody dies. I remember with my mother. It was like a piece of machinery I didn't know I had switched on and . . . things happened." She turned her face away toward the tall window at the far side of the room. "I wish I could shake the feeling that this is a movie. I wish I could go back to last Wednesday night and say something or do something that would change it. He ended up so alone.''

I didn't say anything.

She closed her eyes and squeezed my hand tight. ''I keep seeing his face—''

''Don't think about it, Cindy.''

''How can I not? I loved him.'' She started to sob. ''I loved him, and if I'd taken better care of him, if I'd watched over him the way he watched over me, this terrible thing wouldn't have happened.''

Holding her hand, I leaned toward the bed. ''What happened to Mason, it might as well have happened in a different solar system, on a different star, for all you or anyone else had to do with it.'' I felt a blush creep up my neck, enough of a burn to make me lean back in the chair. ''It just wasn't in your control.''

''That's the way you see it? Like we're on different stars?''

''That's the way I see it,'' I said, wishing I hadn't said anything at all.

That was Thursday. On Friday morning, Cindy Dorn was released from the hospital. I met her at the emergency room, drove her back to the little yellow birdhouse in Finneytown, and dropped her at the door. There were already several cars parked in the driveway—friends come to comfort her and mourn over Mason Greenleaf.

''I'm dreading going in there,'' Cindy said, as she stared glumly at the tiny house. ''I mean, I know they loved him, too. But I don't really want to hear their condolences or display my grief. I just want to sit by myself and be sad.''

''You'll do fine.''

Cindy reached out and touched my hand. ''I'm getting used to you saying that.''

''Did you want me to keep looking into this thing? We still don't know where Mason spent the last week.''

''I've thought about it, and I decided that if he'd wanted me to know where he was, he would have told me. If he took that secret with him when he left, that's the way it should stay.''

"The cops will probably have a few more questions."

Smiling, she said, "I'll be fine." Cindy Dorn leaned toward me and kissed me lightly on the cheek. "Maybe you'll stop in sometime? I've grown sort of fond of you, Harry Stoner."

She opened the car door and walked slowly up the walk, past the hawthorn tree, to her door. As I pulled away, another woman, with blond hair and a long face, came out the door and put her arm around Cindy, guiding her inside.

The next day, a gray Saturday afternoon, Mason Greenleaf was buried at Spring Grove Cemetery. His death and the funeral were well publicized in the papers. I didn't go to the graveside or to the wake that was held at Cindy Dorn's house following the service. But I thought enough of the woman to call her Saturday night. Someone else answered the phone at her house. I could hear the other mourners murmuring softly in the background. When the girl came on the line, I said the usual things. Sorry about her lover, if I could be of any help. I felt stupid saying them, but she seemed pleased that I had called.

After I hung up, I went to a bar in Northside, close by the house of an old friend, a free-lance writer. I was hoping he'd be at his usual spot at the bar. He wasn't there, so I drank for a while on my own, listening to the bar talk and nursing a Scotch. I didn't want to get drunk, but there didn't seem to be much else to do. It had been that way for so long that I'd stopped thinking about it, stopped admonishing myself. Night came, and if I didn't have some sort of surveillance job or if none of the small circle of women that I slept with—Jo Riley, Lauren Sharp, and a few others—were free, I drank.

You get to a certain age, midforties, and it comes to you that this is it, that whatever chance it is that you've been waiting for, the woman, the money, the peace of mind, has come and gone without you even noticing, like a hand that was dealt while you were away from the table, that somebody else bet and folded for you, that you never got to play. You feel cheated—most of us do. But the truth is that everything that's necessary happens to everyone. The trick is showing up. Somewhere in some magazine I thumbed through in some outer office, where I sat waiting for a client to call me in, to find whatever necessary thing it was he thought he'd lost, I read that opportunity used to be pictured as a woman rushing past you, with her hair streaming out in front of her face. If you grab her hair as she approaches, you get a good grip. Once she passes by, there is nothing to hold on to.

That evening I held on to my glass of Scotch. And I didn't think about Cindy Dorn, whom I liked well enough to reach out for, but whom I already knew I was going to let pass by and regret.

The next day, Sunday, I slept in with a hangover. Around two o'clock I made my way into the shower. As I was toweling off, the phone rang. I padded out to the bedroom before the answering machine clicked on, and picked up. It was Jack McCain.

"We got criminalistics on Greenleaf," he said.

"It took you long enough."

"There were complications," McCain said.

"Like what?"

"Like for one, his family wasn't crazy about us doing an autopsy. Have you talked to that bunch?"

"I missed them."

"It was like they just wanted it to go away without any fuss. Anyway, we finally got permission from Greenleaf's brother. Turned out it was hardly worth the effort. Outside of a few contusions on his face, which he probably got from falling down after taking the overdose, there was nothing unusual. Death was caused by barbiturate poisoning, Seconals and booze. It'll be ruled a suicide by the coroner."

"Have you told the girl?" I asked him.

"I thought maybe you'd want to. Of course, I'll be happy to answer any questions she might have."

"I'll call her."

"Good," he said, sounding relieved. "By the way, we still have some of his belongings in the property room. Watch, ring. The girl can pick them up anytime she wants. Just tell her to have the duty sergeant buzz me, and I'll pass her through.''

"I don't suppose anyone ever figured out why he ended up in that hotel?''

"We have him drinking at a bar called Stacie's down on lower Fifth Street earlier that night. He had some company, according to the two witnesses.''

"Christ, don't tell me,'' I said, feeling the ghost of Ira Lessing pass through the room.

"Yeah, they were fags all right. And a pretty noisy bunch. Maybe he had a lovers' quarrel with one of 'em. Anyway, he left alone, sometime around eleven-thirty, and that's the last anyone saw him, before he started stinking up the hotel room.''

"You didn't get the names of his drinking buddies, did you?''

"I guess we could find out. But it'd mean a helluva lot of leg-work, and with the family just wanting the whole thing to go away and the physical being so cut-and-dry, I doubt if the coroner'll want to open that can of worms. Guys like Greenleaf kill themselves all the time, Harry. They just get tired of being fags.''

"This guy was bi,'' I said.

"Same difference,'' McCain said. "It's hard to kid yourself into believing you're half one thing and half another.''

"Maybe.''

"Look, if it'll make it easier to break this thing to the girl, you can talk to the IOs who did the interviews at Stacie's. Segal and Taylor, at Six. They can fill you in on the chain of evidence.''

I jotted down the names Segal and Taylor as I hung up the phone.

THE District Six station was on a Ludlow Avenue hillside just
west of the viaduct, a ranch-style building with a hedge in
front and a fenced lot to the side. Immediately below the
station house, the smoggy industrial flats of Ivorydale stretch north
along the Mill Creek. On a boiling hot afternoon like that Sunday, I
could smell the soap stink of lye all the way around to the front of
the building, where it mixed with magnolia and the taste of hot tar.

A semicircular counter inside the station house door divided the
lobby off from the squad room. I went up to the counter and asked
one of the desk sergeants if I could talk to Detectives˙ Segal or
Taylor.

"Tell them Jack McCain gave me their names. It's about the
Mason Greenleaf suicide."

The sergeant pointed me to a bench, and I sat there for a time,
listening to the beat cops in the squad room taking names and
kissing ass: bad boys and honest cits all treated to the same mono-
tone rhetoric, like a class of slow children practicing arithmetic.
Eventually a husky man in a cheap blue suit came up to get me. He
had a square, tan, heavily seamed face cleft sharply at the chin, and
a mane of white hair streaked with the yellow of old blond.

"I just got the word from Jack McCain that I'm supposed to give
you whatever help you need," he said, smiling so broadly, I could

see the wad of chewing gum at the back of his mouth. He held out his right hand. "Nate Segal."

"Harry Stoner."

As I shook with him, Segal clapped me on the arm with his other hand, pinching the muscle beneath my sport coat like he was chucking a kid under the chin.

"I hear you used to be a cop, Harry."

I shrugged off his hand. "I was with the DA's office for a couple of years, before I went private."

"Yeah?" he said, chewing his gum vigorously. "Is that good money, private?" He didn't wait for an answer. "Let's go on back to the office where we can cut through some of this static."

I followed him down an aisle that ran past the front desk to a back wall lined with doors. Segal opened one with his name on it and ushered me in—this time without laying a hand on me. There was a small bright window at the back of the room, with an air conditioner rattling in it like a card in a bicycle wheel. A desk and long file took up the left-hand wall. The right had a couple of chairs parked against it and several framed commendations with Segal's name on them.

"Have a seat," the man said, settling in behind the desk. Reaching into his mouth, he pulled out the wad of gum and deposited it in a glass ashtray.

"I quit smoking last year," he said, wiping his fingers on his pants leg. "The wife kept hounding me about it. First I couldn't light up in the bedroom, then it was the living room. Before I knew it, I was out on the porch every time I wanted a butt. It got to be such a hassle, I just said fuck it. Now I'm a sugar junkie." He patted the paunch that gathered above his belt. "Gained twenty-nine pounds, teeth hurt. It's like they got it set up so whatever you need to make it through the day is going to kill you. You know?"

"It's a tough world," I said, pulling a chair up across from him.

"I wasn't kidding when I asked about the money you make. I got two more years to retirement, and then I gotta find something to do. I was thinking security, maybe. You do any of that?"

I shook my head. "Just PI work."

"What's that, divorce mostly?"

I didn't feel like going into it. "About Greenleaf?"

"Got it right here." Segal spun in his chair and opened the long file. "I guess Jack already told you that we didn't come up with a whole lot," he said, pulling out a folder and scanning it as he turned back to me. "Greenleaf spent a few hours in a bar called Stacie's, left alone around eleven-thirty, checked into the Washington a little before midnight. And you know the rest."

"How'd you place him at the bar?"

"His car. He left his Saab in Stacie's lot. After a couple of days the bar owner got tired of seeing it sit there and called us. We hauled it to the impoundment lot on Gest Street, by the way, so somebody ought to pick it up before they start stripping it for parts."

"McCain said Greenleaf was seen with some people at Stacie's."

Nate Segal reached into his coat pocket and pulled out a fresh stick of gum. "Yeah, he had company," he said, peeling the foil from the stick. "A couple of adult white males, according to the bartender and one of the waiters. For what it's worth, the bartender said he didn't recognize any of them, including Greenleaf. All he remembered was that the three of them came in together, ordered a lot of booze, and got shit-faced."

I thought about the empty bottle of Chivas in Mason's condo. "Did he give you a description of Greenleaf's friends?"

"The older one was your generic middle-aged GWM. Slacks, sports shirt. Gray hair. Maybe six feet, skinny. The other one was short and blond. A good deal younger than Greenleaf and the gray-haired fag. Late twenties, early thirties maybe. He didn't drink as much as Greenleaf and the older guy."

"Jack said the three of them had words at some point?"

"Yeah. A lot of loud talk between Greenleaf and the gray-haired guy. Nobody at the bar remembered what about—or claimed not to. The younger guy, the blond, supposedly tried to make peace. But Greenleaf got up and left. The other two stayed in the bar for an hour or so. Waiter said the gray-haired guy was fairly upset. Like close-to-tears upset.'' Nate Segal shook his head. "Queers, you know?''

"You didn't do any follow-up on these two?''

"Why?'' Segal said, folding the fresh stick of gum into his mouth. "Why jerk some guy out of the closet that don't want to come forward on his own? I mean, this thing was all over the papers and TV, so there was plenty opportunity to be a good citizen.''

He had a point. "You said Greenleaf left the bar at eleven-thirty and checked into the hotel at midnight. That leaves half an hour unaccounted for, right?''

"Right,'' he said, working the gum.

"You don't have any idea where he went?''

"Not a clue.''

"Any indication that he *had* been with someone?''

"No semen on his clothes or corpse,'' Segal said. "Nothing but booze and Seconals in his stomach. No credit cards missing from his wallet. Still had money in his pocket when the coroner carried him out of the hotel. Look, the guy was apparently having a bad enough week that he didn't go to work or tell his friends where he was staying. He goes to a bar with a couple of fags, gets blasted—blood alcohol of one point four—wanders around for a half hour or so brooding about his life, ends up in a cheapo hotel, and swallows a handful of sleeping pills on top of a bottle of booze. Goodnight, Irene.''

"McCain said there were some bruises on Greenleaf's face.''

"Minor contusions. Nothing like a fight, if that's what you're getting at.'' Segal stopped chewing the gum and stared at me. "*Is* that what you're getting at?''

"I'm just looking for a reason why. Something I can tell the family.''

Segal leaned back in his chair. He was tired of answering questions, and I was tired of asking them. "You got to know we can't tell you why. People get depressed and kill themselves. For the most part, you never know what the final straw was. Obviously this guy Greenleaf had personal problems, emotional problems. And maybe something did happen to him, in that bar or while he was wandering around drunk—something that just screwed him up even more than he already was. But unless the coroner says otherwise, finding out what it was isn't our business. We determined the cause of death, made sure there was no crime committed. And after that . . . well, people can spend their lives asking themselves why somebody does himself in.''

The guy was right. Even though he was trying to make less work for himself, he was still right. Absent a note or a clear chain of evidence, no cop can be expected to explain motive in a suicide. "Okay," I said, getting up from the chair. "I'll pass it on to the family."

"Understand, I'm not trying to be a hardass," he said, looking relieved that I was leaving. "If the family has questions I can help with, I'll be happy to talk to them. But when it comes down to it, they're the ones who are gonna have to figure this thing out."

There was no question in my mind, as I walked out of the station house back into the heat and stink of soap, that Nate Segal and his partner had done a half-assed investigation of Mason Greenleaf's suicide. They'd dug up just enough detail to fit with the coroner's verdict, and that's all they'd done. The fact that Greenleaf was gay, which to your average cop automatically meant deviant, was a large part of it, although suicides in general aren't top priorities with police. They're simply too complex, and often too painful and baffling, to linger over. Although Segal and Taylor had done an unusually superficial job, when it came down to it, there wasn't any doubt that Greenleaf had taken his own life. And that was where the cops and the coroner were content to leave it. Ultimately, I guessed, the family would be content to leave it there, too. There was too much probable ugliness in the details and, for Cindy Dorn, too much betrayal.

Once I got to the car I drove straight down Ludlow to a Frisch's on Spring Grove and phoned Cindy from a stand inside the restaurant lobby. It had been several days since I talked to her, and I couldn't kid myself that it didn't feel good to hear her voice when she answered the phone, even though she sounded sad and worn. I told her that McCain had called and asked me to relay the results of the investigation.

"The coroner is going to bring an official finding of suicide in Mason's death. Outside of that, there isn't much new. A few details about the bar in which Mason spent that last night. A lot of questions still unanswered. If you don't feel up to hearing this, it can wait a day or two."

"No," she said, "I've wanted to talk to you anyway. If it hadn't been for the funeral and the aftermath, I would've called you this morning."

"Should I come out now?"

"Wait till tonight. Mason's brother and sister are at the house right now, and I . . . I just don't want to deal with this while they're around."

"Okay," I said. "I'll come about nine."

"You promise?" she said in a tiny voice.

"Sure. You think I'm going to flake out on you?"

"People do that, you know."

"I'll be there. You can count on it."

TWILIGHT was just descending over Blue Jay Drive, when I pulled into Cindy's driveway at nine sharp. She was waiting for me on the front stoop, her chin on her knees and her hands wrapped around the legs of her loose white dress. Even in her brown study she was more than pretty. It had been a while since I'd met a woman who made me feel like she did—just to look at.

"It's good to see you," she said, stirring as I came up the walk.

"And you," I said, smiling at her.

She reached out a hand, and I helped her to her feet. "I've had Mason's brother and sister here all day."

"How was that?"

She shrugged. "They're nice, rich, stupid people who want to feel bad but don't know how. Neither one of them has an inkling what Mason's adult life was like. They cut themselves off from him once they learned he was gay, so the only good memories they have are of him as a child. That's what they talked about, mostly. What a good swimmer he was. How kind to animals and other children. Actually they were just exercising their nostalgia, remembering themselves as kids, trying to work up a little honest grief. It was depressing and a little revolting, too." She sighed. "I'm probably being unfair. I've been feeling disappointed with people anyway, lately."

"It's normal. You've suffered a loss."

"Have I?" she said with a cynical smile. "What have you lost when you don't know the person who's been taken from you well enough to realize that he's on the verge of taking his own life? Harry, I lived with Mason for three years. I saw him almost every day of those three years. This is something—" She threw her hands to her head and combed her fingers through her curly black hair, pulling it back savagely from her face. "How could I *not* know that something was this badly wrong with him? What kind of person is that blind? And what kind of person would keep this kind of pain secret from his lover?" Dropping her hands, she shook her head disgustedly. "Anymore, I don't know if I knew Mason at all. Or myself."

I tried to look sympathetic, following the etiquette of mourning like friends are supposed to do when people die. But the truth was that she was right about her lover—he was a jerk to have abandoned her like he did—and she was wasting her emotions trying to figure a motive that he himself probably hadn't fully understood.

"I'm sorry to lay this on you," she said, brushing her eyes with her sleeve. "But I've had to play the gracious widow for the last three days. And I'm tired of it. Come inside."

I followed her through the door into the narrow living room. A half-dozen folding chairs had been set up by the couch and along the window side of the room to accommodate the mourners. Paper cups and plates were scattered on the floor. A stack of fresh plates sat on a card table near the kitchen hall, along with a coffee machine and the remains of a tea ring.

"I know it's a mess," the girl said, staring morbidly at the room. "There have been a lot of visitors here. A lot of Mason's friends from school. A lot of current and former students. It's funny how many people loved him."

"Why funny?"

She dropped down heavily on the couch. "Because he obviously didn't know it, or he wouldn't have done this terrible, stupid thing."

I sat across from her on the stuffed chair. "The way that other people felt about him may have had nothing to do with why Mason killed himself. You yourself said he'd been troubled.''

"Troubled, not suicidal.''

Cindy Dorn shook her head. "What the hell happened, Harry? I know Mason had problems. Maybe more than the usual allotment. He worried about AIDS. He worried about being bisexual. He was deathly afraid of cops. But he was not in despair—or no more so than any fairly thoughtful, screwed-up human being is. Hopefulness was his creed.''

"What you said about the cops,'' I asked. "What does that mean?''

She flushed as if the question embarrassed her. "Mason had some trouble with the police about six years ago, before I knew him. Sully's the one to talk to about it. You remember Sully?''

"Vividly.''

"He represented Mason when the charges were brought. It was an ugly, preposterous thing involving a note that Mason had written to a kid at school. Mason was actually locked up for several days before the charges were dropped.''

"He hadn't had any further trouble along those lines, had he?'' I said, trying to make it sound like an innocent question and not succeeding.

Cindy stared at me coldly. "For chrissake, Harry, Mason wasn't a child molester. The whole thing was a terrible misunderstanding. You have no idea how careful teachers have to be around their students these days. Anyone who works with children has to be careful. You don't dare lay a hand on one of them for any reason, for fear some vindictive parent will twist it into abuse. In case you haven't noticed, there has been an epidemic of such charges in this country and in this city. It's paralleled the growth of AIDS, a kind of fundamentalist AIDS.''

"I was just fishing for a motive, Cindy. Don't take it personally.''

"I just don't like stereotyping. People have done it to me, because of . . . well, because I like men. And they did it to Mason all the time. That's precisely why he was charged, because to the cops all gays are potential perverts." She leaned forward on the couch and stuck her chin in her hands. "I don't suppose they found anything useful, the cops?"

"They haven't really done a thorough investigation."

"Of course not," the girl said bitterly.

"It's not just Mason, Cindy. Suicides are always tough for cops. All the CPD really knows is that Mason died of an overdose of Seconals and alcohol. He apparently did the drinking in a bar called Stacie's, Monday night."

"Stacie's?" she said. "I don't think I've ever been there."

I told her the truth. "It's a gay bar, Cindy. Mason was seen there with two other men. A tall, gray-haired middle-aged man and a younger blond man. The older man drank a lot of Scotch."

"Del," she said, falling back against the rear cushions of the couch.

"That was my thought, too."

She sat with her head to the wall, looking betrayed—the way she'd looked on the night we'd searched Mason's condo.

I said, "The police didn't question the two men Mason was drinking with, so it may not have been Cavanaugh. To be honest, the whole inquiry was cursory."

But she was thinking about the depth of Greenleaf's betrayal. "Why would he have done that to me?" she said in a heartsick voice. "When he left Del, he went through an agony of remorse and self-recrimination. He didn't just walk out on him like a stranger."

"We don't know what happened, Cindy. The part about Cavanaugh is speculation."

She put her hands to her face and sat for a moment in silence. "I thought I could let this go. I thought that was what Mason would have wanted—what *I* wanted. But the fact is I was afraid of finding out the truth. I am still afraid."

It was my cue, although I sure as hell didn't feel like picking it up. "I could look into it for you," I said uneasily. "At least I could find out if Cavanaugh was the one in the bar."

Cindy nodded. "Yes. I guess I need to know who he was with—and why."

"The why could be tougher," I said. "You do understand that this could be painful, don't you, Cindy? You may not want to know some of things I find out."

"All I know for sure is that I can't go on like this."

"Okay. But try to remember that I warned you."

I got to my feet, feeling as if I'd gained fifty pounds, as if I'd literally shouldered the burden of Greenleaf's death like a pall-bearer. I could think of all sorts of reasons not to do this thing, not the least of which was the likelihood that, in spite of my warning, Cindy Dorn would end up hating me for what I revealed to her about Mason and herself. But it was a cinch that the cops weren't going to do any more work. And I didn't want to send her to a stranger.

"I'll start in the morning," I said, as I walked over to the door. "You may want to collect Mason's effects. They're in the CPD property room. The cops found his car outside the bar and towed it to the Gest Street impoundment lot. Call Jack McCain if you have any trouble getting a release."

I went out the door and down the drive, knowing that I'd made a bad mistake. It was going to be Ira Lessing all over again—I could feel it in my gut. As I got in the car, Cindy Dorn stepped out on the stoop. She stood there in the moonlit driveway, while all around us the sleepy yellow brick houses dreamed their pleasant suburban dreams.

"I didn't say thank you," she said, coming down by the car. She reached in the window and put her hand on my face. "I've been a bitch tonight, and I'm sorry. If Mason were around, I would have taken it out on him. Anyway, I wanted you to know that it was a lucky thing the day I called you. Lucky for me."

"Let's hope you feel that way when I'm finished," I said heavily.

"I will always feel that way," she said.

Leaning through the window, she kissed me on the mouth. "You know I'm fond of you, right?"

The persistence of her candor made me smile. "I know."

She smiled back at me. "Good. Because I'm depending on you, Harry. You're about all I can depend on, just now."

Pulling her head back through the window, she walked up the driveway with her arms wrapped tightly around her body. I watched the woman go inside the house, then sat there for a few moments, liking her and at the same time feeling burdened by the pain Mason Greenleaf and I were bound to bring her.

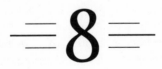

DEL Cavanaugh's home was on Rose Hill in North Avondale. A great stone fortress with ivy walls and a watch tower that rose above the surrounding trees. In the brilliant light of that early Monday morning, it didn't seem like a place that trouble could touch.

I hadn't bothered to phone the man before driving over to his house. I hadn't wanted to give him a chance to say no to an interview. But before leaving the apartment, I'd called Art Spiegalman at the *Enquirer* metro desk and asked him to pull their file on Cavanaugh. There were just two articles in the *Enquirer* archive: one about a tony art gallery the man had run in Hyde Park; and another about the mansion he lived in, which was on the historical register. The article about the mansion mentioned that Cavanaugh's mother was a distant relative of Franklin Pierce and that she still lived with her son in the mansion house. After talking to Art, I called Dick Lock at the CPD Criminalistics Unit and had him do a computerized LEADS search on Del Cavanaugh. There was no record of criminal charges filed against him. I thought about phoning Ira Sullivan to get a little more background on Cavanaugh and, perhaps, to use him as an intermediary. I even went so far as looking up the number of Sullivan's law office in the Dixie Terminal Building. But the truth was, I was anxious to get the thing over with

—to get the Greenleaf case over with. In that sense, I suppose, I was no different than the cops.

It was just a little past ten when I pulled up in the carriage circle of Cavanaugh's fortresslike home. The day's heat hadn't started yet in earnest, but there was assurance of it in the wind that rustled through the tall oaks on the lawn and in the bright blue, cloudless sky. I parked the Pinto in the shade of an oak and walked back up to the pavilion that jutted out from the front door.

A gaunt man with a haggard, near-fleshless face answered my knock. In spite of the heat, he had wrapped himself in a cardigan sweater and held his arms close to his body, as if the chill he felt was enduring and inescapable. There was a distance in his gaze that I had seen before. The thousand-mile stare of dying men.

"Yes," he said in a high-pitched voice. "Can I help you?"

"I'd like to talk to Del Cavanaugh."

"I am he," the man said, drawing himself straight with an effort that was painful to watch.

I knew just by looking at him that he wasn't the man who had been drinking with Mason Greenleaf at Stacie's bar. He didn't have the strength to leave that house.

A white-haired woman in her midsixties with a smart, fine-boned face, so sharply angular it cast shadows on her own flesh, came up behind the man. She was dressed elegantly in an iridescent silk dress. "Who is it, Del?" she said, eyeing me suspiciously. "If you are selling something, we aren't interested."

"I'm not selling anything," I said, feeling the awkwardness of the situation. "I'm a detective working for a woman named Cindy Dorn."

Del Cavanaugh literally staggered at the mention of Cindy's name. The mother stared at him with concern.

"You're here about Mason, aren't you?" he said.

"Yes."

"My son is not a well man," the mother said, pushing roughly past him. "I think you should leave before you upset him."

"I am still here, Mother," the man said, controlling his voice with effort. "I am still capable of making decisions for myself. I'm not yet so far gone as to cede my rights as a human being to you. When I become demented, then you may make these decisions. It is something you can look forward to.''

"Del,'' the mother said with horror.

"Oh, give it a rest, for God's sake.'' Staring at me with his thousand-mile eyes, he said, "Let's go out into the light, Mr.—''

"Stoner.''

He smiled hideously, showing a mouth full of blackened teeth. "Stoner. A good, hard Anglo-Saxon name. Something to bust a knuckle on. I won't ask you to shake hands. There is a fear of contagion with my illness that affects even the most enlightened people. I myself would not shake hands with me.''

Defeated, the mother shrank back in the doorway. The look of hatred on her face as she closed the door on me was something to behold.

"There is a patio around the side of the house,'' Del Cavanaugh said. "We can talk there.''

I followed him down a cut stone path that ran around the side of the house. He was so wobbly on his feet that I stayed directly behind him, to catch him if he fell. But he had developed his own delicate balance, and he didn't fall. The stone path cut through a small sculpted garden. The air was rife with honeysuckle and lilac and heavily shaded by the overarching oaks. In the heart of the garden a tented table and two wrought-iron chairs were set up on a stone tablet. Cavanaugh reached for the nearest chair and virtually collapsed onto it with a long painful sigh.

"Small steps,'' he said, fighting to catch his breath. "I've been reduced to small steps. This is not an easy adjustment for a man like me to make.''

He tried to laugh, but he didn't have the breath for it.

"Everything proceeds in small steps with me now. The loss of weight. Loss of hair. Sight. I'm anticipating the loss of my mind. It is a peculiar feeling, like waiting for water to boil. In the nonce I pass time by recording my descent into the abyss. I've actually videotaped many of my days. And of course I take scrupulous measurements. Energy lost, measured in the time it takes to traverse a given distance. Muscle mass. This can be measured with a scale or ruler. The growth of tumors. This can also be done with a ruler. I am become the sum total of a series of minute daily measurements. Like a growing child marking his height on the wall. Only, I suppose, I'm shrinking. And the darkness is growing.'' The man let his head loll against the back of the chair. He stared up into the oak trees, his gray desiccated face dappled with the shape and shade of the leaves in the sun. "I don't mean to be, but I'm sure I'm disgusting to you. I have no business being with people any longer. A man must defend himself at all times, and I no longer have the strength to defend myself.''

It was like the manual of arms, and it said a good deal about the way he'd lived and the way he was dying.

"Why did you come here?'' he said, looking back at me.

"To ask whether you had seen Mason Greenleaf before he died.''

"And if I had, what possible difference would it make to Mrs. Dorn?''

"She's is trying very hard to understand why Mason took his life. Everyone who knew him is.''

The man started to laugh. "And so I am to be blamed for this, too? What a magically wonderful train of thought that is. Mason visits Del. Mason kills himself. Therefore Del is . . . what? An accessory to murder. You should remind Mrs. Dorn that I did not live with Mason for the past three years. She did. It would, I think, behoove her to ask herself why Mason took his life.''

"Did Mason tell you he was unhappy with Cindy?''

"He didn't have to tell me,'' the man said, looking back at the sky. "I knew him for better than seven years. I knew what he thought and how he felt.''

"Then he did come here?''

"Yes.''

"When was this?''

A shadow of doubt crossed the man's face. "Forgive me, Mr. Stoner, but I'm not as quick with dates as I once was. It was two weeks ago, I believe. On a Thursday afternoon. We sat out here in the garden and talked, just as you and I are doing."

"Did he seem unusually depressed to you?"

The man didn't answer me. "We talked about the old times, when we first met. The days we spent here and at my family's home in Michigan. The fun we'd had. Some of the people we had known who are going or gone."

"Did he know about your illness before he came to see you?"

"Do you mean did he come to see me because I am dying of AIDS?"

"Yes," I said, feeling slightly ashamed of myself. "I guess that's what I meant."

"I suppose that was why he came. He'd known I was ill, of course. That was general knowledge. But I think a mutual friend had told him that I was . . . in decline. It was not an arranged meeting. I hadn't talked to Mason or seen him since our falling out, since he started his *vita nuova* with Mrs. Dorn. I suppose it was quite a shock to him to see me as I am now. When we had our parting, I was a different man." Del Cavanaugh brushed his eyes with bony fingers, then rubbed his thumbs across his fingertips, as if the feel of tears was an unexpected sensation. "I'm not really crying for Mason. He chose to live a lie and was unable to persevere in it. Perhaps seeing me, in my current state, was a blow. As I did not invite him here, I cannot be held responsible for that. But you should tell Mrs. Dorn that what was bothering Mason had little to do with her—or me or anyone else. He had come to the end of his particular road and saw nothing ahead of him but fear and darkness. Tell her no one else is to blame for what happened to him. He made a choice, and choices have consequences."

"He told you he was contemplating suicide?"

Cavanaugh thought about this for a moment, with a finger to his cheek. It came to me that he didn't know why Greenleaf had killed himself, save that he was satisfied that the man had betrayed him and then gone to hell as a result. The vanity of it made me disgusted.

"The man's dead, you know," I said, voicing my disgust.

Cavanaugh looked insulted, as if no one else but him had the right to die. "No, he did not talk about killing himself," he said coldly. "That does not mean that I am mistaken about the reason for his despair."

He crossed his bony hand in his lap and stared at me with his thousand-mile eyes.

"You can go now," he said. "I'm tired of this conversation."

I went back down the drive to where I'd parked the Pinto, got in, and sat there for a time, thinking about Del Cavanaugh, his cattiness, his bitterness, his misery. The image of his illness was horrible and depressing. It had depressed me, and I didn't know or like him. For Greenleaf it had probably been an ordeal. He feared the disease that Cavanaugh was dying from, according to Cindy Dorn. Whether that fear in combination with what it had done to his ex-lover was enough to untrack him, I didn't know. I was certain that Cavanaugh was capable of playing upon that fear and the guilt that it inspired—and probably had. Cavanaugh's own interpretation of Greenleaf's motives didn't impress me. He had blamed the suicide on Greenleaf's choice of lifestyle, which was tantamount to blaming it on his decision to forsake Cavanaugh and live as a straight with Cindy Dorn. It was a savage, self-serving judgment, especially considering the fate that Cavanaugh's own lifestyle had brought him to. Moreover, if it was as simple as that—if Greenleaf had killed himself because he was a homosexual trying to be something that he wasn't—then I didn't see any difference between Cavanaugh's reasoning and that of the cops: just another fag suicide.

At least, I'd confirmed the fact that Greenleaf had paid the man a visit for the first time in years, possibly on the same day he had dropped out of his ordinary routine into the limbo that led to the Washington Hotel. Since the visit with Del Cavanaugh had followed hard upon the company Greenleaf had had the previous night, it was reasonable to suspect that whomever he'd sat on his porch drinking with, late Wednesday night, was the mutual friend that Cavanaugh said had told him about Del's illness. Which pretty much left me where I'd started. Looking for the man who drank Scotch.

I didn't have the stomach to go back into that garden and ask Cavanaugh for a name, so I started up the car and headed downtown, to where I should have gone in the first place, Ira Sullivan's law offices in the Dixie Terminal.

IRA Sullivan's office was on the tenth floor of the Dixie, on the south side of the building, facing the river. Through the large fan-topped windows in the anteroom, I could see the stadium and, beyond it, coal barges cutting downriver in a swath of foam. The anteroom was antiseptic white. White carpet, furniture. The only color in the place came from the view through the window and the few delicate watercolors posted on the walls.

Sullivan's secretary, a goggle-eyed woman with blotchy skin and a taffy pull of bright red hair, asked my name, buzzed Sullivan, then spent the next few minutes chatting me up while we waited for Sullivan to come out of his office.

"He's been in a funk all week," she told me, pecking desultorily at a computer console. "A good friend of his died, and he took it very hard."

"That's why I've come to talk to him."

"You knew Mr. Greenleaf?" the woman said, arching an eyebrow with surprise, as if, to be honest, I didn't look the type.

"I didn't know him. I'm working for a friend of his, Cindy Dorn."

Removing a pair of headphones from her ears and draping them like a choker around her neck, the woman leaned conspiratorially across her desk. "Mr. Sullivan really saved Mr. Greenleaf's bacon a few years ago. He had big problems. Big,'' the woman said, dividing her hands for emphasis.

"I heard he was charged with solicitation.''

"You didn't hear the half of it. They were ready to throw away the key until Mr. Sullivan stepped in.'' The woman cocked an elbow on her desk and rested her chin on it, gesturing with her free hand just as if we were cutting recipes across the kitchen table. "You know I'm not a bleeding heart. But I will tell you for a fact that it is a crying shame the way the police department and the district attorney's office harass certain people.''

As she said this, Ira Sullivan popped his swart face around the corner, making the woman jump. "What're you gossiping about, Cherie?''

Flushing pink, the woman replaced the dictation headphones on her ears and began typing a mile a minute.

Sullivan clucked his tongue ruefully. "You're a shameless washerwoman, you know that?''

The secretary pretended not to hear him.

I'd forgotten how tall and ungainly the man was. Even in a blue pinstripe he looked weird and wroth, with his downturned mouth and upturned hair and electrified eyes.

"Mr. Stoner, let's go on back to my office,'' he said to me. Turning to the secretary, he added: "See if you can manage to hold my calls and your tongue till I buzz you.''

The woman nodded without looking up from her computer screen.

"Look, I want you to understand something,'' Sullivan said, once we got out of Cherie's earshot. "If I'd had any idea that Mason's disappearance would turn out so tragically—well, there's not a thing I wouldn't have done to help him. Not a thing. I want Cindy to know that, too. I tried to tell her at the funeral, but I don't know if she took my meaning. We were all plenty distraught. After what that man went through, to end up like he did, where he did.''

He shook his head sadly.

Sullivan's office was at the end of the hall, a large posh room, painted white like the reception area and accented with modern canvases framed in brass. The one that took up the wall above his liver-shaped desk was an O'Keeffe flower. Unlike most law offices there were no bookshelves filled with case law. Just the big canvases and, of course, the spectacular view through the picture window.

Sullivan waited a moment—to let the luxe room work on me—before sitting down behind his desk. "I don't do much court work anymore," he said, in case I'd missed the point. "Just corporate stuff and a few favors for my friends."

I sat down across from him on an overstuffed chair that gave beneath me like a down pillow. "I understand that you represented Mason Greenleaf at one time."

Sullivan cocked his head and stared. "Before we get into this, I'd like to know what your interest is in this tragedy."

"Cindy's dissatisfied with the police investigation of Mason's death. She feels they've done a cursory job."

Sullivan laughed. "Our police department doing a cursory job? Now, how is that possible? It isn't as if Mason was a nigger." He leaned back in his chair. "What would you say he was, Mr. Stoner?"

He wanted me to use the word *fag*. Since he figured I was thinking it, he wanted me to say it.

"Mason's bisexuality probably was a factor in the investigation," I admitted.

"How could that be in this great land of ours?" Sullivan said sarcastically. "The home of the brave?"

I wasn't in the mood for a civics lesson from Ira Sullivan. "We can weep about the state of society all day if you want to. Or we can try to figure out why Mason Greenleaf killed himself."

"You don't think there's a connection, huh?" Sullivan said with a snort of disgust.

"I'm sure there is. But there are also specific reasons for what happened. The man disappeared for five days for no apparent reason, and then, drunk and injured, ended his life in a rat trap hotel room. It was a miserable finish."

Sullivan looked away, out the blue window. He didn't say anything for quite a time, and when he finally spoke, his voice was heavy with emotion. "A man can take comfort in knowing who he is, Mr. Stoner—even if he is despised for it. Mason was not blessed with such understanding. He walked a line that no one can walk for long. People try, of course. Lock themselves in unhappy marriages or pointless relationships. But sooner or later what you are comes back to haunt you."

"You're saying he wasn't happy with Cindy Dorn?"

"No," he said, still staring out the window. "I'm saying he wasn't happy."

Given what had happened in the Washington Hotel, there was no disputing his point, although I had the sure feeling that, like Del Cavanaugh, Ira Sullivan was one of those men who wasn't content unless everyone else in the world came down with it, too. If he had it in his power, he would sow doubt like a plague.

"You asked me before, if I'd ever represented him as a lawyer," Sullivan went on. "The answer is yes. Six years ago when he was arrested."

"For soliciting."

"That was the charge," the man said, looking back at me. "The actual crime, if you want to call it that, was somewhat more complex. Mason took a personal interest in one of his students. And the boy, who was eighteen years old at the time, returned his affection. In spite of the fact that there was no physical contact between them at any time, the boy's father brought charges of solicitation and indecent carriage."

"The charges were dropped?"

"Not dropped, but substantially reduced. Mason was ordered into mandatory counseling. It would have been much worse if the police department had prevailed upon the boy to testify. But, of course, there was nothing to testify about. They had never been intimate. They had only been friends. The sole evidence in the case was some letters Mason had written, expressing his compassion for the young man, who was then having a hard time in his life. The father found them and assumed the worst. Mason's real crime was showing bad judgment. In spite of a massive letter-writing campaign, which I helped organize, the Cincinnati School Board disciplined him. Which is why he ended up teaching at a private school. Although it is highly unlikely that he would have gotten *that* job had he not been a friend of the headmaster. His reputation was very close to ruined.''

The way Sullivan explained it, the incident sounded a lot more damaging than the ugly contretemps that Cindy had dismissed as vicious, antigay prejudice.

"Mason was living with Del Cavanaugh at this time?"

Sullivan nodded. "Yes. Which was another thing that went against him. The fact that he was then living openly as a homosexual did not play well in court. Del's own attitude didn't help, either. He took the position that there would have been nothing wrong if Mace *had* been carrying on with the boy, who was no longer technically a minor. Unfortunately, he took the position publicly, in front of a TV crew." Sullivan shook his head. "Del's asinine like that. He had other problems, too. But he also had guts. And that's always something to admire in this world. His relationship with Mason ended soon after the trial, and I always thought it was partly because Del felt that Mason hadn't stuck up for himself more strongly. Frankly, a number of us felt that way, given the ridiculousness of the trumped-up charge. It was just another fag witchhunt, flimsier than most. But later on, it became obvious to me that Mason simply didn't have it in him to defend himself."

"Why was that?" I asked.

Sullivan locked his hands together on the desktop. "Who can say why? Each of us handles the burden of his identity in a different way. Mason's way was to be kind and hope for the best."

"I talked to Del Cavanaugh this morning. Mason went to visit him during the week before he killed himself."

Sullivan chewed his lip. "Seeing Del in the shape he's in would have been hard for Mason to take."

"I'm sure it rocked him," I said grimly.

"You know Mason had a phobia about AIDS?"

"Cindy told me he was anxious about it."

"This went beyond anxious. When he was with Del, he had his

blood tested every two or three weeks. Terry Mulhane was Mason's internist. Maybe you should check with him to see if . . . there was some recent problem.''

The thought had occurred to me. So had the consequences it might hold for Cindy Dorn—and possibly for me. Like everyone else in the world, I was wary of AIDS. I wasn't phobic about it, as Mason Greenleaf had been. But after a decade of plague and propaganda, it was there now, in the back of my mind, this unsettling, invasive fear that changed everything.

"Cindy says she practiced safe sex and their last blood tests were negative," I said, trying not to sound defensive.

But Sullivan wasn't buying it. "That must be a great relief to you," he said. "I would still check with Terry Mulhane. I would also talk to the staff at Nine Mile to see if things were going smoothly on his job."

"You have some reason to think that they weren't?"

"No. I just know that Mason took his work very seriously. When the school board finally decided to let him go, he was so despondent that he threatened to kill himself. Of course, he got over it."

"He didn't make a habit of that, did he? Threatening suicide?"

Sullivan shook his head no. "Mason wasn't that unstable. You have to remember that the circumstances of his arrest were humiliating, and the police were still hounding him in spite of the fact that the charges had been reduced. Once they get your name, they can make life quite miserable for a gay man. For a while there they were dragging Mason into every lineup that involved a charge of solicitation or molestation. I actually had to secure an injunction to get them to lay off."

"You don't know if he'd been harassed again recently, do you?" I said, thinking it would make a damn good motive for suicide.

"If he was, he didn't tell me. As his lawyer, I am sure that he would have come to me with such a problem."

But this time *he* sounded defensive, which made me think I should follow up on it. The obvious fact that Greenleaf hadn't confided in him prior to killing himself was bothering Sullivan, just as it was tormenting Cindy Dorn. It occurred to me that Mason Greenleaf hadn't confided in any of the people one might have expected him to turn to—Cindy, Sullivan, or Del Cavanaugh. Outside of the vague malaise he'd voiced to the girl, he had gone to his grave silently, like a man with a secret. Which led me back to Stacie's bar and the only two people I knew for a fact that Greenleaf had talked to before he committed suicide.

"Mason was seen in a bar called Stacie's on the night he died, in the company of two other men, a gray-haired older man who drank a good deal of Scotch and a younger blond man with a mustache. I thought at first that the Scotch-drinker was Del Cavanaugh, but now I'm not sure. You wouldn't know any old friends of Mason's that match those descriptions, would you?"

Sullivan thought this over. "I can't say, the descriptions are so vague. You understand I don't want to put anyone in a difficult position without further checking."

"Meaning that you do know people who would fit the bill?"

"Several," Sullivan conceded. "I'll make inquiries for you."

Under the circumstances it was the best I could have hoped for.

"I appreciate the help," I told him, getting up and holding out my hand.

We shook like old pals.

"I'll call you after I've checked into it," Sullivan said as I left the room.

= 10 =

THE conversation with Sullivan had gone well enough to give me hope that he would eventually help out, especially if he could see his way to naming names. And I had the feeling that in time he would. Like Cindy, he had been wounded by Greenleaf's silence; and, like Cavanaugh, he was vain enough to take it personally.

Sullivan had already helped me in one way: by making it clear that Mason Greenleaf's life and death had had shapes of their own —independent of my bad memories of Ira Lessing's tragic death, and my part in revenging it—and that at their heart was a secret that he hadn't been able to impart to his lover or his ex-lover or his friends. Both Cavanaugh or Sullivan had guessed that that secret was his inability to come to terms with being gay, a fate that he had tried to escape and couldn't. Where Cindy Dorn saw inexplicable betrayal, they saw self-delusion and a sad, inevitable self-reckoning. While their version of Mason Greenleaf smacked heavily of their own biases, it did have the merit of fitting the few facts that I knew. Like it or not, I couldn't get around the fact that Greenleaf had ended up in a gay bar with two gay men.

As I rode the elevator back down to the Dixie Terminal lobby, I plotted a bit of strategy to take me through the rest of that afternoon, until it was late enough to catch the night help who had served Greenleaf and his friends at Stacie's bar. I decided to begin at the beginning, with whatever had been bothering Greenleaf during the weeks before he disappeared. Besides his homosexuality, Sullivan had suggested three possible motives: a fear of contracting AIDS, a terror of harassment by the law, or a serious problem at work. I had already seen what AIDS could do, and it was fearsome indeed. But according to Cindy, Greenleaf did not himself have AIDS, unless of course he'd had his blood tested during the week before he dropped into limbo. Had he, in fact, been diagnosed with HIV, it would have been more than enough to start him in decline. It was the first thing I planned to check when I got back to the office. The other two possible motives, job- and cop-related trouble, could be handled by a couple of quick trips. I didn't have much hope that any of it would pan out, especially since Cindy had already told me that Mason wasn't having a problem at work, and neither Sullivan nor the cops themselves had said that he was having any current problems with the law. But without a solid lead, I had to start somewhere.

When I got back to my office, I looked up Mason's internist, Terry Mulhane, in the Yellow Pages. He had an office on Auburn Avenue in Corryville. I dialed his number and got a receptionist who put me on hold. A few moments later she came back on, full of apologies.

"We've got some sort of flu bug going around, and the phone's been ringing off the hook."

I told her who I was and asked her if it would be possible to talk to Mulhane about Mason Greenleaf.

"I can ask," she said dubiously, as if Greenleaf was a painful subject.

After a short pause, a man picked up the phone. "This is Terry Mulhane," he said. "You say your name is Steiner?"

"Stoner. I'm a private investigator Cindy Dorn hired to look into Mason Greenleaf's death."

"I thought the police had ruled it a suicide," the man said.

"We're still looking for a motive."

Mulhane sighed. "All I can say, and I told Cindy this at the funeral, is that it wasn't because of a medical problem. There was nothing wrong with Mason. I checked him out myself no more than a few days before he did this thing, and he was fine.''

I felt relieved for Cindy—and for myself—and curious about what had motivated Greenleaf to go to the doctor before he died. "Did his complaints have anything to do with AIDS—or fear of AIDS?"

"I suppose in some way all of his complaints had to do with that. Fear of AIDS or fear of retribution—it amounted to the same thing with Mason, I've always thought. What I can tell you for certain is that he wasn't sick when he came to see me. He said he'd been having trouble sleeping. His BP was up. But it was generally up when he came in for a visit. White jacket BP. There was nothing about his condition that indicated suicidal depression. Nothing like that at all.''

I could tell from the tone of his voice that Dr. Terry Mulhane felt guilty about Mason Greenleaf's suicide. As he had probably supplied Mason with the sleeping pills that he'd used to kill himself with, I could understand his pain.

"Was this a regular scheduled visit?" I asked.

"No, he just came in for a quick check. Look, I've got a waiting room full of people,'' the man said, as if he wanted to be done with the conversation—and the bad feelings it evoked.

"I have a few other questions, doctor, if you could spare some time later today.''

"Under the circumstances, I can hardly say no," he said, sounding like no was exactly what he wanted to say. He went off the line for a moment, and I could hear him talking to his receptionist. "I should be free 'round six-thirty this evening.''

"I'll come to the office.''

"Mr. Stoner," he said before hanging up, "I knew Mason as a friend and a patient for better than ten years. And the fact that he did what he did is not easy for me to accept—or talk about. You understand that it was my job to keep him well.''

"If it's any consolation, doctor, he didn't tell anyone how close he was to killing himself.''

"I'm afraid that isn't a consolation," the man said.

I glanced at my watch as I put down the phone. It was just a little past noon, which gave me more than enough time to follow up on Ira Sullivan's other suggestions and talk to Mason's colleagues at Nine Mile School, before returning to Corryville for my meeting with Mulhane. Since the CPD building on Ezzard Charles was more or less on the way to Nine Mile, I decided to stop there first and confirm the fact that Greenleaf hadn't had any recent brushes with the law.

The blue sky had clouded up while I was on the phone with Mulhane. By the time I got back down the street, it had begun to rain—a loud pop-up thunderstorm that only lasted the few minutes it took me to walk uptown to the Parkade on Sixth and pick up the Pinto. By the time I pulled into the 'GUC parking lot across from the CPD building, the storm was over and the threatening clouds had begun to divide.

The pavement was so hot that the rain raised a mist on the sidewalks. It trailed me out of the lot and up the pathway that led, between flagpole and cut stone marker, to the front doors of the penal yellow police building. Inside the shifts were changing, and the traffic on the first floor was heavy with patrolmen in summerweights. I made my way through the throng up to Homicide on the third floor. Jack McCain was sitting in an office carrel off the Homicide squad room, staring morosely at an arrest report.

"Did you talk to the girl?" he said, looking up as I came through the door.

I nodded. "She's still got me looking into it."

McCain dropped the arrest report on the desk and fumbled through his shirt pocket for a cigarette. "Well, good luck. We did what we could, you know."

"I know, Jack. It's a kind of therapy for her, I think."

"So what can I do for you?" he said, lighting up.

"A couple of things. For one, you can check to make sure that Greenleaf wasn't having any problems with you guys. Ask around at Vice, Narco, Munie, and Park. I guess it's possible that he could have been picked up using a false name, so you better give them a physical description, too.''

''I'll tell you right now we've had no contact with him since the solicitation thing,'' McCain said flatly. ''I mean, we did do a little checking, Harry, no matter what the girl thinks. But if it'll make you happy, I'll double-check.''

''Thanks. You guys would make a good motive.''

McCain smiled. ''Why not just face the obvious? He was half gay and couldn't keep living half straight?''

It was the same theory that Cavanaugh and Sullivan had advanced—a man who had painted himself into a spot he could no longer live in and who didn't have the will or the hardness of heart to force his way out. It was tidy and quite possibly true. Only it depended entirely on the assumption that Greenleaf's relationship with Cindy Dorn had been a self-deception. From what I'd seen of the woman, I had trouble believing that she wouldn't have scented that out at the start, although it was a fact that she'd feared Greenleaf's past.

''I haven't ruled it out,'' I said to him.

''What else can I do for you?''

''I'd like to take a look at the jacket from Greenleaf's solicitation bust.''

''Jesus Christ, that was six, seven years ago. What the hell would that tell you?''

''Known haunts, MO, acquaintances—something. I mean, the ground is so thin already, I figure anything could be a lead.''

''All right,'' he said, stretching it out with a sigh. ''Go down the hall. Talk to Rob Sabato in Vice. He was IO on the solicitation case. Tell them I said it was okay to give you the jacket.''

''I appreciate the help,'' I said, getting up from the chair.

He gestured with one of his hands, shooing away the gray smoke that hung between us. ''It's okay. But let's not make this into an industry, Harry.''

''I'm just trying to make the woman happy, Jack.''

I walked out of McCain's office and down the hall to the Vice squad room. A sergeant directed me to Ron Sabato, who was sitting at a desk at the back of the room, feet up, reading a classified section of the newspaper. As I approached him, he lowered the paper and stared at me drearily over the top of the page. He was a thin middle-aged man with an acne-scarred face, hinged like a corner at either side of a hawklike nose. His peppercorn hair was cut short, military style, and like mine was going gray at either temple.

"What can I do for you?" he said, all business.

I told him who I was and what I wanted.

"Yeah, I kinda remember the case. Something along the lines. A fag solicitation thing. Teacher goes after high school kid. Right?"

I smiled at his "headline" capsule. "Right."

Sabato put the newspaper down on the desk and patted it with his right palm. "I read these things every day. You never know what you might find. I once busted a prostie ring had an ad in the Gold Chest."

I laughed.

"It was an escort service run out of Dayton. They come down here in a Lincoln Town Car, as many girls as you wanted, come right to your door. The chauffeur was the pimp. It was a sweet little bust."

He got up from the desk and went over to a long metal file. "What was this guy's name again?"

"Greenleaf. Mason Greenleaf."

Sabato opened a drawer and thumbed through the folders. "Might be the jacket's over at A&D, being from so far back." He came to the end of the drawer and nodded. "Yeah, it's A&D. I can call over there. Have it for you maybe late tonight or tomorrow."

"That'd be fine."

"So what's your interest in this case?" he said, closing the file and going back behind the desk.

"The guy killed himself a week ago. The family hired me to look into it."

"Suicides," Sabato said, shaking his head. "They're the worst. Did he leave a note?"

"No."

"Then I'll tell you, fella, you're wasting your time. Ain't nobody gonna figure out the reason why. I had a friend who killed himself, so I know what I'm talking about. My advice would be to tell the family to try to forget it.''

"I've been getting a lot of that advice."

"It's good advice," the guy said. "You should take it."

I wasn't feeling particularly encouraged as I walked back down to the ground floor of the CPD building and across Ezzard Charles to the 'GUC lot. A lot of people, from Del Cavanaugh to hatchet-faced Ron Sabato, had been telling me to quit. If it wasn't for how I felt about the girl, I probably would have. If it wasn't for the girl, I wouldn't have started in the first place.

NINE Mile School was located in Madeira, northeast of the
Kenwood exit of I-71, a cluster of white stucco buildings,
vaguely Spanish in style, nestled in the wooded hillside
above the expressway. It was a little past two when I got out there.
As I turned onto the access road that led to the complex, I passed a
couple of riders in jodhpurs and boots, urging their horses up a trail
beside the road. It was that kind of neighborhood, that kind of
school.

I parked the Pinto close by the entrance gate and stepped out into
dappled shade, redolent of spruce and horse piss. A couple of kids
standing by a red Mercedes watched me closely as I walked across
the gravel lot to the white stucco buildings—like I was someone
who bore watching. The lot was filled with Mercedes and BMWs.

An archway in the front building led me directly onto a pillared
portico, running around a quadrangle of sunburnt grass. On the
complex side of the portico, windowed doors opened onto airy
schoolrooms. I followed a series of signs hung from the rafters to
the main office.

Inside, a plump middle-aged woman in a flouncy peasant dress
was sitting at a desk behind a countertop. She had a haggard face
and long gray-brown hair, cut in bangs and worn in a ponytail down
her back. The length of her hair—or perhaps the fact that she was

still wearing it that long into her late forties or early fifties—made her look a little desperate. The gold in her smile and the peasant colors added to the air of wilted youth.

Behind her and to her right a varnished wood letterbox, stuffed with memos, depended from the wall. The polished wood caught the sunlight coming through the open windows on the lot side of the building. Everything in the room was bright with sunlight, floors, desk, whitewashed walls.

"Can I help you?" the woman said, smiling amid the glare.

"My name is Stoner," I told her. "I'd like to talk to your headmaster about one of your teachers, Mason Greenleaf."

The woman dropped her eyes to the desktop, like she'd been slugged from behind. "You're a police officer?"

"I'm working for Cindy Dorn, a friend of Mason's."

"Of course. I'm Helen Tobler. Assistant headmistress here at Nine Mile."

"Would you mind answering a few questions, Ms. Tobler?"

"No. I wouldn't mind at all. I was very fond of Mason. All of us here were fond of him. It's a terrible tragedy."

She gestured to a chair in front of her desk. "Please sit."

I came around the counter. As I sat down, I noticed that the fingers of the woman's right hand were stained blue with mimeo ink. She caught me staring at them and shrugged. "Can't afford to Xerox everything."

"I would have thought you could," I said, smiling.

"I know," the woman said. "People see the cars in the lot and the horses on the trails and think we're as rich as our clientele. Well, I assure you we are not. Private schools like ours are run on very tight budgets. Most of our staff and personnel do far less well financially than they could in the public schools."

"Then why do they teach here?"

"We offer them small classes and the chance to work with gifted children. You'd be surprised how attractive that is to a certain kind of teacher. The ones for whom teaching is a calling."

"Like Mason Greenleaf?"

She nodded. "Yes, he was extremely dedicated. I would say he was among the most dedicated and effective teachers we had."

"You think it would be possible for me to talk to any of his students?"

The woman sighed, drumming her blue-stained fingers on the desk. "If it were up to me, I'd see no problem with it. But the headmaster, Tom Snodgrass, might object. Frankly, some of the parents might object, too. You understand that one of the things we're supposed to offer is privacy."

"Perhaps I could talk to Snodgrass myself?" I asked.

She nodded. "He's at lunch, but he should be back shortly."

I cleared my throat, trying to think of some decent way to broach the question of Greenleaf's motive for suicide. But the woman didn't need coaxing.

"Obviously, you want to know why Mason did what he did?"

"Yes."

"Of course, I've thought about it quite a lot," she said, leaning back into a sloping beam of sunlight. "And all I can say is that whatever problems he had, he didn't say a word about them to any of us here at Nine Mile. In fact he was such a sweet, positive soul that it makes what happened especially disturbing.

"Frankly, I can't understand it," she said, dropping her eyes again. "Unless something just overwhelmed him, like somebody dying, or maybe finding out that he had cancer, or Cindy leaving him . . . ?"

There was an undisguised note of curiosity in her voice. And who could blame her for being curious? I told her the truth. "He wasn't ill, and he had no recent problems with Cindy."

I didn't mention Del Cavanaugh—given the clean bill of health that Dr. Mulhane had reported, there was no need to broach the subject of AIDS. But I did bring up the solicitation incident from six years past. The off-chance that he'd been enmeshed in a similar situation at Nine Mile was the chief reason I'd come to the school. "You do know that he'd had a problem with a student some years ago?"

Helen Tobler pursed her lips as if she wanted to spit. "The

school board thing was a travesty. But those are the times we are living in. When Mason came to us after being disciplined, we did not hesitate to hire him—and believe me, our standards are the highest. They have to be—they're what our reputation is founded on.''

She didn't mention that Greenleaf had apparently had an in with Tom Snodgrass. It made her umbrage slightly less impressive.

''You aren't aware of any such incident that might have occurred here at Nine Mile?''

''Absolutely not,'' Helen Tobler said flatly. ''In fact I don't believe there was an 'incident' to begin with—just an overzealous father who had lost custody of his son in a divorce hearing and was trying to score points against his ex-wife. Mason became his whipping boy, thanks to the prosecutor's zeal to persecute homosexuals.''

''Prior to the week that he dropped out of school, did Mason seem distant or preoccupied to you?''

''Not to me he didn't,'' Helen Tobler said. ''But our schedules were such that we didn't see a lot of each other that week. He may have complained a bit about the heat, about having trouble sleeping at night. He didn't look particularly well rested, but then neither do I. I mean it's been hot, and our classrooms aren't air-conditioned. You really ought to talk to Tom. He's a longtime friend of Mason's and would have seen more of him than I did. He should be back any minute.''

I glanced at my watch, which was showing a quarter to three. Since I wanted to talk to some of Greenleaf's students, I decided to wait.

I sat in the office for a good quarter of an hour, watching Helen Tobler run circulars off the noisy mimeo machine. After a while she gathered a bunch of the papers in her blue hands and walked around the counter to the door.

''I'm going to distribute a few of these up and down the quad. You're welcome to keep waiting here until Tom gets in.''

A few minutes after she left, a boy came through the door. He was about seventeen, thin, dark-haired, with a sharp-featured, hand-some face. He stood by the counter for a second, staring at me.

"Where's Ms. Tobler?" he said with a touch of suspiciousness, as if I'd done something to her.

It dawned on me that he was one of the kids giving me the eye in the parking lot.

"She's delivering some forms to the classrooms."

"Uh-huh. Who are you?"

He said it like he had a right to ask anybody anything he wanted. Which was probably how he'd been raised and educated. It gave me a slightly different feel for the nature of the student body than the official version I'd gotten from Helen Tobler. "I'm a truant officer," I said.

The kid smiled. "No, you're not. You were asking about Mr. Greenleaf." I wondered just how the hell he knew that, until he glanced at the open window. "I heard you talking."

"You always snoop at the window?"

"I heard you mentioning his name." The kid ducked his head. "It's awful what happened to him."

"You were a student of his?"

The boy nodded solemnly. "I was in his senior honors seminar this summer. I'm Lee Marks."

He held out his hand across the counter, and I started to feel a little better about his manners.

"Harry Stoner," I said, shaking with him.

"Do you know why he did it?" Lee Marks said, resting his elbows on the countertop and staring at me with an earnestness that was touching.

I shook my head. "No, I don't, Lee."

"I couldn't believe it when I heard," Lee Marks said with emotion. "None of us could. He was such a nice guy. It's so unfair."

It's a hard lesson, that one about what's fair. And it's surprising how often you have to learn it before it sticks, if it ever really does.

"Trimble's taken over the class now," the boy went on. "But it's not the same. Greenie was like a kid himself. I mean, he knew how to connect with his students. He wasn't snotty or condescending like most of them are. He made you feel the relevance of whatever he was teaching. It was a gift.'' Lee Marks shook his head again. ''I won't forget him.''

In spite of the fact that we'd gotten off on the wrong foot, I liked Lee Marks who, as Helen Tobler had said about Greenleaf, seemed to be a sweet, positive soul.

''You're going to college in the fall?'' I asked him.

''Harvard.''

Behind him the door opened and a tall, balding man with a thick-lipped, scowling face came into the room. His knobby cheeks were red and sweaty from the heat, adding to his general look of unappeasable ire, like a Hindu god. No one had to tell me that he was the headmaster.

''Who are you?'' he said to me in a no-nonsense voice.

I told him who I was—quick, like a bunny. ''Your assistant, Ms. Tobler, told me to wait here for you.''

The man turned the thermostat down on the red, irritable look. Taking a handkerchief from his pocket, he tamped the sweat on his brow as he walked around the counter toward Helen Tobler's desk. Almost as an afterthought, he glanced back at the boy.

''What is it, Marks?''

''Nothing,'' the kid said, straightening. ''I was just talking to Mr. Stoner.''

That didn't sit well with Tom Snodgrass. ''Get back to class,'' he snapped.

As Snodgrass turned away from him, Lee Marks gave me an odd, inquisitive look. He was out the door and Snodgrass was in my face before I had a chance to make anything of it. But I figured I'd already heard what I needed to hear—that Greenleaf was as well-liked by the groundlings as he'd been by the staff.

''Helen didn't give you permission to talk to the students, did she?'' the man said, sitting down at the desk.

''No. She said I'd have to ask you.''

''Then let me tell you right off that I'd prefer that you didn't talk to them. When a popular teacher like Mason passes away, it's like a death in the family. And when he takes his own life—well, it's even worse. The kids need some time to heal. So do I.''

"Ms. Tobler told me that you two were friends.''

"We went to grad school together, Mace and I, twenty years ago. He's known my wife, Sheila, even longer than that—since college. Quite frankly, neither Sheila nor I can understand why he did this. He was a survivor, Mason.''

I thought about Del Cavanaugh, who was not going to survive, and said, "Sometimes survivors feel guilty.''

Sighing, Headmaster Tom Snodgrass folded the handkerchief up and packed it neatly into a pocket. "I've said the same thing to myself. A lot of Mace's friends, a lot of our friends, have died recently. It adds to the weight, no question. You get up in the morning and you feel heavier, more burdened. Nothing ages you like friends dying, Stoner. It's the real clock on the wall.''

"There wasn't anything troubling him here at school, was there?'' I asked, already knowing what he was going to say. What everyone had said.

"I don't think there was,'' Snodgrass said. "I mean, I can't know what he didn't tell me, but he wasn't complaining about the job, if that's what you mean.''

"Was anyone complaining about him?''

Snodgrass raised his head sharply as if he caught my drift—and didn't much like it. "You're make a reference to his problems with the Cincinnati School Board?''

"I'm just looking for a reason why he killed himself.''

"Do you know what happened six years ago?'' he said, leaning forward across the desk.

"I've heard several different versions.''

"Well, let me tell you the one that I know,'' he said pointedly, as if he felt obliged to dispel the rumors and false impressions. Given the fact that he'd hired Greenleaf after the incident, I could understand his sense of accountability. "I heard this from Mason himself when I interviewed him for this job. And I had it confirmed by a mutual friend, a supervisor in the public school system.''

Snodgrass made a church out of his fingers and stared red-faced over the steeple. "Mason had a student named Paul Grandin, a senior interested in theater arts. Paul was a troubled kid from a split family. His father was a nasty, brutal man who had physically abused Paul from an early age. His mother was an overweening alcoholic who couldn't say no to her husband or to Paul himself. The kid grew up hating both of them and despising himself. He had no confidence, no sense of purpose, and a conflicted sexual identity. As an adolescent, Mason had many of the same problems, so he strongly identified with Paul and treated him the way he wished he'd been treated at that age—with compassion and intelligence. He found the boy a psychotherapist to help him work through his neuroses; he got him a part-time job at the Playhouse-in-the-Park; he encouraged him to become involved in extracurricular activities at school. Naturally the boy was very grateful and very fond of Mason, as Mason was of him. There was never anything more than a bond of affection between them."

"I was told about some letters?"

"If Mason made any mistake, it was writing those notes to Paul," Snodgrass conceded, sinking behind his tented hands. "Paul had graduated that June and gone off to a theater arts camp in Wisconsin before his freshman year at college. Mason wrote the letters to him while Paul was at camp—just as anyone would write to a friend who was away. Paul brought the letters back home with him when he returned to town. Somehow Paul's father found them.

"If a heterosexual had written such a letter to a friend, no one would have thought twice about it. But as you undoubtedly know, Mason was bisexual and, at that time, involved with a man. Apparently someone told the father that Mason was bi, and the father blew up. The police really put Mason through the wringer, you know. If his lawyer hadn't secured a restraining order, I think they would have hounded him to death. Even at that, if he hadn't found Cindy, I'm not sure he would have survived."

Given the upshot, I didn't have much confidence that his relationship with Cindy had been the answer to his problems, either—or that Mason Greenleaf had ever allowed anyone to know what that answer might have been.

Thanking the man for his time, I got up from the chair.

"I'm sorry I couldn't be more help, Mr. Stoner," Tom Snodgrass said. "I hate to say it, but I'd feel less troubled and confused if Mason had been killed by accident or even murdered."

It was a little shocking to hear it put like that. But as I walked back out to the lot, I realized it was just another way of saying that, like everyone else I'd talked to that blistering July day, he really didn't understand why his friend had taken his life.

= 12 =

FEELING discouraged at having struck out with the cops and at Nine Mile, I drove back to the office to check for messages from Sullivan or Sabato. Neither man had called, leaving me pretty much where I'd been that morning—without a lead or much hope of finding one. Even if I got lucky and found Mason's Scotch-drinking friend or the young blond man he'd gotten drunk with in the bar, I had the feeling I wasn't going to get to the bottom of the suicide. Greenleaf's silence had simply been too complete. In spite of his open relationship with Cindy Dorn, it looked to me as if it had been that way for years—hidden in the folds of his cheerfulness and despair, a core of silence that had never changed. I could nibble around its edges for months, wasting my time and Cindy's hopes, and come up with little more than the simple, self-evident formula that Sullivan, Cavanaugh, and Jack McCain had proposed that morning—that he'd killed himself because he was unhappy with his life. Because I liked her and wanted to help her, I'd been trying to see the thing from Cindy's point of view. But I had the feeling there would come a time when even she would have to accept her lover's silence as final.

Around five-thirty, I grabbed a bite to eat at a Chinese restaurant on Sixth Street, then walked uptown to the Parkade. I picked up the Pinto and headed east on the Parkway through the ruins of Over-the-Rhine to Dr. Terry Mulhane's office in Corryville. The late afternoon sun had laid its hand on everything in the north-side slum, firing the red-brick tenements ash white and driving the men and women who lived in them out of their airless rooms and onto the cement stoops. On the sidewalks their kids jeered and jostled, the older ones slap-fighting and darting out into traffic to touch base with the big boys in the BMWs with the black-out windows and the boom boxes going inside like fireworks.

I followed Reading Road out of the slum, north to Taft and then down to Auburn. Terry Mulhane's office was a block beyond the McMillan intersection—a made-over mansion house with French windows and gray Robin Hood trim. It was only a mile from Over-the-Rhine, but it was a different world.

I parked in a lot at the back of the building and walked through the sunlight, around to the front door. Inside, a lone receptionist sat behind a dry-wall divider with a rectangular opening in its center that framed her like a landscape. There was a good deal of New Age artwork on the walls, dolphins and sunsets and kids looking coy. I guess it was supposed to be soothing, but it made my skin crawl.

Even though the door had chimed when I opened it, it took the receptionist a moment to raise her head and ask what I wanted. It could have been that she was tired—she certainly looked tired—but, given the decor, her lack of haste may have been a deliberate mood-setter too.

"My name is Stoner," I told her. "I'm here to talk to Dr. Mulhane."

She nodded indifferently and waved to the empty waiting area, littered at day's end with magazines. I sat in a padded chair, staring at the dolphins and wondering what Mason Greenleaf's New Age medicine man was going to look like. After a time a tall bearded gent with the suffering, doleful face of a feast day saint came out a door beside the reception desk and scanned the room. He wore a white hospital jacket over Dockers and a checked shirt.

"Are you Stoner?" he said, sounding more the martyr than the saint.

"I'm Stoner."

"Terry Mulhane," he said, nodding hello. "I'll give you a few minutes. Then I'm going to go home, eat supper, and collapse. Okay?"

"A few minutes is all I need."

I followed him through the door into a complex of examination rooms. Mulhane pointed to a doorway and I walked through into a paneled office. To my surprise there was nothing New Age about it, just the usual diplomas on the walls, the picture of the wife and kids, a couple of bookshelves for show. There was a couch to one side of the room and a desk the size of a double-oven stove on the other. I took the couch.

"I don't mean to sound like an asshole," Mulhane said, settling behind the desk, "but I've been going since six-thirty this morning, and I'm beat."

"Like I said, it'll just take a few minutes."

Swiveling in his chair the man cupped his hands behind his head and stared at me with curiosity.

"When's the last time *you* saw a doctor, Mr. Stoner?"

"I don't believe in doctors."

He smiled. "Well, I'd advise you to change your religion. You look like you could use a physical."

"I've been up for a while, too."

"Chasing Mason's ghost," Mulhane said with melancholy "Have you had any luck?"

"Not much. None at all, really."

Leaning forward in the chair, the man dropped his hands and folded them in front of him on the desktop. "The best I can come up with is that he simply broke down emotionally. I didn't see it coming. I should have, but I didn't."

Mulhane sat there for a long moment, looking somber. I didn't for a moment doubt the sincerity of his remorse, but his guilt wasn't going to get me anywhere. Nor was the talk about sudden, inexplicable breakdowns. I'd been hearing it all day.

"He may have been upset by a visit to his ex-lover, Del Cavanaugh," I said, trying to turn him to specifics.

Mulhane looked up at me and sighed. "I'm sure he was. He told me he was dreading it."

"Mason told you he'd gone to see Cavanaugh?" I said with surprise.

"He told me he was planning to go."

"When was this?"

Mulhane shuffled through a folder on his desk. "A week ago last Thursday. The last time I saw him. He stopped in that morning to complain about the insomnia."

Presumably before he went to see Cavanaugh that same Thursday afternoon. It wasn't much of a chronology, but it was a start.

"Did he tell you how he'd heard that Cavanaugh was dying?"

"I think I may have told him myself when he came to the office. Del is also a patient of mine."

It certainly blew hell out of my theory that the Scotch-drinking stranger Greenleaf had met on the Wednesday night before he disappeared had told him about Cavanaugh's illness. And it maybe blew hell out of the idea that Cavanaugh was part of the reason for his despair. Whatever had been bothering Greenleaf had clearly started *before* he'd seen his ex-lover, although I supposed the news that he was dying and the subsequent visit to his home could have accelerated his decline.

"If you've been talking to Del," Mulhane went on, "you may have gotten a wrong impression about why Mason went to see him. Del's a bitter man just now. Actually, he's been a bitter man most of his life. And Mason breaking up with him was a blow he never got over. Anyway, Mason didn't go to him because he was still holding a flame. He went out of kindness and a sense of obligation, to say good-bye to a friend."

"It will help Cindy to hear that," I said. "She's tormented by the fear that Mason betrayed her."

"It's natural for her to feel that way, given what Mason did. But I honestly believe that he was happy with her. In fact, Mason once told me that the thing he was most afraid of was losing Cindy. He had in his mind that whatever made him happy wouldn't last very long."

"Why?"

The doctor shook his head. "I guess when people have been telling you that you're undeserving of love for most of your life, it begins to sink in."

The way he was putting it, it sounded like Mason Greenleaf had been primed for suicide for a long time. Which made Mulhane's surprise that he'd gone through with it a bit mystifying.

"If he was this chronically depressed," I said, "why wasn't he in therapy or on medication?"

"Mr. Stoner," Mulhane said, "Mason wasn't clinically depressed. He functioned quite effectively given the load he had to bear, and he did so with unusual grace and good humor. The fears he had were reality-based. Certainly he had every reason to be terrified of AIDS, especially given what has happened to Del. He had reason to fear the loss of love—his past was checkered with broken relationships. It bothers me that people, even many professionals, automatically assume a pathogenesis because someone is occasionally and reasonably unhappy. Mason Greenleaf was not without considerable resources."

It was the first time he'd sounded like a guru. But it was an enlightened kind of guruism, based on close, affectionate observation of his patient. Clearly Mulhane was the kind of doctor who treated the "whole" person. And just as clearly, Greenleaf had been his friend. Which must have made his suicide especially painful.

"Something must've happened during that week after I saw him," he said, as if he'd been reading my mind, "some awful blow. I have to believe that whatever it was hit him where he was weakest, where he was most afraid."

"That he would lose Cindy," I said, completing the thought.

"That's my best guess."

It was a new theory and, on the surface, not a particularly persuasive one, given the fact that Cindy Dorn hadn't even hinted at a possible breakup.

"When he came to see you on Thursday afternoon, did he talk about any trouble with Cindy?" I asked.

"Not specifically," Mulhane said. "But looking back on it, I can't help thinking there was some sort of coded message in Mason's complaints. Something that I just missed at the time. I've gone over it again and again, trying to decipher it. But frankly, save for the fact that the visit was unscheduled, it was so much like his usual office check-ups that I can't be certain that I'm not reading my own remorse into what he said."

"What exactly did he say?"

"He complained that he was tired, that he hadn't been able to sleep. He said he'd had a number of bad dreams."

"Did he tell you what the dreams were about?"

"Cindy, Del, Ralph Cable."

"Who is Cable?"

"Mason's college roommate at Rutgers. Mason had a love affair with Cable, and Cable took advantage of it to more or less blackmail Mason into giving him cash and other possessions. It was a particularly crushing experience for Mason—one that set the tone for many future disappointments."

"Do you know if he saw Cable again recently?"

"Cable is dead," Mulhane said. "He was killed in Viet Nam in 1971."

The next question was obvious. "You think it was possible that someone else was blackmailing him?"

"I think that would be the sort of thing you would be best equipped to find out. But I'll say this, Mason was not the naïve, trusting soul he'd been when he was a college kid. I doubt if anyone could have extorted money from him simply by threatening to reveal that he was homosexual or bisexual."

In light of the storm he'd weathered after the Paul Grandin scandal, I doubted it, too. Still it was the first thing like a lead that I'd come across—something I could easily check out by examining Greenleaf's bank statements.

"At the time I thought the dreams were symptomatic of Mason's usual complex of anxieties. He tended to convert them into physical complaints, and fatigue and sleeplessness were nothing new. I gave him a prescription without thinking twice about it."

I could see where the Seconals had become a major regret. "He could have gotten the sleeping pills anywhere."

Terry Mulhane stared at me blankly. "What are you talking about?"

"The pills you prescribed. Seconals."

"I didn't prescribe Seconals," Mulhane said defensively. "Mason was a heavy drinker, and I'd never prescribe sleeping pills for a drinker. I gave him Buspar, a tranquilizer that isn't potentiated by alcohol."

"The coroner's report said he died of barbiturate poisoning."

"You're sure?"

"Yes."

Looking surprised, the doctor sat back in his chair. "Where the hell did he get the Seconals?"

"He didn't see any other doctors, did he?"

"Not that I know of."

I wasn't sure what to make of it, save that it was something else to look into. I got up from the couch.

"You've been a help," I said to Mulhane. And he had been.

Terry Mulhane scrubbed savagely at his beard with the back of his hand. "I'm still mystified by the Seconal thing. I just assumed Mason overdosed on alcohol. You think you could get me a copy of the coroner's report, so I can double-check the finding?"

"Sure, I can."

"I gotta tell you, Stoner, you're not the kind of man I thought you would be. I was afraid you were taking advantage of an ugly situation, taking advantage of Cindy."

"Believe me, doc, I'll be happy to get this thing over with."

"We all will," he said.

= 13 =

MASON Greenleaf's bad dreams about an ex-lover turned blackmailer didn't constitute much of a lead, but they were what I had. Besides, I figured it wouldn't take much work to check them out—just a quick look at Greenleaf's bank books. To do that I was going to need a key to Greenleaf's condo, which meant I was going to have to talk to Cindy Dorn. Since I wanted to talk to her anyway, I went back to the office and dialed her at home. I didn't plan on raising the possibility of blackmail with her—not until I came across solid proof. But it had also occurred to me that finding a money trail might tell me where Greenleaf had spent the last four days of his life. Anyway, that was the excuse I was going to use.

A man answered Cindy's phone on the second ring. "Yello," he said. "Cindy Dorn's residence."

There was enough Tennessee in the guy's voice to make me guess he was Greenleaf's brother.

"Can I speak to Cindy?"

"Sure can."

He went off the line and Cindy came on. "I'll handle it, Sam," I heard her say off the line before she said, "Hello."

"Cindy, it's Harry. You've got company, huh?"

I could hear her cup her hand over the receiver. "You don't know the half of it."

"I may need to get into Mason's condo again."

"Why?"

"Nothing important," I said. "Just a routine check of his bank statements—see if he had any unusual expenses before he died. Something I should have done a long time ago."

"All right. If you pick me up, I'll go with you over to Mason's. Maybe we can get Mason's car, too, on the way back. Anything to get the hell out of this house for as long as possible," she said, dropping her voice to a whisper.

"I'll be out there in about thirty minutes."

After finishing with Cindy, I went through the messages on the answering machine. Ron Sabato had called to tell me that he'd located Greenleaf's jacket and that I could pick it up at Vice after eleven that evening. Someone else had called but hadn't left a name or a message. There was no word from Ira Sullivan.

I took the elevator down to the street and headed west up Sixth to the Parkade. Although I was hungry again, I could wait until after I checked Greenleaf's condo before eating. Later in the night I'd stop at Stacie's and try to get a name.

I caught the expressway on Sixth Street and pulled up in front of Cindy Dorn's house a little past nine. There was still enough light in the sky to fill the yard with the barbed shadow of the hawthorn tree, twisting across the grass and walk.

A car was parked in Cindy's driveway, a red Seville burnished cinnamon in the sunset. A tall gray-haired man was bent behind it, shifting luggage around in the trunk. As I pulled in, he turned around and stared. He was wearing yellow hunting glasses, with the sunset reflected in each lens.

When I got out of the Pinto, he strode down the driveway to greet me. His loud voice and long shadow got to me before he did.

"Hey, there!" he said. "I guess you must be Harry Stoner." He held out his hand. "Sam Greenleaf, Mace's older brother."

I shook with him.

In the face he looked a little like his brother, only more robust and less bedeviled by life. He was taller than Greenleaf had been, judging from the one photo I'd seen of Mason. Hair cut short at the sides, military-style. There was a good deal of barracks in the way he held himself too, ramrod straight with his feet a pace apart and his hand folded at ease behind his back. He was dressed as if he'd just stepped off the links—checked pants, white belt, white shoes, golf shirt.

"Been wanting to meet you," he said in his hale, too-loud voice. "I hear you've done a fine job for Cindy."

"I haven't done anything yet," I said, wondering where the hell he'd gotten that notion—or whether he was just blowing hard. He had that air about him.

"We stopped in to say good-bye to Cindy. Firm up a few things about Mason's estate. Terrible thing, this thing about Mace. Terrible." He cast his burning yellow eyes down to his white leather shoes. "I guess Cindy's told you we weren't a particularly close family. Maybe we haven't seen as much of each other as we should've done, living in different cities like we all do. But as you get older, you drift apart. Life just works out that way. Nobody's to blame."

It occurred to me that that had been the point of his foray: that nobody was to blame. But I was wrong.

"Look, I want to say something to you before we go inside," he said, lowering his voice and leaning his head toward me, close enough that I could smell the stink of cigarettes on his breath. "This thing's been a real blow to my sister. Hell, it would've killed my parents if they were still alive. I mean, it would've killed them. The point here is, we don't really need to know all the gruesome details. What happened is bad enough, without dragging Mace through some mud patch. Like I told the police, let the dead bury the dead."

He didn't know what I was going to uncover. But he'd clearly seen enough of Mason's life to fear the worst—and the publicity that could possibly attend it. It was another unfortunate echo of the Lessing case. Ira Lessing's family had wanted to disown the truth, too, along with their dead son. It made me feel sorry for Mason Greenleaf, who had lived and died an outcast of his own kin.

"I'm working for Ms. Dorn," I said. "You'll have to take it up with her."

"I know who the hell you're working for," the man barked, and then smiled like his teeth hurt—to cover the outburst.

"We're Mason's closest kin, me and my sister," he said, moderating his tone. "And we'd just as soon you left this situation alone. That's all I wanted to say. Take it for what it's worth."

"I'll keep it in mind," I said.

The man shifted uneasily on his feet. Having said his piece, he was finished with me—like an officer who's given an order to a subordinate.

"Y'all a friend of Cindy's, huh?" he said, trying small talk. He smiled again, but the smile wasn't entirely friendly and neither was the way he'd put the question.

"I just met her a few weeks ago."

Sam Greenleaf chose to let that drop, along with his aspersion and any further attempt to make conversation.

"Well, let's get on inside, then." Greenleaf waved his hand at the front door, as if he'd taken possession of Cindy's house.

I followed him up the short path to the front door. Inside I could hear a woman talking nervously in a high-pitched southern voice.

I stepped out of the twilight into Cindy Dorn's narrow, oblong living room. Cindy was on the couch, staring with a glazed look at a smartly dressed blonde sitting on the chair across from her. The woman, whom I took to be Greenleaf's sister, had the tan, high-cheeked, drum-tight face of an aging Junior Leaguer. One of those moneyed, half-pretty women who do good and drink. The room was still a shambles of plastic plates and folding chairs, leftover food and coffee.

"Found me a penny," Sam Greenleaf said, bending down and picking a coin off the shag rug. "Must be my lucky day."

Cindy flinched. "I haven't had time to do a lot of cleaning."

"Don't have to apologize," Greenleaf said, putting the penny down on the coffee table in front of the couch.

"Heavens, no," the blond woman said, casting a reproachful eye at her brother. She turned to me, smiling. "I'm Cassie Greenleaf. Mason's sister. And you're Mr. Stoner. Cindy said you'd be coming. I want to thank you for the help you've been to Cindy and to us. The past few days have been so awful."

She put a trembly hand to her brow. "So awful."

"Cassie," Sam Greenleaf said sharply, "don't let's start up again. We got a long trip ahead." Turning to me, Greenleaf said, "Sit down, Stoner."

He took the other end of the couch, leaving me a folding chair beside the door. Cindy Dorn gave me a hapless look.

"You know what I don't understand?" Cassie Greenleaf said, as if she were picking up the strand of a previous conversation. "How can the police be sure that Mace intended to do this thing? How can they be sure it wasn't an accident? People do have such accidents, don't they? Drink too much and take a sleeping pill. Isn't that what happened to—who was that woman, that gossip columnist used to be on TV?"

"Kilgallen," Sam Greenleaf said quickly, as if it were a rerun of a quiz show.

"Yes, that's right. And there have been lots of others. Sometimes people have accidents that can kill them."

The brother shook his head. "It wasn't an accident. You know it, and so do I. Mace has been lost to us since he left home. And there wasn't a thing we could do to bring him back."

Cassie Greenleaf laughed scornfully. "Like you even tried."

Sam Greenleaf flushed with embarrassment. "Now ain't the time to go into this, Cassie."

"Why, because we got a stranger in the house?" the sister said with a practiced malice that made me certain that they'd played this scene any number of times before, over any number of things. "Not once since he moved away did you show him any kind of love or understanding. Not once. He respected you, Sam. You were his older brother."

Cindy Dorn put her hands to her face, as if her head were about to split open and she were trying to hold it together by main force. "Please," she said. "Could we please not do this again?"

The brother and sister stared at her for a moment, then looked away at opposite sides of the room.

"I'm sorry," Cassie Greenleaf said in a whisper. "We're not usually like this, if you can believe it. And I wouldn't blame you if you can't."

"There has been a lot of strain," the brother said in what was, for a man like him, close to an apologetic tone. "No one wanted this to happen. No one." He looked over at me. "You didn't ever find out who he was with there at the end? At that bar?"

"No."

"Surely somebody ought to find out," he said unthinkingly, before he realized where that line would lead him.

"The men he was with in the bar didn't leave with him," I said. "Mason was by himself when he died."

"Alone," Greenleaf said dismally, as if that was less of a comfort than he'd expected it would be.

The sister started to cry openly. The brother put a hand to his brow.

"I think we better call it a night," Cindy Dorn said, getting up from the couch.

"Yes, we should go," Sam Greenleaf said to his sister, who was still weeping. "We got a six-hour drive to Nashville." He turned to Cindy. "I'll come up in a week or so and settle Mason's affairs. If there's anything you want from his house, you just . . ." He looked down at the floor. "Anything you want."

It took another ten minutes to get the Greenleafs out of the house, into the car, and on their way to Tennessee. Cindy maintained a thin-lipped show of politeness almost to the end. But when Cassie Greenleaf tried to kiss her good-bye, she simply turned her face away. Trembling, the sister started to cry again, as the brother led her by the hand to the Seville.

"You see what you've done," she moaned to Sam Greenleaf. "Now she hates me because of your bullying."

"Just get the hell in the car," he snapped. "You can run to your shrink when you get home. Tell him any goddamn thing you want."

"Jesus Christ," Cindy whispered, as we watched them pull out of the driveway and off into the night. "Can you imagine being related to them? That braying jackass actually had the nerve to tell me that Mason's problems were all in his head, like a brain tumor."

"He's certainly washed his hands of him at this point. The brother more or less told me he didn't want me to continue to investigate."

"Of course he doesn't want to continue. The blood might end up on his front door." She blew some steam out of her mouth. "You said you needed to get into Mason's condo?"

"If you can handle it."

"After that crew, I can handle anything."

On the way over to Mount Adams, I filled Cindy in on the little that I'd learned that day. Just going over it in my own mind reminded me of how vague it really was—speculative and inconclusive opinions, divided somewhat depressingly between gay and straight. The only good news—and it *was* good news for Cindy—was that it didn't appear that Greenleaf had been betraying her with Del Cavanaugh. I'd expected her to be greatly relieved, but she didn't react with relief. Instead she curled up in the car seat and didn't say a thing.

After a time I asked her what was wrong.

"Everything," she said miserably. "Seeing his brother and sister, how ashamed they are of him, even now. Hearing what his gay friends said about him—about me. Like they're gossiping about some dead actor and his fag-hag moll, when he was just this shy, decent, mixed-up man. It's disgusting to be everybody's meat."

"It doesn't change who he was," I said, "or who you are."

"Everything's changed," she said angrily. "*He* changed everything by what he did. And now I've got to live with it. With the ugly inconclusive horror of it. I mean, you were in that hotel room with me. You saw what he looked like—what Sam and Cassie are so embarrassed to call their own. What Sully and Del say he was doomed to come to. What the rest of them are wondering if I drove him to.''

I didn't say anything.

''I mean, so what if he wasn't with Del? So what? He left me alone, without a word.''

''You want to forget about this, Cindy?'' I said.

''Yes, I want to forget about it. But I can't. I can't sleep, and I can't stand to be awake. So what do you suggest?''

By then, we were at the foot of Mount Adams, climbing the hillside. Instead of turning onto Celestial, I drove up past the bar district and parked beneath some maple trees, in a little cul-de-sac overlooking the river. It was dark and fairly quiet, save for crickets and the distant bar noise.

''I'm sorry,'' Cindy said, after sitting there in silence for some time. ''I'm just fresh out of inner resources. All the people who've been parading through the house. Seeing my dirty socks, my dirty house, my dirty, screwed-up life. I feel completely exposed.'' She hugged her arms around her breasts. ''And alone.''

She leaned her head back against the seat and looked over at me. I felt a surge of protectiveness run through me like a current. Without thinking, I pulled her to me and kissed her on the mouth. After a moment she drew back and stared at me uncertainly.

''Are we going to do this thing?'' she said, asking it more of herself than of me—although it was a damn good question.

''Do you want to do it?'' I asked.

''I don't know. My needs are pretty enormous right now.'' She stared at me uneasily. ''I could fall in love with you, Harry.''

''What would be wrong with that?'' I said, knowing full well that there could be plenty wrong with it—for me as well as for her. A part-time drunk who'd been living without real hope or attachments for the better part of a decade.

''It's what I used to do when I had a problem,'' Cindy said in a small voice. ''Fall in love. Usually with the wrong guy.''

I inched back in the seat. ''You have to do what's right for you.''

''Don't be mad. I wasn't talking about you. I was talking about me.''

"I'm not mad, Cindy. You're right to be careful. You should think about this. Maybe we both should."

She gave me a shy, sidelong look. "What you said at the hospital, about being on different stars, scared me. You live in a cold place."

"I've seen a different side of life than you have," I said, feeling more stung by what she said than I had any right to be. What she had said was true.

"I didn't say it scared me away. It's just—there are some things about me you don't know. Things you *should* know, maybe. I mean aside from the fact that my last lover was bisexual."

I didn't say anything.

"That doesn't bother you?"

I told her the truth. "Yeah, it bothers me. But you had safe sex. And I haven't wanted to take a chance on anyone for so long, I figure I can't let it matter."

"You're honest enough." Leaning over, she caressed my cheek, then kissed me on the mouth. "I'm not a cock tease, you know. You don't know me very well yet, but believe me, I'm not."

Smiling, I said, "I believe you."

I started the car, nervously feeling as if I'd actually taken a chance for the first time in about ten years—reached out and grabbed the Opportunity I'd always seem to let pass by. It was unsettling, because the old familiar drunk in me had planned to let her pass by, too. Apparently, the rest of me had different priorities.

☰ 14 ☰

IT was past ten by the time we pulled up in front of Mason Greenleaf's condo. After what had begun in the car, I'd expected Cindy to react badly when she saw the place. But if she felt any guilt, she held it in. At least, at first she did.

We parked on Celestial and walked through the salty white patches of street light over to the Chinese red door. Cindy opened it with a key she had taken from her purse. The breath of that burning summer breathed out of the dead house. The smell of heat and dead plants and Mason Greenleaf. Cindy turned away.

"I don't know if I can go in," she said, leaning heavily against the jamb.

"Then let me do it."

I went through the door into the dark, burning living room. Navigating by memory I found the spiral staircase leading to the second floor, and a wall switch that shot a focused spot directly down the staircase. I climbed up through the light to the bedroom. His enameled desk was on the right. I went over to it and flipped on a lamp. I already knew where the bank books were. I'd seen them in the desk drawer the first time I'd searched the room—a leather-bound check register and a savings book mixed in with his school papers. I took them from the drawer and laid them on the desktop, then sat down in his chair and started to go through them.

The savings book was current through the week of July 10, the week he had disappeared. Even though I knew the man came from money, the balance staggered me. It was in the high six figures. Every month a deposit of three grand had been made to the account —probably his paycheck from Nine Mile. Every three months there was a much larger deposit of ten thousand dollars, possibly from a trust fund or another savings account. The withdrawals were just as consistent—weekly transfers of from five hundred to a thousand dollars.

The check register showed me where the savings transfers had gone. He had kept a constant balance of three or four thousand dollars in the checking account. All expenditures were neatly laid out in a fine hand. The week before he disappeared, he'd spent his usual amounts on groceries, credit cards, phone bill, CG&E, tickets to the summer opera, Playhouse-in-the-Park, and Riverbend. On Tuesday, July 12, two days before he'd dropped out of sight, he'd made his last entry: a check made out to cash in the amount of a thousand dollars. It was a fairly large sum, but there were several other such checks scattered throughout the previous months. As far as I could see, there was nothing in his records to indicate that he was being blackmailed or that he was planning any kind of major change.

As I was flipping back through the checkbook, examining earlier months, Cindy Dorn came up the stairs.

"They're still delivering his mail," she said shakily. "I've got to call the post office and tell them to stop."

She went over to the bed, sat down, and put her face in her hands. I went over and sat down next to her, putting my arm around her shoulder.

"I'm okay," she said, sounding not at all okay. "Did you find anything?"

"No. Nothing. Just an ordinary week with one slightly larger than usual check made to cash on Tuesday. No other entries."

"We were supposed to go to the opera on Friday. *Werther.*" She laughed dully. "Appropriate, huh?"

"I don't know much about it."

Cindy smiled. "I didn't either. It was Mason's passion, opera and theater."

"Yeah, I saw. Riverbend, the Playhouse. He kept you busy."

"He was fun. He knew a lot about a lot of things."

"And he was rich," I said, feeling overmatched.

"That didn't matter. I was never into rich. Neither was he. I mean, it was nice to go all those places, but I just went to be with him. I'm kind of a homebody, really." She glanced at me nervously. "Jesus, let's get out of here. I'm beginning to feel uncomfortable again—and guilty."

"Okay." I helped her up.

"Do you think we're ever going to know what happened to him, Harry?" she said as we walked over to the stair.

"You want the truth?"

"Always."

"No, I don't."

Cindy sighed. "Then maybe it's time to stop."

The police impoundment lot was located on Gest Street, near Dalton. To get there, I had to circle back down through town onto the Ninth Street overpass, through the west side industrial flat. As soon as we got off the hill, Cindy relaxed.

"It was just being there," she said, trying to explain her nerves. "Seeing the letters, knowing he would never read them."

"It's bound to happen. You loved him. You still do."

"Yes," she said. "But I honestly don't know if I can forgive him. We never lied to each other, Mason and I—that was the basis of our relationship, that was why he was so dear to me. The other men I've known—the ones that I loved—I was always the one who was up front, laying myself open like a fool and getting burned for it. With Mason there was a mutual trust. That's the thing that's so hurtful. I *did* trust him."

It probably wasn't in my own interest, but I said it anyway. "Nobody who I talked to today thought that he didn't love you."

"Then why did he kill himself?"

"It didn't have to do with you, Cindy. It had to do with him. He had a lot of fears, a lot of conflicts. Seeing Cavanaugh dying of AIDS, maybe, triggered a panic. He'd been to the doctor that week already on Thursday, complaining about fatigue, insomnia, bad dreams.''

"Mason's bad dreams," she said, as if they were a familiar subject.

"He'd had them before?"

"When he was stressed out at school, during exams or the opening week of classes. Bad dreams about me, Del, Sully, Ralph Cable. Cable was often in them.''

"Do you know why?"

"I guess because he associated Cable with school. He was Mason's college roommate. They had a rocky relationship that ended when Cable went to Viet Nam. Unfortunately, he got killed over there. His death seemed to haunt Mason. He always thought Cable had volunteered to prove a point about his manhood after Mason threw him out. Anyway, Mason felt partly responsible for what happened. The bad feeling between them when they parted was something he could never go back and undo.''

He'd dreamed about friends who had failed him, friends whom he had failed, friends with whom he wished to make amends. Dreams he'd had before, when he was under stress on the job. Only he hadn't been under any stress at work—at least, none that I could discover. No trouble with the cops, either. And in spite of what I'd said to Cindy, I wasn't really convinced that Del Cavanaugh and a fear of AIDS had triggered Mason's depression—not after talking to Mulhane. I didn't know what had driven him to kill himself. And as I told Cindy, I wasn't sure that I ever would. But it was moot now that she had decided to call it quits. It was a healthy step away from bad memories, I thought, for both of us: Greenleaf and Lessing.

I turned onto Gest Street. Up ahead I could see the fenced impoundment lot. A tin-roofed plank shack by the front gate served as a watch post. I pulled through the gate and parked by the door of the shack.

"Do you have keys and registration?" I asked.

Cindy nodded. "Mason gave me a spare set of keys. I took the registration with me that day—when we went to the hotel."

I got out on my side, Cindy on hers. Together we walked through the white glare of the spotlights, up a short stair to the open door of the guard house. Inside a lanky cop with a SWAT cap on his head was sitting behind a battered desk, working a crossword puzzle and listening to a Reds game on a table radio.

"Can I do for you?" he said listlessly.

Cindy handed him the registration. "It's my friend's car," she said.

The cop swiveled around and pulled a clipboard from a nail on the wall, turning back to us as he ran a finger down the impound-ment sheet. "We've had it for a while. Hauled it in a week ago last Wednesday from Stacie's parking lot. Got a twenty-five-dollar tow-ing charge and twenty-five dollars a day storage." Looking up at Cindy, he said, "Tell your friend there are cheaper ways to park."

He glanced pointedly at me, as if he thought I was the unnamed friend.

While Cindy wrote out a check for the impoundment fee, I went out into the yard to look for the Saab. The cop had it located near the northwest corner of the lot. The spotlights didn't cover all of the grounds, so it took me a while to find it—parked on the Dalton Street side, in a dark, weedy patch of gravel. Like the other vehi-cles, it had the license number and date of impoundment soaped on its back window. Like the other vehicles, it was covered with days of inner city dust and grime.

I dug a rag out of a heap of tires and junk parts stashed by the fence and wiped off the front windshield. I was working on the back window, when Cindy came up.

"You want to drive it back to your place?"

She shuddered. "I'd rather you did. Just seeing it, abandoned like this . . ."

"Okay. You follow me in the Pinto."

Cindy dug through her purse for the spare keys and handed them to me. I unlocked the driver's side door and hopped in, handing her my keys.

"If you have any trouble with the Pinto, flash your lights."

"What kind of trouble?" she said suspiciously.

"It's got its quirks," I said with a laugh.

Looking like she didn't think it was very funny, Cindy walked off, making her way through the jumble of abandoned cars.

After four days in the sun, the interior of the Saab stank strongly of overheated vinyl and leather and something like rot. I opened the windows to air it out, then got in and turned on the ignition. On the third try, it turned over with a gargle and spit of exhaust. I backed it out of the parking spot and weaved my way to the front gate. Cindy was sitting there in the Pinto, ready to go.

"I'll catch the expressway on Ezzard Charles," I called to her. "That okay?"

She nodded.

I coasted out of the lot with Cindy right behind me. I stayed on Western up past the Terminal, cutting under the expressway to the entrance ramp at Liberty.

It wasn't until I got on I-75 that I began to notice the other smell, the one I'd thought was dry rot. I might not have noticed it at all, if I hadn't rolled up the windows to cut the wind noise. But in there with the heat and leather and July smog was something else—faint, familiar, and disquieting. The too-sweet smell of decaying blood.

I almost jerked the car off the road, but we were halfway to Finneytown by then. I rolled down the window again to let some air in and glanced nervously around the interior of the car. I didn't see any blood on the leather seats or dash. It was too dark to get a good look at the floor. I had to live with the stink for the ten more minutes it took to get to the yellow brick house.

As soon as I pulled in the driveway, I flipped on the interior lights of the Saab and began searching the car. I was halfway into the backseat when Cindy pulled up behind me. The sudden flash of the Pinto's headlights through the Saab's rear window lit up the interior, and that was when I saw it. Dried brown streaks of blood down the back of the driver's side seat, on the backseat itself, and a dried pool on the backseat carpeting with a froth of fungus growing around it like a bad spot on bread. There wasn't a great deal of blood—as much as might come from a broken nose and split lip. If the car hadn't been locked in the merciless heat for four or five days, it probably wouldn't have grown so rank.

Cindy flipped the Pinto's headlights off, and the Saab's interior went dark again. I heard the Pinto door open and shut as I backed out of Mason's car.

"What is it, Harry?" Cindy said, coming up the driveway.

"There are some bloodstains in the backseat," I said, straightening up.

"Blood," she said, throwing a hand to her mouth.

"Yeah."

"What should we—should we call the cops?"

If there had been more of it, I wouldn't have hesitated. But there wasn't enough to prove homicidal mayhem. Nothing like the charnel of Ira Lessing's front seat. All the bloodstains demonstrated was more sloth on the part of the IOs, Segal and Taylor, who had obviously had the car towed without checking it out. Greenleaf had had contusions on his face and body when the cops found him. It was entirely possible that he'd fallen down outside the bar—or gotten into a fight with his argumentative friends—and simply sat in the car for a time, drunk, dazed, and bleeding. It struck me that Stacie's was where I had to go—to straighten out a good deal of Mason Greenleaf's last few hours on earth. It also struck me that I *should* get a copy of the autopsy report for Terry Mulhane, to see what he made of those vague contusions that the cops and the coroner had dismissed as meaningless. Since I had to pick up the arrest report on the SCPA thing anyway, I decided to stop at CPD and get the coroner's report, too, before heading on to the bar—and wherever else that took me.

Cindy was still standing with her hand to her mouth, looking appalled. "What're we going to do?" she said again.

"I'll talk to Jack McCain tonight," I told her. "Tell him what we found. He's probably not going to be overly impressed—I mean, Mason did have some bruises on him when he was found in the hotel. If he agrees to send an IO out, fine. If not—well, we can get a specialist of our own to do phenotyping if it comes to that. In the meantime, I'm going to make some inquiries at the bar where the car was parked. If Mason was involved in some violence, it looks like it would've happened there.''

"He got . . . beat up?''

"Cindy, I don't know. I suppose it's possible, although the hotel clerk at the Washington didn't say that he looked beat-up when he registered.''

It occurred to me that that was another stop I should make—the Washington Hotel.

"I don't get it. Why didn't the cops find this? I mean, this changes things, doesn't it?''

"We know why the cops didn't find it,'' I said with disgust, "and it doesn't change the fact of his suicide. But it sure as hell might have a bearing on the sequence of events that led up to it. I just don't know enough to say.''

Cindy slapped her hand on the car. "I don't want you to stop, Harry. I want you to keep going until you find out the truth of what happened to him. I owe that to Mason.''

I didn't want to get into the question of what she owed to him. But the truth was, the bloodstains *did* change things enough that I couldn't honestly talk her out of continuing the investigation, even though it pulled us both back into the past.

15

I WENT straight downtown to the CPD and looked up Jack Mc-Cain in Homicide. I told him about the blood I'd found in the backseat of Greenleaf's car. He stared at me blankly for a long moment, then snatched the phone up off his desk.

"Larry," he barked into the receiver, "I want a criminalistics team sent out to—" He cupped his hand over the mouthpiece and glared at me. "What's the house number?"

I gave him Cindy's address on Blue Jay Drive.

He repeated the street number over the phone. "Talk to the woman. Cynthia Dorn. Get a blood sample out of the backseat of the Saab in her driveway and dust the whole damn car for prints. If Segal and Taylor are still on duty, get them to oversee it. If they're at home, wake their asses up. The lazy sons-of-bitches should have done this job in the first place."

McCain hung up the phone with a bang. "Satisfied?"

"Yeah."

"You should be," he said, looking pissed off. "This doesn't make a goddamn bit of sense. The guy killed himself. Whether or not he had a bloody nose in the backseat of that car, he still killed himself."

"It should have been done, Jack. You know it, and so do I."

"Yeah, it should've," he conceded. "That's why I'm sending

those cocksuckers out there. But this doesn't mean anything like I'm reopening the case. You understand that?''

"I understand.''

"You gotta make her understand it, too, Stoner. Because this is it. No more from us. We'll run your prints and your blood. What you do with the results is up to you.''

I stopped at Vice to pick up Greenleaf's jacket and put in a request for a copy of the coroner's report through hatchet-faced Ron Sabato—I didn't have the nerve to ask Jack McCain. The folder Ron gave me was going to take a while to parse: arresting officers' reports, investigating officers' report, witness interviews. The one thing that caught my eye as I thumbed through it on the way back to the car was a Polaroid snapshot of a blond kid with a pale, peroxided mustache. The IOs' report identified the boy as Paul Grandin, Jr., of 243 Rue de la Paix in Clifton—the student that Mason Greenleaf was accused of soliciting in 1988. The photo was six years old, and I had no idea how six years might have changed Paul Grandin's appearance. But if he still wore a mustache and hadn't dyed his hair, he fit the description of the younger man who had been drinking with Mason Greenleaf in Stacie's bar. Then again, so did the guy I passed on Elm Street, pushing a shopping cart full of empties to the recycling center.

It was almost midnight when I pulled into Stacie's lot on lower Fifth. The bar was located in a deserted dell beneath the I-71 distributor—a converted office building with an ornate Sullivanesque facade. To the west, up Fifth Street, the city ended in a rubble of red brick, like a fallen wall. To the east, a dark stretch of Broadway ran haywire through the pillars of the overhead distributor. There were no other buildings nearby.

As I got out of the car, three men came out the door of the bar and down a short staircase to the parking lot. The one in the middle was so drunk, he had to be held up by his buddies on either side. I watched them walk toward the south end of the lot. Once they cleared the pale of the neon beer signs flashing in Stacie's windows, I had to strain to see them—the lighting was that poor. With the noise coming from the bar and the overpass above it, it was difficult to hear, too. All in all, a good spot for a mugging.

I walked over to the staircase and up to Stacie's front door. The closer I got, the louder the noise grew—a typical bar racket of voices, glassware, and music. Through the front door, another flight of stairs led up to the bar proper. The place was crowded with men, most of them dressed in ordinary summer wear. A scattered few sported the cliché motorcycle leather jackets, caps, and chains, still dressing up like Brando in *The Wild Ones*. But they were the exceptions. Most of the men had the tame, buttoned-down look of United American bookkeepers. Middle-class professionals, looking for privacy and safe company in the age of AIDS.

I found a table to myself near one of the side windows. While a waiter in a white shirt with a garter on each sleeve brought me a beer, I looked around. The bar occupied two stories, with the second floor torn out and made into a landing that surrounded the first. Upstairs a rock band was going like a storm siren. Downstairs the room pulsed with talk. To my left, a long, mirrored bar with a chrome rail and chrome-edged stools ran halfway down the room. The liquor bottles lined up behind it were lit softly from panels below. Outside of a few baby spots, it was the brightest light in the place. It occurred to me that Greenleaf and his friends would have to have been making quite a ruckus to stand out in that dim, noisy room. Either that, or someone who knew him or his friends had been keeping an eye on them.

The waiter came back with the beer. Polishing the table with a washrag, he set the bottle and glass down in front of me. He was a thin, pale, black-haired kid in his early twenties, with heavy-lidded eyes and a scraggly mustache that had been filled in with mascara to make him look grown up.

"Two bucks." He had to shout to make himself heard.

I handed him a five. "Keep it."

He nodded. "You're new to Stacie's, aren't you?"

"You know all the customers by sight?"

"Pretty much. Most of 'em. You just get into town?"

"This month. I was looking for a friend."

"Aren't we all?" the kid said, smiling.

"The guy's name is Mason Greenleaf. You know him?"

The waiter thought about it for a moment. "I don't know the name. What's he look like?"

I described Mason to him.

"Still doesn't ring a bell," he said. "You should talk to Maxie, the bartender." He nodded toward the long, dim bar. "He's been here forever. If anyone could tell you, it's him." The kid slapped his washcloth over his shoulder. "You can't find your friend, maybe you'd like to have a drink with me. I'm off at two-thirty."

He walked into the crowd, glancing at me heavy-eyed over his shoulder, like it was WWII and we were saying good-bye at the railroad station. As soon as he was out of sight, I downed my beer, then went over to the bar. As I sat down on a stool, the bartender came over to get my order. He was a huge, fat man with a curly red beard and red hair cut in a crew on top and tied in a short pigtail in back. He wore a gold earring in his right ear and a bib apron with a picture of Paul Prudhomme on it.

"What can I get you?" he said.

"I'll take a Cutty, straight up."

Turning to the bar, he grabbed a bottle with a chrome snout and flipped an ounce of booze into a shot glass. "There you go," he said, setting it down in front of me like a chess piece.

I decided to cut to the chase with this one—the small talk with the waiter had been too depressing. Pulling a couple of twenties out of my wallet, I slid them across the bar.

The guy laughed. "Where've you been drinking? State prison?"

"It's for some information."

"There are magazines, you know?" he said, still grinning. "Classified ads. Cost you a lot less than this." A doubt crossed his face, killing the smile on its way down from his eyes. "Unless, of course, you're a cop." He tugged thoughtfully at his gold earring. "Are you a cop?"

"When's the last time a cop gave you forty bucks to answer a few questions?"

The guy smiled again weakly, showing a mouth of mossy teeth, grayed like a baby's teeth with mother's milk. "You've got a point." He laid his fat forearms on the bar, stroking the two twenties with his right hand like he was petting the cat. "All right. So what do you want to know?"

"A week ago last Thursday, three men came into your bar. Early in the evening. One of them was gray-haired, middle-aged, drank a lot of Scotch. The second was young, blond, had a mustache. The third one had dark hair, fair skin, blue eyes, lean face, late thirties. The gray-haired guy and the dark-haired one got into an argument—"

The guy started nodding his head. "Sure. Helluva argument. Shouting, finger-pointing. I thought the gray-haired one was going to get physical. He was one angry drunk."

"This place is pretty noisy," I said, glancing over my shoulder. "How come you happened to notice? Had these men caused some trouble before?"

The bartender thought about it for a moment. "Look, you know and I know that the one guy is dead, right? I mean, the cops were here about this, a week or so ago."

"Yeah, he's dead. He killed himself."

"So what's your interest? You're like . . . what? A relative? A reporter? A friend?"

"I'm a friend of a friend who wants to know why he did it."

The man sighed. "I wish I could help. I knew a fella killed himself not too long ago. It's a hard thing to take."

"You're saying you didn't recognize any of these guys?"

"No, I didn't. They just made a lot of noise. Knocked over a chair. I think maybe somebody complained. That's why I kept an eye out."

I shook my head. "I don't know if that's worth forty."

He pressed the money under his right palm, as if that cat he'd been petting were struggling to get loose. "Look, I can ask around for you. Maybe somebody else recognized them. Only thing is, it was early on a slow night. I don't think there were a whole lot of other people around. What I'm trying to say is, I wouldn't hold your breath. Your friend, either.''

"After the three of them had the argument, the dark-haired one left?''

He nodded. "Yeah. Just stormed out. All pissed off.''

"How drunk would you say he was?''

The man looked puzzled, like I'd thrown him a curve. "How drunk?''

"I mean, was he falling-down drunk?''

"I don't remember him being drunk at all,'' the bartender said uncertainly. "It was the other one—the guy with the gray hair—who got loaded.''

"You're telling me the one who left wasn't drunk?''

"I dunno. Could be I'm not remembering it right. Maybe he *was* kind of loaded.''

But he looked and sounded exactly like someone who had said something he shouldn't have said, although I'd be goddamned if I knew why he'd be holding anything back.

"The guy who left—he left alone?''

"Yeah. The other two stayed in the bar for another hour or so.''

"Did they have any more arguments? Say anything you remember?''

"Naw.'' He shook his head. "They just drank a few more drinks and . . . I dunno where they went.''

"Was there any commotion in the lot that night? A fight, maybe?''

He shrugged. "Nothing I heard or saw.''

I dug through my wallet and pulled out a plain business card with my name and phone number on it. "What's your name?'' I said to him.

"Max Carlson.''

"You think over what we talked about, Max. You search your memory. Ask around. Something new comes to you, you come up with a name for the other two men, you call me. If it pans out, there's a reward in it. Couple thousand bucks.''

"Couple thousand?'' the guy said, his eyes getting big.

After examining the man's bankbook, I figured Mason's estate could afford it. "Yeah."

The bartender studied the card, then tucked it in his apron pocket. "I'll think about it," he said. "What about the forty?"

"Earnest money," I said, turning for the door.

= 16 =

I WAS sure that Max Carlson would do all that he could to find the names of the two men who'd been drinking with Mason Greenleaf on the night he died. The two thousand dollars were weighing on him like a pang of conscience. I could see it in his eyes, a wonderful change of heart.

Max had made me curious about Mason Greenleaf's sobriety, or lack of it. When I'd first asked him, he had said Greenleaf wasn't particularly drunk. The second time, he'd acted like he'd been caught in a lie. If Greenleaf *hadn't* loaded up at Stacie's, it could change things slightly. To end up with a blood alcohol content of one-point-four, Mason would have had to put away a good deal of booze in that hotel room—or in the half hour between the bar and the hotel. It was an odd thing to do—to get drunk *after* leaving a bar. Unless what had happened in Stacie's—or in Stacie's lot—had upset him so much that he couldn't stand to think, or be Mason Greenleaf, one more minute.

As I walked out to the lot, I decided to stop at the Washington before calling it a day. Drunk or sober, if Greenleaf had come to harm in Stacie's parking lot—and the bloodstains in the Saab indicated that he had—he would have been wearing the bruises when he checked into the hotel. Nobody at the scene had mentioned bruises, not the cops or the desk clerk. But by this point no kind of mistake or oversight would have surprised me, the investigation had been so slipshod.

The Washington was only a couple blocks north and west of the bar, easy walking distance even if you were drunk and a little banged up. As I climbed Fifth Street to Elm, I glanced back down at Stacie's, trying to imagine what Mason Greenleaf had been thinking on the night he died. He reportedly left the bar at eleven-thirty, then either fell down or was knocked down in the lot after having words in the bar. Hurt, he'd crawled into the backseat of the Saab. Maybe he'd even passed out. In any event, it was possible that he'd been in the car for the half hour that had elapsed between his leaving Stacie's and checking into the Washington.

It had been a particularly bad week for Greenleaf. The dreams about old betrayals that wouldn't let him sleep, the visits to Dr. Mulhane and to Cavanaugh, and then four days of silence and the rocky night at a bar that he shouldn't have been in, with two men he shouldn't have been with. When he got his head together, he didn't drive home from the parking lot, even though home was only a mile or so away. Instead he got back out of the car and climbed the hill that I just climbed—heading for oblivion.

It was close to one o'clock, about the same time of night that Greenleaf had checked into the Washington. Looking across town from where I was standing, at Fifth and Elm, I could see the string of streetlights stretching west—and little else. Uptown or downtown, there was nothing to catch the eye. No bars, no restaurants, no shops open late on a weekday night. Nothing but the Washington Hotel two blocks north, with its crummy little arcade announcing ROOMS BY THE DAY OR THE WEEK in flickering neon. It was either there—or back down the hill to the noisy bar beneath the overpass and his angry friend.

I walked up to the Washington, in and out of the soft-edged patches of streetlight and darkness, crossing over to the west side of Elm at Sixth. I could hear the neon frazzle of the hotel sign from a block away. Beneath the arcade, rows of bulbs cut a broad circle out of the night. The hotel door was ajar, propped open with a rubber stopper. I eased through it down a short wainscoted hall decorated with postcard photographs of the city framed in dusty glassless frames. A television was going in the common room at the far end of the hall, lighting the dim lobby with a flicker like firelight. I could see a couple of nodding old men and one pretty young black woman dressed in shorts and halter—in out of the heat, on a night with no trade—sitting on the couches and chairs, staring mindlessly at the TV.

The stout middle-aged man drowsing behind the desk was the same guy who had ushered Cindy and me up to Mason Greenleaf's room. He was still wearing the Reds cap he'd had on the week before, brim pulled down over his forehead to shade his eyes against the bare bulb hanging above his meshed-in cage. He stirred from the chair as I came up to the desk, squaring the hat up with one hand and rubbing the sleep out of his jaws with the other.

"Sorry, buddy. Got no rooms left," he said, barely conscious. "Welfare took 'em all. Won't have anything available for several weeks."

He yawned, patting his open mouth like a tom-tom. He didn't remember me.

"Human Services uses you for temporary shelter?" I asked.

The clerk nodded. "We never know when they're gonna call." He sat back down hard on the metal chair, propping his elbows on the counter and his head on his hands. "This used to be a nice hotel, you know that?" he said to nobody in particular, to himself. "We had a bar and a restaurant. Good food." He sighed. "Every once in a while I actually rent a room."

He looked up at me again, struggling to keep his eyes open. "Did I tell you we ain't got no vacancies?"

"I don't want a room. I want some information."

"You're a cop?" he said without surprise, as if cops were no strangers to the Washington Hotel.

"No. I'm a private investigator looking into the death of the man who killed himself in your hotel."

"Oh, yeah. The guy on the fifth floor."

I got out my wallet and took out another couple of twenties, placing them on the hardwood counter. The man stared at them suspiciously, as if they were pictures of money.

"What do you need to know?"

"The man who killed himself," I said. "What kind of shape was he in when he checked in that night?"

"Drunk. Looking for a place to flop."

"I thought you didn't have any rooms to rent?"

He looked puzzled. "Must've had a few that night. Sometimes they open up when they find the niggers a place to stay permanent. Now that I think about it, the front room on the upper floor was open. We try to keep that open—just for emergencies."

"What kind of emergencies?"

He shrugged. "Somebody you know gets kicked out by his old lady, that kind of thing. Of course, we can't always do that. Depends on the Welfare."

"So the front room was open that night?" I said.

"Yeah. Must've been. Top floor, front."

"You're sure this guy was drunk?"

The man laughed, showing a mouth full of gold and empty spaces. "That's one thing I know about."

"Did he have a bottle with him?"

"I didn't see one if he did. Course he could have had it in his coat pocket. We did find one in the room, when we found him next day." The clerk puckered his lips and fanned his face furiously, as if he was clearing the air. "Man, what a stench in that room."

I remembered. I had been there.

"He came in by himself? On his own power?"

"Yeah," the clerk said, "I guess so. I didn't actually see him come in. I was taking a crap." He nodded to a door marked Private behind the desk. "When I come out, he was standing right where you are, bobbing and weaving like a featherweight. He dropped some money on my desk and says, 'I'd like a room upstairs.' I gave him the room."

He shrugged as if he didn't see the mystery in it.

"Did he look like he'd been beat up or taken a bad fall?"

"I don't remember that," he said uncertainly.

But by then, I was pretty sure that he really didn't remember much at all. It had been late that Monday night. He'd been sick to his stomach and as sleepy as he was when I'd come in a few minutes before. Moreover the guy was conditioned not to look at anyone too closely. That was the etiquette of transient hotels like the Washington. Everyone's business was his own. Hell, he hadn't even remembered my face—and less than a week before, he'd ridden me upstairs to identify a dead man.

I heard a john flush, and the door behind the desk opened. The old man I'd seen on Tuesday stepped out, his pants hanging open. When he saw me, he smiled a shameless, broken-toothed smile.

"Jesus, put your pants on, Pat," the clerk said, glancing back at him.

"I'm trying," the old man said, struggling gamely with his suspenders.

I took out a business card and laid it on top of the money, pushing it all over to the clerk.

"If anything else comes to you, call me." I said it for the old man's benefit, too, figuring he'd get the word out to everyone in the hotel.

"Couldn't take your money," the clerk said, plucking the card off the twenties. "Not after what happened."

I nodded at him and pocketed the bills. The old man frowned as if his heart were breaking.

"Harry Stoner," the clerk said, reading off the card. "That'd be you?"

"That'd be me."

"Well, I'm sorry about what happened. That man seemed like a nice man."

I walked back down to Stacie's lot and picked up the Pinto. I was tired and hungry, and outside of the fact that the cops' main witnesses weren't terribly reliable, I hadn't really learned anything new. Nothing I could make a lead out of. I'd just have to wait and see what fell out from Stacie's and the Washington. As I was pulling out onto Fifth, a blue-and-white cruiser rolled by, making the usual inner city rounds. He was the first cop I'd seen in that neighborhood all night.

I circled back around Broadway to Sixth Street, then uptown through the dead streets to the Riorley Building. Outside of the cop car on lower Fifth, the only sign of life was the flurry of traffic around King's News, where the touts were double-parking to run in and pick up the fresh racing form. It was past two when I pulled up in front of the Riorley. I parked on the street and went upstairs to the office.

The light on the answering machine was on, flashing the news that I had three messages. I flipped on the desk lamp, sat down, and played them back.

The first call was from Ira Sullivan, asking me to phone him at his office the next day. "There could be something odd here," he said in an odd-sounding voice. "I found an old friend who talked to Mason. I'd best wait before jumping to conclusions." And that was it.

His tone of voice had been so strange that I decided to phone him right away, even though it was going on two-thirty. I looked him up in the white pages and dialed the number. I let it ring five times, and when no one answered and no answering machine came on, I hung up. His message had to have come in late, after my first stop at the office around eight. Could be he was off talking to the "old friend" he'd referred to in the message. Cindy had said Sullivan was a night owl.

The second call turned out to be almost as odd. There was a long silence and then a boy's voice: "This is Lee Marks. Mr. Greenleaf's student from Nine Mile. I want to tell you something. I'll be home tomorrow, all day." He left a number, with a Kenwood exchange. I jotted it down on a notepad.

The third message was from Cindy, asking me to return the call as soon as possible. "After talking to those cops, I'm not going to be sleeping," she said. "So call anytime."

I dialed her number.

She answered on the second ring. "Oh, man, I'm glad to hear

your voice," she said, sounding shaken enough to make me ask if anything was wrong.

"It's just that the cop treated me like I was a jerk when he came to check Mason's car. Some guy named Segal. A real *momzer*."

"He was the IO on Mason's case."

"I told him about the bloodstains, and he told me it didn't make a difference. Mason killed himself, and the blood in the car didn't change that. The bastard had all sort of explanations for what it meant: Mason bumped his head getting in the car—apparently there was quite a dent in the car roof. Or he fell in the lot and then bumped his head. Anything to avoid lifting a finger to find out why he died. I don't even know why he bothered to take the samples."

I knew why—because he'd been ordered to. "Be patient, Cindy. There are some things that may break our way."

"You have news?"

"Possibilities."

There was a moment of silence on the line. Having done with Mason, we were left with each other—our own possibilities.

"You wouldn't want to come out here, would you?" she said tentatively.

"Yes," I said, thinking about her. "I would."

"Good," she said, sounding so relieved that she said it again. "Good."

═ 17 ═

I T was almost three when I pulled into the driveway of the little yellow brick house and parked behind Mason Greenleaf's Saab. Cindy opened the door a short time after I knocked. She was wearing a white T-shirt that stretched down to her thighs. Passing her hand through her curly black hair she smiled at me sleepily.

"Hey," she said.

"Hey, yourself." I kissed her on the lips.

"I must've dozed off," she said, stepping aside to let me in.

I went over to the couch and sat down wearily. Cindy knelt down beside me on the floor.

"I'm glad you're here," she said. "You want anything? Food or anything?"

"I'm fine."

There was a moment of silence, as we both settled into the newness of being together.

"Did I tell you about that cop, Segal?" she asked.

"Yeah, you did. Might as well just accept the fact that the case is officially closed. Anything we find, we'll have to find on our own."

She laid her cheek on my leg. "Did you learn anything at that bar?"

"No, but Ira Sullivan left a message that sounded promising.

And a kid from Mason's school apparently has something to say. We'll see tomorrow.''

We sat there for a while. Two vaguely haunted people in a haunted house.

"This is more awkward than I thought it would be," Cindy finally said. "I mean, you don't really know me."

"How much do you know about me?"

"I have some ghosts, Harry. More than Mason."

"You think I don't?"

"Yeah, but mine are doozies." Folding her hands on her breasts, Cindy laid her head back against the edge of the couch. "I want to tell you a story about me. I wanted to tell you earlier tonight. There just wasn't any time for it. Now that you're here . . . you should hear this before you decide whether you want to be with me. Because it's something you should know. Something that matters."

"Cindy, we could trade horror stories all night."

"I want to say it."

"All right," I said.

Cindy closed her eyes. "Before I met Mason, I was with a guy, Jerry. I'd been with him for better than a year. And I was in love with him, even though I knew that he didn't love me. He liked me in bed—he liked that part a lot. After Randy and the divorce, I was willing to settle for that, to settle for anyone who had a need for me.

"Lovemaking was a game with Jerry. 'Let's pretend under the covers.' He'd turn off the lights and tell me to close my eyes, then start whispering to me: what he wanted me to do to myself, what he wanted me to think about while I was doing it. Most of his fantasies had to do with seeing me make love to other people, men or women. I didn't mind—or told myself I didn't. I wanted to please him, and I've never been a prude about sex. Then he started bringing it out of the bedroom. We'd go places—bars, parties—and he'd push me off with other men, friends of his. I knew what he was doing, what he wanted me to do. But it's one thing in fantasy and another in reality. I loved him and I wanted him to love me, but I was never a party girl. He kept at it. We had a fight. A bad one. And

I could feel we were coming to the end of each other, that I was about to lose him.

"One night, right before the end, we were in a bar and we ran into this friend of Jerry's, a guy named Dave. I'd seen him before at several parties, a nice-looking guy who liked me and didn't disguise it. That night the three of us ended up going home together— back to Jerry's house. There was a lot more drinking, some lines of coke, suggestive talk. It got late and all three of us were stoned. We ended up on the couch. Jerry started in on me, not even hinting anymore, just telling me to make it with Dave, to let him make it with me. At that point I was so drunk and desperate to hang on to him that I told myself that I didn't care anymore. So I kissed Dave. He started undressing me, handling me. I got hot and just went with it while Jerry was watching.

"After he finished, Dave told Jerry what a great piece of ass I was and left. Then we just sat there, Jerry and I, for the longest goddamn time, naked, with the television going and this stink of disgust and contempt filling the room up like a gas leak. I gave him what he wanted—I even enjoyed it, like he wanted—and he hated me for it. Jerry told me to get dressed and drove me back here. It was the last time I ever heard from him or saw him. I left a dozen messages for him that night. Wept on the phone. Begged him to forgive me—for what, I don't know. He never called again.

"The next day I couldn't even get out of bed. I just lay there, wishing I was dead, thinking about how to do it so it wouldn't leave a mess. I was like that for maybe a week. As close to the edge of my life as I've ever been—even after Randy, and that had been bad. I didn't eat. I didn't answer the phone. I just sat in bed and cried with shame. Eventually a friend of mine who I taught with, Alice Connelly, came to the house. She fed me, cleaned me up, got me dressed and out of bed.

"The next week there was this teachers' conference in Louisville. Alice insisted that I go with her, even though I didn't want to go anywhere that people were. But she wouldn't take no. So I stuffed myself with antidepressants and went. I thought I could handle it with the drugs in me. But I couldn't. Couldn't stand to be around people. I ended up making a scene at a cocktail party—just burst into tears and ran back to the hotel room. Mason happened to be standing in the hall when I came off the elevator.

"I don't know what he said to make me trust him—I was so distraught, I don't remember much of anything. Just that he was kind, and gentle, and nonthreatening—just what I needed. Someone who would love me first, then make love to me. All my life it's been the other way. Even as a kid.

"Mason was kinder to me than anyone I've ever known. And I loved him for it. I still do. When we made love, I knew he loved me. I grew to depend on that assurance. Now . . . I'm afraid I'll lose myself in you, Harry. You see, I know it's still part of me—the willingness to do anything to please, to love without being loved back."

She turned her head toward me and opened her eyes. "So, you see the kind of woman you're getting. I'm going to be in love with you, and I want you to know it—up front—before we go upstairs. Because once we start, I'm little girl lost. And if you're not prepared to make a commitment, I'm likely to get hurt."

I stared at her for a long moment. "I wouldn't hurt you, Cindy."

"I just want you to be honest with me. That's all I want."

She got to her feet and held out her hand. In the backlight I could see all of her through the thin cotton shirt. Her high round breasts with their long dark nipples, the heart of auburn hair that covered her sex, her long brown legs below the hem of shirt.

I took her hand, and she led me up a half-flight of stairs to a landing above the garage. The door on the right led to her bedroom. She pulled me through it over to a large brass bed, sitting beneath a window that looked out on the driveway. Arching her back, Cindy stripped off the T-shirt and lay down in the middle of the sheets. She was brown all over, save for narrow strips of white at her breasts and hips.

I unbuttoned my shirt and pants.

"You look nice," she said, watching me undress.

I lay down beside her on the cool sheets. Shimmying closer to me, Cindy ran her hand down my belly. I reached down and began touching her.

Squeezing her eyes shut, she shuddered up and down her spine. "Just your touch," she whispered.

She wriggled out of my arms and reached over to the night table. Opening the drawer, she pulled out a condom and handed it to me. Flipping off the lights, she slid down the sheets.

Sometime in the night I heard her get up. Opening one eye, I saw her walk naked across the room and out the door to the bath. I thought to myself, even as I was falling back asleep, that she was very beautiful and that I wanted her. Feeling a little uneasy at wanting her as much as I did, because she was a bit screwed up and very vulnerable. Because I wasn't used to wanting anyone that much.

I woke up with the same mixed feeling of desire and uneasiness, alone in her bed, with the morning sun pouring through the window. The light glinted off her vanity mirror and off the polished wood of the dresser across from the bed. A drawer stood open atop it, with a leg warmer dangling over its edge. I could smell the night on the sheets. Lying in bed, I thought about her—thought about how we'd connected so strongly physically.

Naked, I wandered out into the hall, into the bathroom, and stuck myself under a hot shower. I found my clothes, washed and pressed, hanging from the doorknob of the bedroom. I slipped them on and went down to the living room. The card tables were folded up and gone, along with the chairs and plastic plates. The room smelled of coffee and cooking.

I went into the kitchen and found her standing by the stove, arranging a tray full of breakfast. She turned to me with surprise as I came into the room.

"You got dressed! I heard you in the shower and was going to bring your breakfast upstairs." Smiling, she picked up the tray and set it down on the Formica breakfast table. "Eat," she said.

I was hungry and I ate, while she watched.

"Are you okay? You seem so quiet."

"I'm okay," I said.

Her pretty face bunched up with worry. "What is it, Harry?"
She sat down on the kitchen chair, facing me.

I put down the fork and stared into her face. "I'm forty-five years old this November. I'm a part-time drunk. I have virtually no friends except for a few ex-cops. I sleep with three or four women, all of whom I've known since the early seventies. All of whom have other attachments. I haven't had a serious relationship in better than ten years, and I'm not used to being in love."

She started to smile. "Meaning what? That you're in love with me?"

"I've been half in love with you since I first saw you. It was a pleasant fantasy. I didn't think it would come true. Now . . ."

"What?"

"Now we're sitting here, and I'm thinking that I'm too old for this, that I'm bound to disappoint you or lay myself open to being disappointed."

She reached across the table and stroked my cheek. "I'm willing to take the chance if you are."

"I don't think I have a choice," I said, picking up the fork and starting to eat again. Out of the corner of my eye I saw her smile.

After breakfast, while Cindy did the dishes, I called Ira Sullivan from the kitchen phone. His secretary, Cherie, told me that he hadn't come into the office yet.

"He doesn't have any appointments today, so he may not be in at all. I'd tell you to try him at home, only he doesn't always answer the phone."

"Does he call in for messages?"

"Sometimes," she said without confidence.

"If he does call, tell him to phone me at my office. If he doesn't get in touch by this afternoon, I'll stop at his place—sometime after five."

I hung up the phone, got out my notebook, and dialed Lee Marks at the number he'd left on the answering machine. A woman answered in a harried-sounding voice, "Yes?"

"Could I speak to Lee?"

"Who is this?" she said, putting a little sweetness in her voice, as mothers do when they want to get the lowdown on their kids.

Before I could answer, someone picked up an extension. "Mom," a boy said, "is this for me?"

"It's Harry Stoner, Lee."

"Mom, please get off the line. This is important. It's about school," he added, as if he knew that would turn the trick.

Which it did. His mother hung up.

"You called me, Lee," I said to him.

"Yeah. Look, I don't think it's a good idea to talk on the phone. I mean, she might pick up again any second. And . . . I don't want her to hear this."

"Is there someplace you'd like to meet? The school?"

He laughed. "Definitely not the school. You know the Kenwood Mall?"

"Sure."

"I'll meet you there in a half an hour. Down by the theater. Okay?"

"Lee, what's this about?" I said, wondering if he was pulling my chain.

"It's about Mr. Greenleaf. I wanted to tell you yesterday, but Snodgrass came in."

"All right," I said, "I'll meet you at the mall."

But I still wasn't convinced that he was on the level, even as I kissed Cindy good-bye and walked out the door.

= 18 =

IT was close to noon when I got to the Kenwood Mall, on the northeast side of town. I parked the car close to a Lazarus department store and walked across the lot to the mall entrance. The doors opened onto an enclosed concourse with a little fountain in its center and corridors radiating off at compass points around it. The place was surprisingly crowded for a weekday noon. Aside from a few power-walkers scurrying along—heads down, eyes fixed, like Alice's rabbit—the crowd was mostly teenagers, out of school and on a tear. They darted eagerly in and out of the stores that lined either side of the long walkway, nosing right and left as if they were following scent, plastering themselves against windows, against each other. Like dogs in the backseat of a car.

I found a ''You are here'' sign in the south corridor that looked like a map of Los Angeles and managed to navigate a good half-mile farther south to a balcony overlooking a plaza. Below me, a band was playing light rock too loudly and with no discernible ensemble on a small step-up stand. All around them, more kids were mobbing cafeteria-style food booths—ordering everything from pizza to Chinese, served on paper plates and eaten on your choice of stool.

As I went down the staircase toward the band, I spotted Lee Marks beside the marquee of a Loew's theater, making time with a tall, pretty brunette in a leotard and neon yellow bicycle shorts. When he saw me walk up, he waved, then said something to his girlfriend. Glancing my way, she walked off a short distance and pretended to stare at some lingerie that even a teenager would have been ashamed to wear.

"Mr. Stoner!" Lee shouted to me over the din.

With the rock band and the kids playing with their food, I could see it was going to be impossible to talk.

"Is there someplace we could go?" I shouted.

He nodded. "Follow me."

He led me down another corridor that sprang from the headwaters of the eateries. Eventually we got far enough way from the chaos to hear each other speak—some secret, unused segment of the mall where bookstores were lined up like ducks on a pond. We found a resting place, a couple of varnished benches, and sat down. Up the way, clinging to the shadows of the storefronts, I could see Lee Marks's neon-colored girlfriend. He could see her, too.

"Oh, for God's sake," he said, looking embarrassed. "She thinks she's gotta keep an eye on me."

"Why?"

"Because of you, I guess."

It was true I was over forty, but I was a clean old man.

"What does she think I'm going to do—kidnap you?"

He laughed. "Yeah, I think that's exactly what she thinks."

"What's her name?"

"Gloria," he said. "She's okay, really. She just watches too much TV."

It appeared to me, from his manner, that Lee Marks didn't. Which was something of a relief.

"Well, we're here, Lee," I said. "I haven't kidnapped you yet. What exactly do you have to say?"

He bit his lower lip, raking it under his front teeth, as if he'd gotten his audience but wasn't sure he could go through with the performance. "I honestly don't know how important this is," he admitted. "I mean, it's such a little thing. But when I saw you yesterday and you told me that the police still don't know why Mr. Greenleaf killed himself—I just thought maybe I should tell you.''

''Tell me what?''

''It's something I saw, about three weeks ago. Right after an assembly at school. You know, one of those 'for-your-own-good' things that everybody's got to attend. There was a lecture and a play, dramatizing the danger of drugs and AIDS. Anyway, after it was over I stuck around the auditorium to wait for Gloria to pick me up. I was standing outside the lobby when I heard some loud voices coming from inside the door. Everybody else had left. At least, I thought they had. Anyway, I went inside to look. It was pretty dark—they'd shut off the lights. But down by the stage I saw Greenie talking to a blond guy with a mustache. I'd never seen the other guy before. I couldn't hear what they were saying, except that the blond guy looked upset. I started to feel embarrassed about spying on them, so I went back out to the lobby.

''After a while Greenie came out by himself. He had his head down and his face was . . . I mean, he looked sick. When he saw me, I asked him if he was okay. He smiled and said sure, he was okay. He didn't know I'd seen him with the other guy, the blond one. We talked a little about the summer session and about me going to Harvard. I said I'd write him a postcard when I got settled in at Cambridge, and then he made this funny face and told me not to do that. I mean, it was a strange look. He said just to drop by the school and say hello to him when I got into town at the Christmas break. He said he was proud of me and that he was sure I would do well.''

''He didn't say anything else?'' I asked. ''About the man he'd been talking to?''

Lee Marks shook his head. ''No. He just walked off, out to the parking lot. I don't know why, but I had the funniest damn feeling that I wasn't going to see him again. Just . . . something about the way his voice sounded when he told me he was proud of me and that I would do well. Like he was saying good-bye.''

''Did you see him again?''

The boy laughed. ''Yeah. The very next day in class. He acted like nothing had happened. Lectured about *The House of Seven Gables*. I tried to talk to him after class. But he didn't stick around like he usually did. The day after that, I guess that was Thursday, he didn't come in. I never did see him again. None of us did. Until the funeral parlor.''

He dropped his head.

By then, his girlfriend had gotten close enough to spit at. When she saw the boy drop his head, she rushed over to the bench and sat down beside him, reaching out for his hand and glaring at me like I was a dirty bastard. Love in bloom. Hell, I knew the feeling.

"This is Gloria," Lee Marks said, blushing.

"Hello, Gloria," I said.

"Hi," she said in a clipped voice. Like time was money.

"How good a look did you get at his blond man?" I asked Lee Marks.

"I was pretty far away, Mr. Stoner."

"If I showed you a photograph, do you think you might recognize him?"

"I'm not sure. Maybe."

"How 'bout coming out to the parking lot and taking a look."

"You have like a mug book or something?" he said with surprise.

"I have a photo."

The kid glanced at his girlfriend. "Sure, why not?"

We went back up the corridor—Lee, Gloria, and I—up the stairs where the band played on, up to the top level and out into the lot. After the air-conditioned shade of the mall, the sunlight was almost blinding, the heat ferocious. It took me a while to find my car—to the amusement of the two kids.

"My mother had to call the cops once," Gloria admitted, as we wandered through row after row of gleaming chrome.

We finally came to the one that wasn't gleaming, my rusty Pinto. Lee had already seen my hulk, but Gloria's jaw dropped.

"Is that an *American* car?"

The Marks boy laughed. I unlocked the passenger side door and pulled out Mason Greenleaf's jacket. I found the photograph of

Paul Grandin, Jr., unclipped it from the arrest report, and showed it to Lee. He stared at it for a moment, holding a hand above his eyes to cut the glare.

"The man I saw was older than this. In his twenties. And his mustache was a lot darker."

"The picture was taken six years ago."

He looked at it again. "I can't be sure. But, yeah, I guess it could be this guy."

He handed the photo back to me.

"Who is he?" he asked.

I gave him the short version. "Someone Mason used to know. You never saw this man at the school before?"

Lee shook his head. "I thought maybe he was one of the pre-school parents. Only I'd never seen him at any other assembly."

"How was he dressed?"

"Casual. Sport coat, shirt, jeans. He kept wiping his nose with the back of his hand, like he had a cold."

I smiled at the kid. "You'd make a good detective."

"He's going to be a doctor," the girl said, chasing that idea with a broom.

I stuck the photo back in the jacket. "You've been a big help, Lee."

"When you find out why he killed himself, then I'll know I've helped."

I told him I'd tell him when I found out.

As Lee Marks and Gloria wandered off, back to the playground of the mall, I got in the car and stared at Mason Greenleaf's jacket. I hadn't even bothered to bring it inside Cindy's house the night before. Now it seemed like a good idea to look at the whole file.

It was too hot to sit in the car, so I drove out of the lot to a chili parlor on the other side of Montgomery. I found a table in the back of the restaurant, ordered a coffee, and read through the strange case of Mason Greenleaf and Paul Grandin, Jr.

The complainant in the arrest had been the boy's father, Paul Grandin, Sr. He had an address on Madeira Road in Indian Hill. On the afternoon of September 3, 1988, Grandin Senior found five letters written by Mason Greenleaf to his son, hidden in his son's desk at the home of his ex-wife in Clifton. There was no explanation of why the father had been looking through his son's things— or ransacking his ex-wife's house. According to Grandin's complaint, Greenleaf had solicited sex from his son in three of the letters and had referred to a previous instance of consensual sex in two others. Armed with the letters, Grandin Senior had gone to the school where Greenleaf was teaching on the morning of September 4, 1988, hauled him out of the classroom, and assaulted him right there in front of the kids. The police were called, at which time Grandin Senior made his charges against Mason. Mason counter-charged him with assault. According to the IOs at the scene, Mason took a pretty good beating.

Greenleaf's half of the case was then referred to the vice squad. Two detectives, a man named Art Stiehl and my new pal Ron Sabato, were assigned to the investigation. Various interviews were held at the school itself, with other students and teachers. Grandin's mother was interviewed, and so was Grandin himself at his mother's home. Although Ira Sullivan had said that Grandin never cooperated with the cops, the IO report indicated that, on the initial interview, Paul had "expressed guilt" about his relationship with Greenleaf without explicitly confirming a sexual liaison. Whatever Paul Grandin, Jr., had said was enough, in combination with the letters themselves, to send the case to a grand jury. Which, in this town, with this kind of charge, meant an automatic indictment.

Stapled inside the back of the jacket was a frontal mug shot of Greenleaf, taken on the day of his arrest, on the day that Paul Grandin, Sr., had worked him over. I hadn't paid attention to it when I'd first skimmed the jacket. This time, I did. Behind the bruises—and he was badly banged up—Mason Greenleaf looked like a man who had been condemned to death.

I closed the jacket on his haunted face. There was a phone stand by the restaurant door. I went over to it and called Dick Lock at CPD Criminalistics.

"I need another LEADS search," I said. "Paul Grandin, Jr."

I gave him Grandin's last known address, at his mother's home on Rue de la Paix in Clifton.

"What're we looking for, Harry?" Dick asked.

"Anything. Misdemeanor, felony, warrant. And a current address, if you can get one."

"I can cross-check with the state BMV for that."

"Call me at my office when you have the results. I'll be in after five."

After hanging up on Dick, I paid my chit and walked back out to the car. Paul Grandin, Sr., lived a couple of miles from where I was standing. Even though it was half-past two on a weekday afternoon, I decided to pay him a visit on the off chance that he was home. If he wasn't, I would leave him a card with a note to call me.

═ 19 ═

THERE was a gold Mercedes 450 sitting in the carriage circle in front of Paul Grandin, Sr.'s, Indian Hill home. I could see it gleaming through the hedgerow in front of his estate as I turned off Madeira Road into his driveway. Then I saw the house. A huge brick Georgian with a stern Tory look to it, red-cheeked and disapproving.

A good amount of timbered ground spread out behind and around the house, enough square acreage to convince me that Paul Grandin, Sr., was top United American Soap management or big money law. Way out in the green distance, shimmering like a mirage, a boy was riding a lawn tractor. I watched him loop around a stand of cherry trees, trailing a jet of cuttings behind him that sparkled in the sunlight like the plume of a speedboat.

The front door was oak and brass with a scalloped window above it set with ruby glass. I lifted the knocker and let it fall. I waited a moment, and when no one answered, I dug a business card out of my wallet, penciled a message to call me on its back, and stuck it in the mailbox. As I turned to the car, I heard a girl shriek with laughter. Her voice startled me enough to make me whirl around. Someone else, a man, shouted, "Goddamn lucky!" And I realized the voices were coming from behind the house.

A cut-stone path led from the door around the north side of the mansion. I followed it to a concrete landing, where a canopied stairway began its descent to a fenced tennis court in a dell below the house. I listened to the flap of the canvas awning above the stairs and the distant sound of the tennis match and, figuring the worst the Grandins could do was call a cop, started down.

As I got closer to the court, I could hear the two voices more clearly, along with the pock of a tennis ball and the squeak of shoes on a clay surface. The girl was riding the man mercilessly for losing point after point. From the bile in his voice, he didn't much like it. As I got to the bottom of the stair, the girl spotted me. She was a very pretty kid, maybe seventeen or eighteen, dressed in blinding white. Ball in hand, she lowered her racket and stared as if I were a unicorn.

"Serve the goddamn thing," the man called out to her angrily.

He couldn't see me because of a tarp that was strung along his half of the fence, blocking his view of the staircase. But when I got down to ground level, he saw me.

"What the hell!" he shouted.

Stalking across the court, he came straight at me. He was a tall man with thin gray hair and a broad, tan, pugnacious face. He wore his hair in a comb-over that he held in place against the breeze with his left hand. He swung the tennis racket menacingly in his right.

"This is private goddamn property," he said at the top of his lungs, as he came up close.

"There wasn't any sign posted," I said.

"The hell there isn't. Right at the top of the stairs, below the azaleas."

"I must have missed it."

The man lashed at his comb-over as if he was planting a tent stake. "All right, you're here. Now what it is you want?"

"I was looking for Paul Grandin."

He slowly lowered his hand from his head and stared at me through sun-streaked eyes. "You're talking to him. Grandin Senior."

"My name is Stoner, Mr. Grandin. I'm a private investigator. I wanted to ask you a few questions about your son, Paul Junior."

"Christ almighty," he said, wincing as if I'd stabbed him with a knife. "I took an ad out in the *Enquirer* three years ago, making it clear that I am no longer responsible for Paul's debts. What more do I have to say? His problems are his to solve. I've done all I can."

"This has nothing to do with debts. I'm working for a woman named Cindy Dorn."

"What did he steal from her?" Grandin asked bitterly.

It was obvious that Paul Grandin, Jr., had meant nothing but trouble for the man for quite a long time.

The girl had started over toward us. As she came close, I could see that she had the same tan, broad-featured face as Grandin Senior, only what looked pugnacious on him looked like free-spirits in her.

"Who is it, Dad?" she asked.

"A private detective, asking about your brother," he said miserably.

"I need to get in touch with him," I said to the girl.

"Why?"

I thought about trying to dodge the question, but there was no way around the truth without making the interview more painful than it already was. "Mason Greenleaf killed himself about a week ago. Your brother may have been one of the last people who talked to him before he died."

I knew as soon as I said it, there was going to be trouble. Grandin's face flushed red to the roots of his thin gray hair. Alarmed, his daughter reached a hand out to him.

"Jesus wept," the man said in a voice shaking with rage. "You dare to drag that scum who poisoned my son's life into my house! I ought to kill you!"

He raised the tennis racket like a club. I grabbed his arm before he could swing at me.

"Don't," I said, staring into his trembling face.

"Dad, please," the girl said in a terrified voice. To me she said: "I think you better leave."

I let the man's arm go and turned for the stairs. Grandin walked directly over to a phone, hung from a fence post. "I'm calling the cops, you son of a bitch."

I had so much adrenaline going, I didn't much give a damn what he did—as long as he kept his distance from me. I was already to the top of the stairs when I heard footsteps behind me. I looked back and saw the girl.

"Wait, please. He won't call the police."

"Yeah? What makes you so sure?"

"Look."

She pointed down to the court. Grandin was sitting on a white stool by the fence, his face in his hands. Even at that distance, I could tell from the movements of his back that he was weeping.

All the anger drained out of me in an instant.

"I'm sorry," I said. "I was just doing my job."

"You didn't know about Paul and . . . that man?"

"I knew there had been some accusations made, several years ago."

"That man ruined my brother's life and destroyed our family," the girl said flatly. "You can't expect us to care if he's dead. We wished him dead."

"I only wanted to talk to Paul."

"Paul has nothing to do with him anymore. Not for years. It's crazy to think differently. Who said he was talking to that man?"

"Someone said he thought he'd seen them talking."

"Then he's mistaken," she said. "You should go. And please don't come back. We don't want to hear that man's name again."

I went over to the car. The girl watched me as I got in.

"Leave my brother alone," she called out as I pulled away. "Leave my father alone."

I drove off with her voice ringing in my ears. In the space of a few minutes, I'd managed to alienate a young woman and reduce her father to tears of rage—just by mentioning Mason Greenleaf's name.

It had been my plan to stop at Rue de la Paix on my way to town and talk to Paul Grandin, Jr.'s, mother. But after the fiasco in Indian Hill, I decided that there had to be a better way to find the boy than through his family. In spite of all the things I'd heard to the contrary, it appeared to me that the Grandins—or at least the father and daughter—honestly believed that Mason Greenleaf had corrupted Paul. The kind of hatred I'd seen in Grandin Senior's face, the bitterness in his daughter's voice weren't equivocal testimony. Of course the daughter had been a child when the episode with Mason occurred, and her memories of it had undoubtedly been shaped by her father's prejudices. Still, the depth of their anger was impressive—and unsettling.

I stopped at the CPD building on my way to the office to pick up the coroner's report from Ron Sabato. Sabato wasn't in. Another cop named Atkins found what I wanted in a file on Ron's desk.

Since I was in the building, I stopped at Criminalistics and asked Dick Lock if he'd finished the LEADS search.

"Computer's been down most of the afternoon," he said. "I did the BMV for you before it crashed."

He handed me a printout on Paul Grandin, Jr. According to his license application, the boy lived on Klotter Street in Over-the-Rhine. It was a far cry from Indian Hill, so far that it made me wonder if Dick had the right guy. But his age matched up correctly. So did color of hair.

"This is current?" I asked.

"Fairly. Renewed two and a half years ago. What's the problem?"

"The kid comes from money, is all."

"Well, it's hard times now, Harry," Lock said.

═20═

LOWER Klotter Street runs west off Ravine, on the northern edge of Over-the-Rhine. At one time it, too, had been a slum of crumbling brownstones like most of the north side, but throughout the eighties urban developers had moved in and begun to gentrify the uphill side of the street, the side with the city views. The downhill side, overlooking the burnt-out shell of McMicken, was still mostly Appalachian poor. It made for an odd mix, reflected in the parked cars on the street—half Mazdas and half junkers—and in the pedestrian traffic. As I drove up the block looking for Grandin's address, I saw a middle-class woman in a business suit unlocking a stout iron gate that barred the door to her condo. Across the block a ten-year-old kid with a cigarette drooping from his pale, old man's face led a muzzled German shepherd around by a rope.

Grandin's house turned out to be on the renovated half of the block, a red brick three-story townhouse with freshly painted white trim, sitting on the upslope side of Ravine. A steep stone staircase led to it, through an iron gate that someone had left unlocked. I parked beneath the house in the sawtoothed shadows of the tenements and picked my way up the stairs to a concrete landing. Another staircase, freshly constructed out of treated lumber, led up to a second-story front door. I climbed the second set of stairs and knocked.

A moment passed, and a man who was not Paul Grandin answered. He had a tough, handsome, blue-eyed face and long blond hair that he wore combed back from a widow's peak and tied in a ponytail that ran halfway down his back. There was a gold earring in his right ear, a Semper Fi tattoo with globe and anchor on his right bicep. Behind him, from inside the house, I could hear a stereo playing a recording of blues guitar.

Scowling as he opened the door, the man craned his neck around the side of the building and looked down the stairs toward the street. "How'd you get through the gate?"

"It wasn't locked," I told him.

The guy grabbed his head, then his hips—as if he didn't know where it hurt worse. "How many times do you have to tell the electricians to lock the goddamn door?"

He blew some steam from his mouth, then crossed his arms at his chest and stared at me like what was done was done. Like I was done.

"So what is it?" he said, leaning arms crossed against the jamb. "You selling something? Insurance? Magazines?"

"I'm looking for Paul Grandin."

"Paul doesn't live here anymore."

"Do you know where I could find him?"

"Mister, I don't even know who the hell you are."

I dug through my wallet for a card and handed it to him. He stared at it curiously. "You're Stoner?"

"Yeah."

"Tim Bristol," he said, nodding hello. "I don't think I've ever met a detective before. A few cops, but never a detective." He tucked the card in his shirt pocket. "So what is it, Paul's in trouble again?"

Like Paul Grandin's father, trouble had been Tim Bristol's first thought.

"He's in no trouble. He may have some information that relates to a case I'm working on."

"What case would that be?"

Since I needed his help to find Grandin, I went ahead and told him about Greenleaf's unexplained suicide. "Paul may have been one of the last people Greenleaf talked to."

Tim Bristol chewed this over for a moment. "It's possible, I guess. The guy always liked Paul, for all the good it did him."

The man's bitterness was undisguised and unmistakable. "I thought you and Paul were friends?"

"Friends?" He shook his head. "Uh-unh."

"Didn't you say he used to live here?"

"He did. Last summer he conned me into rehabbing the house. 'Long about September, he got tired of doing the work, fished around for a better offer, and moved out." The guy laughed like the joke was on him. "How's that for friends?"

"Do you know where he went after he left?"

"I know where he wanted to go. Back home to live off his old man's money. Get his sister and his mom to wait on him hand and foot. But of course that ain't going to happen. Not in this life." He stared at me curiously. "Have you talked to his old man?"

"Briefly."

"Well, don't, for chrissake, mention my name to him. He hates my guts. Thinks I corrupted his fucked-up little boy—me and that poor son of a bitch who killed himself. Paul never got around to telling him about the fifty others that came after us. And during. The little whore always goes with whoever can give him the sweetest ride and the least amount of trouble. He's a taker, you know?"

Unfolding his arms, Bristol extended his hands and spread his fingers. "Take, take," he said, clawing the air. "That's all Paul understands. He had a tough time of it as a kid, so he figures it's owed him—whatever he wants, whenever he wants. If somebody can't fork over, well then, 'Fuck you, buddy, it's time to move on.' "

Tim Bristol glanced through the open door of the townhouse—at a piece of unpainted drywall forming the side of a staircase. "I sank every penny I had into this fucking place to please him. What a dumbass cocksucker, huh?''

He turned back to me and laughed another empty laugh.

Hearing Tim Bristol complain about his lazy, faithless, manipulative boyfriend, I could see why Grandin Senior considered his son's life a ruin. His life sounded like a ruin to me, too. And if Mason Greenleaf had started him down the road to that life, I could see where Grandin Senior might easily hold a grudge. Judging from Bristol's description, he'd certainly fallen a long way from the hapless, abused kid that Tom Snodgrass had described and that Mason Greenleaf had supposedly taken under his wing—if Paul Grandin, Jr., had ever been that kid. According to Bristol, he had been a rotten son of a bitch from the start.

''Did Paul ever talk to you about Mason Greenleaf?'' I asked him.

''Yeah, once in a while,'' Bristol said. ''He used the old bastard just like he used everyone else. I mean, it was pathetic. Whenever he didn't have a bit part at the Playhouse or couldn't con a dollar out of one of his other rich johns, Paul would run over to Mount Adams and play the poor misunderstood kid for Greenleaf. You know, he'd swear he was going to clean up his act, quit the whoring around and the partying, and settle down to being an actor, making a career. Greenleaf bought it every fucking time! Five hundred. A thousand. He once gave him three grand when Paul conned him into thinking he had a screen test and needed the money for plane fare and hotel. I don't know why he kept believing him. I mean, Paul had proved how insincere he was a thousand times over. I guess he wanted to think he could make a difference.'' Bristol slapped himself lightly on the cheek, as if Paul Grandin was a dream he couldn't quite shake. ''Look, who's talking, huh?''

But I was thinking about the little bits of money that Greenleaf had been feeding his friend. There had been regular withdrawals from the checking account in the amounts that Bristol mentioned, even as recently as the last week of Greenleaf's life. Which meant he might have been subsidizing the kid for years—out of guilt or affection or some combination of both.

I studied Tim Bristol for a moment, knowing that what I wanted to ask him next was a question he might resent. But it had to be asked. "Was Paul soliciting this money from Greenleaf for sex?"

"What do I know?" Tim Bristol said, flushing. "I always got the impression it was more of a father-son thing. God knows, Paul didn't have much of a real father. And God knows if there was something between them, Greenleaf wasn't the first. Paul was turning tricks in high school down on Fourth Street."

It was an ugly picture that he was painting of Paul Grandin, who appeared to be more of a victimizer than a victim—perhaps from the start of his relationship with Greenleaf. It wouldn't have been the first time that Mason had been manipulated and taken advantage of by someone he'd loved. At the same time, I knew that Bristol was a jilted lover who'd lost his stake in Grandin and the house when Grandin had left him.

Bristol must have heard the vengefulness in his own voice, because he began to show some remorse. "Look, I've probably gone a little overboard about Paul. Leaving me in the lurch like he did—well, I'm not feeling real charitable. I honestly don't think he means to use people up the way he does. He just never learned how to care about anyone but himself. You know, with his mom and sister he could do anything, and they'd just take him right back, give him a few bucks, a place to crash. And with his old man, it was like nothing he could do was right. Bouncing around between them for most of his life, he survived on charm and snake oil. I don't think he ever tells the truth, but he's such an attractive liar that you end up laughing it off—until somebody gets hurt."

"Tim, do you have any idea where I can find Paul?"

Bristol took a deep breath. "Yeah, I know where he went," he said heavily. "The Playhouse had a new production starting up last fall. A morality play about AIDS that toured the city schools this year. Paul got a bit part in it, and one of the actors, a young guy with a few movie credits, cruised him during rehearsals. Paul, he just went with it. You know, no more rehab, chance at the big time, so long, Tim. He claimed it would be better for his health—he had these allergies to things like sawdust and nails. It was such horseshit. He just got tired of pulling his share of the load. The guy's got a house in Mount Adams on Ida. Freddy Davis is the fucker's name. I don't know the address. I stopped caring what Paul did the moment he stepped out of this door.''

But he certainly didn't look like he'd stopped caring. Bristol put a hand over his eyes, although there wasn't a drop of sun falling on that shaded porch. ''I don't deserve this,'' he said, fighting to control his voice.

There wasn't a thing I could say that made a difference. So I said nothing.

I left Tim Bristol standing there with his hand to his brow and walked down to the sidewalk, shutting the iron gate behind me. The sun was glaring fiercely on the tarmac, on the windows of the sandblasted townhouses and crumbling brownstones.

I got in the car, the sweat coming out all over me, and thought about Paul Grandin, Jr. The play Grandin had been performing in— the play on AIDS—would explain what he had been doing at Nine Mile School, when Lee Marks had spotted him talking with Greenleaf after the performance in the deserted auditorium. What it didn't explain was what they'd been talking about—or what the continuing bond was between the two men. Clearly, in spite of what Grandin's sister had said, there *was* a bond that had continued after Greenleaf's arrest and prosecution. Some sense of obligation or remorse or appetite that had kept Greenleaf feeding the kid money. If Greenleaf had a long-standing sexual relationship with Grandin, the fight with the gray-haired man at Stacie's bar could have been a three-way lovers' quarrel. Given Tim Bristol's description of him, the kid was certainly promiscuous enough to have provoked such a scene. Why such a quarrel might have driven Greenleaf to suicidal despair was something only Paul Grandin could tell me.

Before heading for Mount Adams and Freddy Davis, I looped around Clifton and dropped off the coroner's report with Terry Mulhane's secretary. Mulhane was still seeing patients—the waiting room was stacked up like a lumberyard—so I left a message for him to call me when he was free.

I found a phone stand on Auburn Avenue, outside the office, and called my own answering machine to check for messages. But nothing had come in—from Ira Sullivan or Max Carson or anyone else. I dug another quarter out of my pocket and dialed Sullivan's office. I got taffy-haired Cherie the Secretary.

"What can I tell you?" she said with a laugh. "He never came in. You oughta try him tonight at home, is what I would do. There's a nice widow woman lives up the hall from him, Marlene Bateman, keeps an eye out for Mr. S. when he's had a few too many. You try her, if he doesn't answer the door."

Knowing what a gossip she was, I decided to pump her for information about the message Sullivan had left the previous night.

"He called me yesterday," I said putting a note of mild complaint in my voice, "and said that he'd spoken to a friend of Mason's. But he didn't give me his name."

She didn't even hesitate. "Let me think now—who all was through here yesterday?" I heard her paging through an appointment book. "When'd he call you, morning or afternoon?"

"It was in the evening, sometime after eight."

"I got nothing here for last night. He saw Mr. Connors late in the afternoon."

"Who's that?"

"He's an assistant DA. Mr. Sullivan handles most of his legal work."

It didn't sound particularly promising.

"Nothing else?"

" 'Fraid not, hon'," she said, like they were out of that kind of pie. "He saw him around four. They were still in his office talking when I went home at five-thirty."

"All right. Connors, district attorney's office," I said, writing it down on my pad.

"You want his home address?"

She was a dangerous woman. "Sure."

"He lives at 1673 Celestial Street, up on the hill. Real close to where Mr. Greenleaf lived."

It was a short drive from Terry Mulhane's office, through the late afternoon sun, to Mount Adams. I followed Elsinore up the hill, under the Ida Street bridge and through its arching shadow, circling around to Parkside. The Playhouse sat on a knoll above the Seasongood Pavilion—a squat red brick structure undulating along the hilltop like a Cyclopean wall. I parked in the lot behind the Marx theater and made my way through the shade of the elm trees to a side door marked "Actors Only."

I knew the building well enough to find the rehearsal halls, which were deserted at that hour, save for a pudgy, balding stage manager in overalls and sneakers hammering at the back of a set. I told him I was looking for Freddy Davis.

"He's not here," he said, lowering the hammer.

"It's kind of important I talk to him," I said.

"Well, he's booked pretty solid just now, buddy. He got a TV part a few months ago. A real nice break for him."

"He's out of town?"

"He was. I don't know if he's back now or not. Have you tried his agent?"

"It's a personal thing."

The man gave me a look of disbelief. "You're a friend of his?"

"No. I'm looking for a guy, Paul Grandin. I heard he was living with Davis."

The stage manager shook his head. "I don't think Fred has had a thing to do with Paul for quite a while. I know we sure as hell don't anymore."

"He doesn't work for the Playhouse?"

"Our director, Steve Meisel, fired him about two, three weeks ago. Too much trouble."

"What kind of trouble?"

The man turned back to the set. "That's not for me to say."

"You don't know where Paul's living, then?"

He began pounding nails into a two-by-eight. "Scrounging, I guess, like he usually does. Sponging off friends—I don't know what else and don't want to know."

"You wouldn't know Davis's address, would you? Just so I can double-check."

"Some place on Ida," the guy said over the hammering noise. "Take a look at the bulletin board in the actors' lounge. There's probably an old cast list with the number."

= 21 =

I FOUND Freddy Davis's address where the stage manager said I'd find it, posted on an old call sheet in the shabby actors' lounge. Since his house was almost directly across from the Playhouse, I left the car in the lot and walked down the short slope to Ida Street. Davis's bungalow was near the Pavilion side of Ida, a two-story townhouse with a pitch roof and a cantilevered porch in back looking out over the east side of town. I was prepared to find nobody home, but a moment after I knocked, a short, handsome, black-haired man in his late twenties answered. He was wearing white shorts and a white tennis shirt that matched his pearly teeth and set off his deep California tan. An ornately furnished living room spread out behind him like the train of a robe.

"Can I help you?" he said, smiling like a sunburst.

"You can if you're Fred Davis."

"I'm Davis. Who are you?"

I told him who I was and who I was looking for. The sun set in the man's face when I said Paul Grandin's name. But I was getting used to that reaction.

"Why are you looking for him?" Davis asked.

"A friend of his killed himself. Paul was one of the last people he spoke with."

"What an exit!" the man said with a sharp laugh. "I pity him."

"You think I could talk to you about Paul for a few minutes?"

"There isn't much to say. I haven't seen him in several months. Not since April."

"He moved out?"

Davis planted a hand on the doorjamb, as if he felt the need for anchorage. "Yeah, he moved out. I let him room here for a few months when he was down on his luck and sick with bronchitis, and he moved out. That's about the whole of it. I don't know where he went and don't care."

"Did he have any other friends at the Playhouse that he might have turned to?"

The man smiled a weary smile. "You know that old adage about burning your bridges behind you? Paul set fire to them while he was still standing on them. I don't think he had a friend left among the actors at the Playhouse. Steve Meisel used to carry him on the payroll for old times' sake, but from what I hear even Steve finally got sick of Paul's shenanigans and let him go." Davis stared out at the sunburnt street. "He's out there somewhere. Causing trouble. You can bet on that."

"He never mentioned a man named Mason Greenleaf to you, did he?"

Davis gripped the doorjamb a little more tightly, as if he could feel that anchor slipping. He didn't want to talk about Paul Grandin, and I didn't blame him.

"Yeah, he might have mentioned him. An old friend of his. Why do you ask?"

"He's the one who committed suicide."

"That's too damn bad," Davis said, lowering his eyes. "I guess he was one of the only people Paul knew whom he could count on in a pinch. At least, it seemed like Paul used to turn to him whenever he was in trouble. Now that he's gone—Paul must really be alone." Reddening, Davis looked over his shoulder at a sliding-glass window at the back of the fussy living room. Out on the sunlit porch I could see someone in white, sitting in a lounge chair.

"I don't really want to talk about Paul anymore," Davis said.

"I'm sorry about his friend. I sure as hell hope that Paul didn't have a hand in it."

But he didn't say it with much hope in his voice. Turning away, Fred Davis closed the door on me—and my questions.

I walked back across Ida, up the grass hill to the Playhouse. I went into the building through the main entrance and found a pretty blond usher stacking programs in a ticket booth. I asked her where I could find Steve Meisel. She smiled at me as if I was a little lost boy.

"Through that corridor," she said, pointing to her right. "The last office on the left."

I followed her directions to Meisel's office, down a hall filled with framed posters of past Playhouse productions lit softly by a skylight. The door to Meisel's suite was half open. Through it I could see a tall, gangly man with a lumpy face sitting at a desk, reading a script. He had a pair of half-frame glasses on the tip of his nose, with a chain lavaliere attached to either earpiece. I knocked lightly.

"I'm busy just now," the man said, without looking up.

"I'll only take a minute or two," I said, edging into the room.

Meisel turned toward me, the pages of script drooping in his hand.

"My name is Stoner," I said before he could get started. "I'm looking for an employee of yours, Paul Grandin."

He was primed to get angry—I could see it in his face. But at the mention of Grandin's name, the anger seemed to evaporate. Reaching up, he lifted the reading glasses from his nose and let them drop on their chain at his chest. He put the script down, too, delicately on the crowded desktop.

"Are you with the police?" he asked.

"I'm a private investigator."

"What has he done, now?" the man said in a dead voice—sounding like Grandin's father, like Tim Bristol, like Freddy Davis.

"I just need to talk to him. A friend of his committed suicide, and I need to talk to him."

Meisel shook his head. "I can't help you. I let Paul go about two and a half weeks ago."

"May I ask why?"

"All sorts of reasons. He seldom showed up for work, for one thing. He was in a production we had staged for the schools—a little piece of propaganda about AIDS and drugs. It wasn't a stretch, but it was a steady paycheck for a very small amount of work. Sometime late this spring, Paul decided that even that was too much of a demand on his time. Once or twice a week he'd make the performance. The rest of the time, we had to have his understudy fill in. Paul claimed he'd been sick with the flu, but he was never too sick to make the scenes in the bars—or to steal whatever wasn't nailed down around the set. Frankly, he'd caused so much trouble over the past two or three years that I should have fired him a long time ago."

"Why didn't you?"

The man smiled ruefully. "Paul has a way of making you feel responsible for his problems, even though you know rationally that you're not. It's the kind of wounded helplessness that children have, when they're hurt or bewildered. You feel the need to help them, even if they've brought the trouble on themselves. It was Paul's peculiar charm. And I guess I was a sucker for it."

Mason Greenleaf had fallen for the Grandin charm, too. Only in Greenleaf's case there was a mixed history of guilt and obligation behind it that had apparently made Paul Grandin's appeal undeniable.

"Can you tell me why you asked me if I was a cop when I first came in?"

"That's not something I'm at liberty to discuss," the man said uneasily.

"Did it have something to do with why you fired him?"

"Not really. It had to do with Paul alone, and a comeuppance that he had been courting for too long. For most of his life."

"Did this happen recently, this thing with the law?"

"I told you, I can't discuss it. And I won't." The man picked up the script and placed his reading glasses back on his nose.

"You don't have any idea where Paul is living now, do you?"

Meisel shook his head. "I haven't seen him since I let him go. And don't expect to see him again. Unless I go to his funeral. Which I probably would do. What Paul is isn't all Paul's fault. He had some encouragement along the way."

As I walked back out of the office I wondered whether, wittingly or not, Mason Greenleaf had been part of that encouragement.

It was almost seven when I got back to the office. There was a message from Cindy, asking me to call. Before phoning her, I dialed Dick Lock at CPD Criminalistics. I wanted to know exactly what the trouble was that Steve Meisel had been hinting at. It didn't take long to find out.

"Yeah, I ran a LEADS on the kid," Dick said, after I asked him whether he'd pulled Paul Grandin's rap sheet. "Turns out he's a right nasty little customer. The computer came back on line a couple hours ago and spat out a list of priors. Two solicitations and three possession busts in six years."

"Possession of what?"

"Grass and cocaine. On the grass, he got off with a couple of speeding tickets. The coke, he got probated. The first solicitation was dropped. The second one is currently pending. He's got a prelim next month."

"How come the first charge was dropped?"

"He was eighteen when it happened, so maybe his age was a factor. Also he comes from a political family. His dad's a bigwig Republican, Paul Grandin, Sr. Ran for council once, about ten years ago."

"The first solicitation bust," I asked. "When was that?"

"August 31, 1988. In Mount Storm Park. The kid brushed up against the wrong guy in a public john—an undercover cop from Vice."

Paul Grandin, Sr., had assaulted Greenleaf on September 4, just a few days after Grandin, Jr.'s, arrest for soliciting a cop. The father's fury made better sense against the background of the son's solicitation bust. It also explained why he had torn through his wife's apartment and his son's effects. He was looking for a reason —for something or someone he could blame for his son's disgrace. He'd found those letters and found his man in Mason Greenleaf. Whether his suspicions about Greenleaf were justified was still an open question. But I doubted that the father would have needed much incentive to leap to conclusions about him—or to hold fast to those conclusions, even in the face of his son's subsequent misbehavior. It was a lot easier than blaming himself.

"This second bust," I said to Dick. "When did it occur?"

"About a month ago. June 29. In Mount Adams. The kid was in a bar and cruised the wrong guy again—an undercover cop out of Vice. He was in the clink overnight and is currently free on bond."

Clearly that was the trouble that Steve Meisel had refused to talk about. And it was big trouble for Paul Grandin, Jr. It was probably what he'd been discussing with Mason Greenleaf on the afternoon that Lee Marks had seen them in the Nine Mile auditorium—at least the timing was close to right. It must have shaken Greenleaf to the core. Paul Grandin coming to him with a solicitation charge hanging over his head could only have brought back terrible memories. Some of the worst memories of Mason Greenleaf's life. It made much better sense of that week he'd spent before he disappeared, his restlessness, his bad dreams. And the fact that he'd ended up in that bar with Grandin on the night of his suicide suggested that Paul had somehow succeeded in making his problems Mason's problems again. I wondered if perhaps Greenleaf had posted bond for him—made himself legally responsible for the kid.

"You don't have any indication of who went bail, do you?" I asked.

"Just a second," Dick said.

He came back on a moment later. "His mother. Sarah Grandin."

"Is she still on Rue de la Paix?"

"Check."

After I finished with Dick Lock, I returned Cindy's call. Given the unremitting ugliness of the last few hours, it was a pleasure to hear her voice.

"I was just checking in," she said, "to see how you were."

"Better, now that I'm talking to you," I said.

I started to tell her about Paul Grandin, then decided against it. I didn't really know what part he'd played in Greenleaf's suicide—just that he'd played a part. Until I knew the details, I didn't want her to have to face another betrayal from another lover.

"You'll be coming here tonight?" she asked hopefully.

"I'll try. I still haven't talked to Ira Sullivan."

"Look, if you don't want to spend the night, I'll understand," she said, trying out her candor again—or pretending to. "This thing's happened pretty fast between us, and maybe you need some time to think it through."

"I told you how I felt this morning."

"You didn't have to say that, you know. I don't need to be reassured all the time."

"For chrissake."

She laughed. "Actually, I do need to be reassured all the time. Seriously, if it gets too late, you go ahead and crash at your place."

"Why don't you just come to my apartment? Make things simple?"

"Come, like for the night?"

"For as long as you want. Go home, come back. Like you did with Mason."

She thought it over for a moment. "Yeah. I'd like that. Being here alone, with the card tables and the tea rings and the bad memories has been exhausting. It would be nice to be somewhere new for a while. To be with you. Meet your things."

"You'll find them everywhere," I said. "You'll also find a key under the welcome mat."

"That's not very detectivelike."

"I'm not always very detectivelike. Make yourself at home. I'll call if I'm going to be late."

"Harry," Cindy Dorn said, "you don't have to do this, you know? I've been living with somebody for three years, but this is a big change for you."

"I want to do it," I told her. "I want a change."

=22=

I WENT down to Wah Mee's on Sixth Street and had some supper without my usual double Scotch chaser. I had a single Scotch instead.

There were some things about myself I couldn't change as quickly as I had a roommate. Some things Cindy Dorn would have to accept. Or so I told myself. But I did feel a little like I had suddenly developed an eye over my shoulder. It wasn't an unpleasant feeling. I hadn't felt like anybody'd been watching for years. Who wants to watch somebody drink?

It was close to eight when I stepped back out onto Sixth. I walked west up to the Parkade, through the powdery twilight with its mix of late sun and early streetlamp. The temperature had dropped to a velvety touch with a breezy promise of rain in the air. I figured I'd stop at Sullivan's brownstone and check the office again for messages, before going home. It had been a long time since I'd thought pleasantly about going home. It was where I went when I couldn't go anywhere else. Last call of the day.

I got the car out of the garage and headed north up the Parkway —all the way to Ludlow. Dark was falling in earnest, as I coaxed the Pinto up the steep hill to the gaslight district and circled around Telford to Sullivan's building. I parked in the ivory pale of a fluted gas lamp and walked up to the front door of the bundled-up apartment house. There was no one in the dim lobby. Just in case, I went over to the brass mailboxes and looked up Marlene Bateman, Sullivan's nanny. She was in apartment 21, two doors down from Ira.

I climbed the marble stairs to the second floor and walked down the hall to Sullivan's door without hearing a peep. Not the cricketing of television sets, or the dull drum of stereos, or even the rattle of bolts being shot in answer to my footsteps. The hallway was as still as a still life. It was a good place for a man like Sullivan to hide out.

Given what Cherie the Secretary had said about him, I figured that Ira was as unlikely to answer his door as he was to answer his phone, so I rapped hard. When no one responded, I sidled two doors down and knocked again. A black-haired woman with dark eyes and a high-cheeked, vaguely Indian-looking face answered my knock. She was wearing a robe cinched tightly at her waist.

"Can I help you?"

I told her who I was and who had sent me—like I was trying to get into the back room of a pool hall. She smiled as if she were used to fielding calls for Ira Sullivan.

"I haven't seen Sully since last night," she said. "He went out around ten-thirty, just as I was coming in from the movies. I waved at him in the parking lot, but I don't think he saw me."

"Was he alone?"

The woman laughed. "Nooo. He had a man with him. Gray hair, rather distinguished. I must admit, I thought he was a little too distinguished for Sully."

Clearly she found her friend's company amusing, although if she knew anything about the Greenleaf case, she wouldn't have. I didn't know how Ira Sullivan had found him, but the man sounded like the older guy from Stacie's bar. I was almost certain that the younger blond had been Paul Grandin himself. If Sullivan made the same connection, it could explain why he had thought there was something odd about Greenleaf's last night on earth.

"They drove off together," the woman went on. "I assume Sully must've come back late and gone out again early, because his car was gone this morning."

The woman gave me a searching look. "You're being so mysterious, Mr. Stoner. Is something wrong?"

"I don't think so. I just need to talk to Ira."

I dug into my wallet and pulled out a card.

"If Sullivan comes back later tonight, would you mind phoning me? It's rather important."

"If it's not too late, I'll tell him to call you," the woman said.

I hadn't wanted to confront another Grandin so soon after the scene at the tennis court, but given his legal problems, it had occurred to me that Paul might stick closer to home. According to Tim Bristol, Mom had always been a port in a storm—and she had already gone bail for him. Luckily, the woman's condo was only a few long blocks to the south of Telford, back down Ludlow in a little hairpin cul-de-sac pretentiously called Rue de la Paix. Rue de la Paix didn't exist until up to ten years ago, when a contractor decided to build a posh highrise overlooking Cincinnati Technical College. I always assumed the fancy French name was meant to console people for the view—and the bite out of their wallet.

I parked on the street in the too-sweet breath of a honeysuckle and walked up a short cement stair to the apartment house outer lobby. I found the woman's name on a buzzer box and rang her number. After a moment she answered in a weary, vaguely boozy voice. It was a sound I knew too well. The sound of five or six straight shots on an empty stomach.

"What is it?"

"My name is Stoner, Mrs. Grandin. I'm looking for your son, Paul."

"Are you the police?" she said, as if that was the one and only natural response to his name.

Since it sounded like that would get me in—and I had strong reason to believe the truth wouldn't—I told her I was a cop.

"This is about the bond I posted?" she said almost hopefully.

I told her it was about the bond and she buzzed me in.

The inner lobby was a far cry from Ira Sullivan's old mahogany address. Plate glass and tessellated tile, overhead fluorescents, flock wallpaper, stainless fixtures—like something unfortunate and modern in a Jacques Tati film.

Sarah Grandin lived on the twelfth floor, near the top of the highrise. The woman was waiting for me in the hall just outside the elevator doors. She had big, strawberry blond hair inflated in a bouffant around her small, nervous triangular face. Her hair was so large and her face so tiny, she looked like a child's foot in an oversize shoe. She wore a red silk kimono over a gold silk camisole—and smelled like juniper and Chanel.

"I thought this had all been taken care of by my lawyer," she said, rocking a bit unsteadily. Her blue eyes were heavy with drink, and she kept blinking them open, alarmingly wide, as she struggled to focus.

"There are some details," I said, not liking the lie but stuck with it.

"Well, c'mon."

She turned around, almost buckling at one knee, and walked ahead of me up a hall to a door that opened on a white-on-white living room, as fleecy as down lining.

"Sit," she said, pointing to a couch that framed a glass coffee table. There was a bottle of Gilbey's sitting on the table—no glass or tumbler—and a pair of tufted mules and a book, *Striptease,* on the floor beneath it. The woman waggled over to the couch and dropped like a piano onto pavement.

"That's better, huh?" she said, encouraging herself. She blinked wide at me and asked, "What is it? You said the bond?"

"Some questions. Routine questions."

She nodded as if I made sense.

"When's the last time you saw your son?"

She stared at the gin, as if the answer was inside—like a note in a bottle.

"A few weeks ago," she said. "After he was arrested. He came . . . he needed some money. I gave him what I could."

"He's not staying here with you now, then?"

"Is he supposed to?" she said with a pained look, afraid she'd inadvertently given him away.

"No. He just has to stay in the city."

Maybe out of a fear that she was going to say something else that damaged her boy's chances, she made an effort to summon up sobriety. I watched her do it, blinking her eyes, stretching her mouth, straightening up on the couch.

"Wha'd you say your name was?" she asked.

"Stoner. Harry Stoner." I had an old deputy's badge that I saved for these occasions. I showed it to her, pocketed it without pride, and took out my notebook. "At the time your son was arrested, do you know where he was living?"

"Here and there. He had several friends in Mount Adams. I don't remember the names." She extended one arm along the top of the sofa, in a ludicrous attempt to look more relaxed. "You know this whole thing was a terrible mistake. This thing in the bar. Paulie wasn't . . . he was just joking."

"He was arrested for soliciting once before, Mrs. Grandin."

"That charge was dismissed," she said immediately.

"There was also an incident with a teacher of his—Mason Greenleaf?"

I expected her to turn red, like her husband had, at the mention of Mason's name. To my surprise she had just the opposite reaction, shrinking back into the couch with a shiver, as if she'd felt someone step on her grave.

"I could use a drink," she said with a grotesque smile. "How 'bout you?" She didn't wait for an answer, patting around the coffee table like she'd misplaced her glass. I spotted a tea tray on the opposite side of the room, near a picture window looking out on the illuminated green oval of the CTC parking lot and the dark night that surrounded it like a woods. I got up and fetched her a tumbler, setting it down by the bottle.

"Thank you," she said, sounding genuinely grateful.

She poured a stiff shot and brought the glass to her mouth with both hands, shutting her eyes as she drank. It was enough to bring her back into focus, although I knew from experience she'd drift away again before long.

"Mason Greenleaf?" I said again.

She nodded, setting the glass back down. "It was a tragic thing. Very tragic. You know we were all so upset about . . . when Paulie was arrested in the park. And we didn't know what to do, or why it had happened. And Paulie was so frightened, so very frightened." Her voice filled with sympathy for her son. "The policemen had told Paul Senior that in cases like Paulie's, there was always an adult who . . . someone who . . ."

She couldn't bring herself to say it, so I said it for her. "Seduced the boy?"

She nodded and took another drink. "You know, Paul Senior was always such a disciplinarian. He never tried to understand Paulie's needs. Or anyone else's needs," she said with casual bitterness. "I couldn't live with a man like that. Neither could my son. So I left him and took Paulie with me. But Paulie suffered without a man's guidance. I couldn't give him that. And of course his father wouldn't help unless Paulie did things his way. So when this other man, Mason Greenleaf, took such an interest in Paulie, why, I thought it was a blessing. Paulie just seemed to blossom after he befriended him. He blossomed. But then this thing happened, this mistaken thing in the park. And Paul was so angry, and Paulie was frightened. And the police were so sure there had been—what you said. They told Paul that it wasn't Paulie's fault, that if we found this other man, they would drop the charges. And Paulie . . . he finally admitted who it was to Paul."

She smiled a sick smile. "I never would've guessed it was Mr. Greenleaf."

The way she'd told the story, I suspected that it had come as a surprise to Greenleaf, too. It sounded to me as if he'd been deliberately sacrificed by the boy's father—and possibly by the boy himself—to keep little Paulie out of the newspapers. But the fact that he'd been set up didn't mean that Mason hadn't been guilty of some kind of misbehavior with Paul Grandin, Jr. Indeed, his subsequent behavior toward Paul was hard to explain as anything but an admission of guilt—or partial guilt.

"There were some letters Greenleaf wrote," I said.

Sarah Grandin smiled fondly. "Beautiful letters. I read them over with Paulie several times. Full of confidence in him. And affection. And of course, he kept sending Paulie money, too. Little sums to buy himself treats and to treat his friends.'' Her smile went away. ''Of course, Paul never gave Paulie a dime. I don't know how many times I've had to give him money out of the alimony payments, because his father is so cheap and vindictive toward me.''

I suppose I could have asked her a dozen more questions and gotten the same vague, boozy, dishonest answers. But it was Paul Grandin, Jr., I needed to talk to.

''Mrs. Grandin,'' I said, ''it's very important that I talk to your son. Do you know where he is staying?''

''He's in town. He's with friends.''

''Which friends?''

She shifted her eyes wildly, as if she were coming to the sharp edge of that corner I'd backed her into. ''I have it written down. Do you need me to . . . ?''

''Get it,'' I said coldly, like a cop.

=23=

THE address that Sarah Grandin gave me was on St. Paul Street in the nice part of Eden Park, a well-tended Cape Cod bungalow with white clapboard siding and sky-blue trim that ran around doors and windows like the bunting on a sailor suit. I'd just made it up from the street and onto the stoop when it began to rain. I had felt it gathering as I drove across town from Rue de la Paix. The first wave hit as I knocked on the door, washing up and down St. Paul in heavy windblown gusts.

I knocked at the door again—hard—and a short, trim, gray-haired man with a thin birdlike face and darting birdlike eyes answered. He was wearing the day's end remains of a business suit—white dress shirt, gray pinstripe slacks, red bowtie still knotted at the collar twelve or thirteen hours after he'd put it on. A sheet of newspaper dangled from his right hand like a hankie he couldn't shake loose.

"What is it?" he said in a high-pitched, nervous voice.

"Are you Charles Rodner?" I asked.

He nodded.

"My name is Stoner, Mr. Rodner. I'm a private detective."

I reached into my coat and pulled out my wallet, showing him the photostat of my PI license. He took it in with astonishment, making a little O with his mouth and capping it with the tip of his right hand.

"I'm looking for Paul Grandin, Jr.," I said, pocketing the ID. "His mother, Sarah, told me I could find him here."

The man's face went pale. "You say his mother told you he was here?"

He chewed his lip, as if that was hard to believe or as if he just didn't want to believe it—that Paul's mother was handing out his name and address to detectives.

He wasn't what I'd expected, either. I thought I'd find Grandin with another version of Tim Bristol. But Rodner was closer to my age—midfifties, actually—and as respectable as a church deacon. I figured him for P&G bookkeeping, which would account for the pallor and the obvious case of nerves when I showed up asking for Paul. It passed through my mind that Rodner fit the description of the well-dressed older man that Greenleaf had been drinking with at Stacie's bar.

I stepped a little to my right to dodge the rain that was coming off the eaves in a steady stream. "Look, I'm getting soaked here, Mr. Rodner. Do you think I could come inside?"

The man shied away from the door as if I'd thrown a punch—as if that was how anything disagreeable affected him. I could already see what Paul Grandin, Jr., liked about him: he didn't know how to put up a fight. It made it less likely that he'd been the angry man in the bar.

"Come in," he said, waving the newspaper.

I stepped into a short hall. To my right, a portal opened on a parlor, furnished in antiques and near-antiques. A lot of rich mahogany with well-turned legs and tapered feet. A lot of faded floral print on tuxedo sofa cushions and chairs. Persian throws. A heavy sideboard with a quart of Cutty sitting like a teapot on a silver tray, surrounded by cut crystal that glimmered in the lamplight. Photos framed in silver on the mantel and sideboard, too. Landscape oils on the wall, one of them a Constable. The room smacked of money scrupulously saved and scrupulously spent, of nostalgia and loneliness. One of the photos on the sideboard pictured an older woman with fine-spun gray hair and Charles Rodner's chiseled birdlike features. It took me a moment to realize that all the photos were of the same woman, taken at various points in her life from childhood to stately old age.

Rodner saw me looking at one of them and ran a finger across the top of its silver frame. "My mother," he said fondly. "She lived with me here for forty-nine years. This was her house before it became mine."

"You've lived here a long time," I said, brushing my slacks off before I sat down gingerly on one of his flowerbed chairs.

He sat down across from me, resting his chin on his right fist. "Yes. I should move, really. The neighborhood's changed so much —it's become dangerous. But I like being near the park. And I do rent the upstairs rooms to boarders, so I'm not completely alone."

Frightened perhaps by the storm, a black cat wandered in, curling like ivy around the legs of the sideboard. It wandered over by Rodner, who dropped his left hand over the side of his chair and petted it idly.

"I might as well tell you right off that I don't know where Paul is." He scooped the cat up with both hands and deposited it in his lap, stroking it down its back. "In fact, I'm appalled that he gave his mother my address. I assume you are working for his mother?"

It was a fair assumption, and as it seemed to be agreeable to the man, I confirmed it with a nod.

"Truth be told, I haven't seen Paul in several weeks. Before he showed up that Sunday afternoon, I hadn't seen him in months, not since he roomed upstairs."

"When was he a boarder here?"

"In the late spring of this year. As I said, I occasionally rent the upstairs to young men and women. Particularly youngsters who are involved with the theater. I'm a patron of the Playhouse, and I always try to do my bit to help young actors out. I guess I wanted to be an actor myself."

He shot a dark look at Mom, still sitting on the mantel as she'd sat on his ambitions. "Anyway, Paul was one of the youngsters I've tried to help. I met him at a Playhouse function. Someone told me that he was a talented boy and that he was having a hard time making his way as an actor. So I offered him a room in exchange for doing some household chores and maintenance.''

Charles Rodner shook his tiny head. "He was not—I'm afraid—a good worker. So our bargain didn't last very long. Paul was full of charming excuses but not dependable and somewhat dishonest. I felt sorry for him and was perhaps overly generous at first when it came to lending him money. But he never repaid me and, in fact, began to steal things from my home to pawn or sell. He did other things too—dishonest things, hurtful and petty. I won't be taken advantage of.'' He glanced down at the cat and repeated it firmly, as he stroked its glistening back. "I will not be taken advantage of.''

I assumed that that was about as resolute as Charles Rodner got. While writing people off didn't seem in character for him, I had the feeling that once they were written out, they stayed out. Which meant that Paul Grandin must have been awfully damn desperate to have returned to the man's house.

"Do you remember what day it was that Paul showed up here?''

"Yes. It was July fourteenth. I remember because it was my mother's birthday, and I'd intended to spend the evening alone. Out of the blue Paul appeared on my doorstep. Apparently there had been some . . . unpleasantness and he'd spent a night in jail. Anyway, he was desperately in need of a place to stay. I allowed him to remain here for the night.'' He held up a forefinger. "Just the night.''

"Did he tell you why he'd gone to jail?''

Rodner stroked the cat and smiled a dainty smile. "Paul had managed to get himself in a bit of trouble in a bar, flirting with the wrong company. I think he was hoping that I would help him settle the matter. Quite frankly, I had the feeling that I was not the first person he had turned to in his hour of need. Later that evening, he admitted that he'd spent the weekend visiting other friends, hopping from house to house, looking for someone to help him. He seemed fairly desperate. He didn't look at all well, either," the man said cheerily. "He said he'd been ill."

"Did he mention visiting a man named Mason Greenleaf?"

"Greenleaf? Who would that be?"

"An old friend of Paul's. He lives in Mount Adams, too. On Celestial Street."

"He may have mentioned him, among others whom he'd visited before coming to me. Frankly, I wasn't paying a great deal of attention to his ramblings. I confess I rather enjoyed seeing Paul Grandin humbled."

"I don't suppose you know where I could find Paul now, do you?"

Rodner laughed disturbingly. The sudden noise made the cat hiss and leap from his lap. Apparently it scratched him as it jumped to the floor because he kicked at it angrily and cursed: "You hurt me, you bitch!"

His face twisted with pain and the embarrassment of showing it. Blushing, he rubbed his pant leg and bit his lip.

"I'm going to have to put some peroxide on this," he said with a whine.

"I just have a few more questions."

Struggling to his feet, he stared at me as if *I'd* clawed him.

"There is nothing more to say. Paul came to me because he had nowhere else to go. In all his life he was never truthful to anyone, and in the end his lies were repaid by ordinary contempt. He had approached many people over the weekend, and in each case he met with the same scorn and rejection. He was no longer the fair-haired boy blessed with the devil's own looks and charm. That time had passed. He was twenty-six, and he looked ten years older. Hair greasy, teeth green, clothes slept in, his charm reduced to a most pathetic attempt to play on my affection, in order to get himself out of yet another jam. But I knew Paul and saw through him and would not allow myself to be taken advantage of again. I got what I wanted from him. He got nothing from me."

Rodner put a hand on his knee, wincing as if the pain from the scratch were intolerable—a weak, effeminate man with an ugly streak of vindictiveness that he'd gotten his chance to exercise in full, like a boy who'd held his breath long enough to get his way. "Now I want you to leave. And please inform Paul's mother—and Paul himself, if you see him—that I never want to see his shabby face again."

I walked back out to the car, through the rain, thinking about Paul Grandin's desperation. He'd been arrested on the twenty-ninth and spent the night in jail. A week and a half later, he'd met with Mason Greenleaf at Nine Mile, probably looking for the same kind of help that he eventually sought from Rodner. What had passed between them, no one but Paul Grandin knew. But I couldn't see Mason involving himself in another criminal solicitation case—no matter how responsible he felt toward the boy. For that matter, I didn't know what kind of help Mason—or anyone else—could have been to Grandin. Short of trying to bribe the police into dropping the charges, there was little that anyone could do for the kid. He was going to jail this time. That was obvious.

Whatever Paul Grandin had wanted from Mason, he clearly hadn't gotten it, or he wouldn't haven ended up with Rodner on Sunday night, six days later. The very fact that he'd ended up with Rodner at all, a man who hated him, bespoke his desperation. The kid must have lost his job soon after he talked to Greenleaf. He had no permanent place to stay. He'd been bouncing from old friend to old friend, wearing out a welcome that was already threadbare. His mother had handed his case over to lawyers. His peculiarly childish charm, that wounded helplessness that had kept Meisel and quite possibly Greenleaf himself in his corner, was failing him. Greenleaf himself was failing him.

But then something had changed in Mason Greenleaf.

Two days after he'd spoken to the kid, Mason had dropped out of his ordinary life, reemerging on the following Monday night to meet with Paul Grandin again and his gray-haired friend at Stacie's bar—and subsequently, to check into the Washington Hotel and kill himself.

Something had happened to him over that weekend, some change of mind or heart that had led him back to Paul Grandin and to his death. I didn't know what had ultimately broken Greenleaf's spirit, but I did know that finding Paul Grandin was the key.

≡24≡

IT was past eleven when I pulled up in front of the apartment on Ohio Avenue. There was a light in my bay window that I hadn't turned on when I left the house. I parked on Warner and walked up through the rain to my door. I could hear Cindy moving around inside, then I saw her through the curtains, as she walked over to the couch. I watched her for a while through the window, liking the fact that she was there—the freshness of it. I liked the way she looked as she cozied up on the couch, tucking her feet under her butt, holding her curly hair back from her forehead, reading a letter she held in her right hand.

As I unlocked the door and stepped into the narrow hall, she dropped the letter, jumped up, and ran over to me, smiling.

I kissed her mouth and kissed her again.

"My Lord," she said. "That was a nice welcome."

"I'm glad you're here."

"Yeah? I'm glad I'm here, too. I like your things. Your books and records. We had a little get-acquainted chat while I read."

I glanced at the couch, where a pile of mail was sitting on the cushions.

"I stopped at Mason's house," she said, "on my way over here. I just couldn't stand the thought of all those unopened letters piling up on his porch."

"I don't suppose you found one from Paul Grandin, Jr.?"

She gave me an odd look. "Why did you say that?"

I went ahead and told her what I suspected. "I'm pretty sure he had something to do with Mason's suicide."

I explained what I'd learned about the first solicitation bust immediately preceding Mason's arrest, about the money that Mason had been doling out to the boy, about Grandin's second arrest in late June, about his meeting with Mason at Nine Mile soon after, about the kid's desperate search for shelter during the week that Mason had disappeared, and about their subsequent meeting at the bar on the night of Mason's death. The way the case was shaping up, there was no way around Paul Grandin, Jr.—and his relationship with Mason Greenleaf.

As I spoke, Cindy sank down on the couch, staring morbidly at the far wall. "Mason didn't talk about Paul much," she said when I'd finished. "But I knew that they were still friends. I even saw him at the house a couple of times, just after Mason and I first met. Once Mason and I started living together, Paul didn't come by. Still, there was something between them. I'm not sure what. But Mason always acted guilty when Paul's name came up. At first I thought maybe he *had* slept with him—sometime that summer after the kid graduated from high school, before he went off to drama camp. But once I got to know Mason I realized it was so out of character for him to do something like that that I began to think it was something else—something that stretched way back into Mason's past. The kid was very lazy, self-centered, and manipulative, I could see for myself. And Mason was no dummy when it came to being manipulated by lazy, self-centered friends. What I ended up thinking was that Paul reminded Mason of his roommate, Ralph Cable, and that he put up with the kid's shenanigans as a kind of penance for turning his back on Ralph."

"Did Mason take the blame in the solicitation case as an act of penance?" I said dubiously.

"Mason was living with Del at that time, so I don't know what happened there. But Sully used to say Del was very aggressive about being gay. He believed in acting up—you know, coming out of the closet, being gay and being proud of it. Mason was never like that. He was never comfortable being bisexual. He didn't believe in kidding himself about it, but he wasn't a proselyte.''

"Are you saying that Del may have had an influence on Paul Grandin?''

"I guess I am,'' Cindy said. "Paul used to spend a lot of time at Del's house. After all, that was where Mason lived half the time. Being around Del, hearing him preach about gay pride, it might have had an effect on Paul, who was apparently very unhappy about himself and very impressionable. This thing about Paul getting arrested the first time in a park—that was something Mason said Del used to do before they met. Go to the parks and have anonymous sex in the public johns. Even after AIDS he used to do it. It was like a point of honor with him. He wasn't going to be scared out of being who he was or living the life he wanted to live. It was one of the main reasons that Mason broke off with him—he was afraid that Del had contracted AIDS because of his promiscuity.''

I stared at Cindy, and she looked away at the pile of letters sitting beside her on the sofa cushion. She reached over and picked up one of the letters, handing it to me.

"I was reading it when you knocked on the door.''

I stared at the letter, which was written on plain paper and post-marked Columbus, Ohio. It was dated July 19, the Tuesday that Mason's body was found in the Washington Hotel.

> *Dear Mason,*
> *I'm grateful for all that you did for me yesterday. Nancy knows I'm here, although she doesn't know that you helped me, of course. I talked to her late last night on the pay phone. She says she's going to try to come up and be with me whenever she can. My mother doesn't really give a damn. And Dad . . . well, you know exactly how impossible that is. I tried to find another way out. Believe me. I went everywhere I could think to go. But nobody wanted any part of me, except, finally, you. I've brought you so much trouble, Mason. I hope you'll find a way of forgiving me for that. If I have to come back, I will. But*

maybe everybody'll get lucky and I won't have to. I tried call-
ing you late last night, too, and didn't get an answer. I could
use some money for smokes and the phone. Nancy's going to
bring some. Maybe you could mail some up. You know the
address. I'm sorry about Del. Tell him thanks, too.

Love,
Paul

"What the hell?" I said out loud.

"It looks like Mason helped him," Cindy said. "Or gave him money to hide out."

"It must've been that night in the bar," I said, knowing that still didn't answer the question of who the accomplice was that Mason and Paul had been drinking with and Sullivan had apparently contacted, or what he had to do with getting Paul out of town, or why Greenleaf had immediately afterward gone from that bar, up that damn hill, into that hotel and killed himself.

"Who's Nancy?" Cindy asked.

I assumed that was Paul Grandin, Jr.'s, sister. At least, that's what I told her.

I took another look at the envelope, but there was no return address on the flap. The kid said that Mason knew the address, but Mason was dead.

I went over to the phone in the kitchen nook, called information, and got Paul Grandin, Sr.'s, phone number. I scribbled it down in my notebook as I hung up. I'd no sooner put the phone down than it rang, startling me and making Cindy jump. I picked it up and said hello.

"Mr. Stoner," a woman said in a very nervous voice, "this is Marlene Bateman. Sully's neighbor?"

"Oh, yes, Ms. Bateman. Did he finally get in?"

"Something's wrong, Mr. Stoner. The police have just called."

"What is it, Ms. Bateman?" I said, knowing already from the sound of her voice that the man was dead.

Her voice began to shake. "They've found Sully's car on I-71, near King's Island. There's been an accident." She started to cry.

"Sully's dead. They want somebody to come there to—identify the body. They said they're having trouble getting him out of the wreckage. Frankly, I don't think I can do it. I know it's terribly presumptuous. But I couldn't think of anyone to call. And since you're a law enforcement professional, I was hoping . . ."

"I'll take care of it," I told her.

"Tell them to take him to Weiderman's Funeral Home. I'll . . . make the arrangements."

At first Cindy insisted on going with me. Sullivan was her friend, and she felt an obligation to come along. But I managed to convince her that it was a bad idea. She'd seen enough death already. And she knew it.

"You'll probably be a while, right?" she said as I got ready to leave.

"Yeah. Maybe you should go home. These things have a way of dragging out, and I may not be back until morning."

"I'll stay. It would be too depressing at home with Sully dead, too." She gave me a questioning look. "You don't think this has anything to do with Mason?"

"Sullivan said he'd talked to someone who'd seen Mason, and last night his landlady saw him with a guy that fits the description of the older man at Stacie's bar."

Cindy tapped her foot nervously. "I don't like this. It's frightening."

"It's unsettling," I agreed.

"You know, I haven't felt scared up till now. Just angry and suspicious. But it's too strange, Sully getting killed." She looked around the unfamiliar room and shuddered up her spine. "Paul had something to do with both of these deaths. I feel it."

"I think we're going to have to find him."

"How?"

"Possibly through his sister. She apparently knows where he is— or was, as of a week ago."

"Why did he mention Del in that letter?"

It was a question I'd wondered about myself. "It's something else to look into."

Cindy reached out for me suddenly, grabbing my arm as if I'd lost my balance—or she had. "Maybe you shouldn't, Harry. Maybe we should stop."

I sat down on the arm of the sofa and pulled her to me. "Cindy, I can take care of myself. I'm pretty good at it, actually."

"I know that. But I couldn't stand it if something happened to you, too, because of Mason. His death is terrible. I regret it, I mourn it. I always will. But I won't let you get hurt because of it—because of me." She stared directly into my eyes. "I'm not kidding, Harry. Mason would have felt exactly the same way."

I kissed her on the forehead. "I'll have to make sure that nothing happens."

She smiled, but she didn't look confident.

"This is a part of life I've successfully avoided up till now," she said

"Which part is that?"

"Your part. The dangerous part."

I smiled. "Living with Mason Greenleaf wasn't exactly a safe bet."

"Yes, it was. In most ways it was exactly that. Safe sex. Safe haven. No chance of getting hurt." She laughed mordantly. "I'm beginning to understand just how unrealistic that whole idea is."

I stood up and went over to the door. "I'll try to call, if I can. If you get lonely, the girl upstairs is a good soul."

Cindy arched an eyebrow. "Oh, yeah?"

"She's twenty-two years old. A grad student in English. Her name is Linda Fine. Tell her you're a friend of mine. My new roommate."

It took me about twenty minutes to make my way out 71 to King's Island through a driving rain. I spotted the accident a mile before I got there—a cluster of flashers blinking on the left side of the highway, the south lanes going toward Cincinnati. As I got closer, I could see a white car, a BMW 633, sitting in a grassy decline on the far shoulder. A telephone pole was bent above its hood. Two state patrol cars were parked on the embankment, above and below the Beemer. An ambulance with its flashers going was parked alongside it, its back doors open. Flares spilling sulfur yellow sparks at their tips were posted on the highway around the wreck.

I had to drive a few miles north to find a turnaround. Traffic was backed up above the accident, so it took me another fifteen minutes to work my way back down to the BMW. When I got to the first flare, I pulled off on the embankment and parked behind the state patrol car. A cop in a yellow rain slicker came up to me before I could open the door, signaling with his hand for me to roll down the window.

"This isn't a spot for sight-seers," he said, giving me a tough look.

"I'm here to identify the body."

Straightening up, he stepped back from the door. "Watch yourself when you get out."

I opened the door and sidestepped my way up toward the Beemer. The headlights from the stacked-up traffic flooded the roadway with white light, diffused by the rain and a thin mist crawling along the ditch where the front of the car was sitting. As I neared the BMW, the cop fell in step beside me.

"Is he still in the car?" I asked him.

"No. We got him out and into the ambulance a few minutes ago."

I glanced at the wreck. There was a star fracture in the front windshield with a hole in its center the size of a man's head. There was some blood on the glass and on the hood.

"His head went right through it and slammed into the pole," the cop said, following my gaze. "We think he had a blowout." Turning toward the highway, he pointed to some heavy skid marks on the pavement. "Anyway, he lost control. He'd had a bad night, so maybe he wasn't concentrating a hundred percent."

"Why do you say that about a bad night?"

"There was a fresh speeding ticket in the front seat. He got it just outside Columbus, about nine forty-five."

"Was there anything else inside the car? Papers, briefcase?"

"Whatever we got is in the ambulance, along with the body." He cleared his throat uneasily. "You want to take a look?"

I nodded.

Two paramedics were sitting on the rear bumper of the ambulance, smoking cigarettes and talking in the rain. They looked up as we walked over. One of them dropped his cigarette on the wet pavement, stubbing it with his foot, then climbed up into the ambulance. He flipped on an interior light, and I saw the gurney with the body bag sitting on the cobble-metal floor.

The one sitting on the bumper said, "Are you here to identify the body?"

"Yeah."

He stood up. "Watch your head." He opened the doors fully and backed away, shielding his cigarette with a cupped hand.

I climbed into the ambulance. The first paramedic was standing at the head of the gurney. Stooping, I went up beside him.

"You're a friend of his?" he said.

"Harry Stoner."

He picked up a clipboard and wrote my name down, then reached over and unzipped the top part of the body bag. I took a look and nodded.

"It's Ira Sullivan."

The paramedic zipped the bag up over Sullivan's battered face.

"Did you find anything in the car?" I asked him. "Personal belongings?"

"Wallet, watch."

"No papers?"

He shook his head. "Nope. Casual way he was dressed, it didn't look like he was on business. Maybe he was just visiting a friend."

= 25 =

I GOT back to the apartment around three-thirty. Cindy was asleep in the bed. She'd left the radio in the living room on a talk station—probably to comfort herself with the sound of a voice. I flipped it off and sat down on the couch for a while, thinking that in the morning I was going to have to do something I didn't really want to do. But with Sullivan gone, I didn't see where I had a choice. Too many people had suffered, directly or indirectly, because of Paul Grandin, Jr.

I flipped off the lamp and stared out at the streetlights, smeared by the rain. On a normal night, on a case like this, I would have drunk myself to sleep. That night, I went into the bedroom and lay down next to Cindy Dorn and held her tight.

I woke up early—startled by a thunderclap. The last of the night was still there outside, graying and clamorous. I left Cindy sleeping and walked into the kitchen, making coffee in the sink with hot water and crystals, then taking a quick shower. Morning began to break as I toweled off, enough so I could see the wet streets through the bedroom curtains and the first spate of traffic starting like a fuse in the half-dark. It was still only a little past seven.

She woke up as I began to dress, propping herself up on her elbows and smiling at me groggily.

"I took a pill," she said. "I don't usually do that. But I was afraid I wouldn't be able to sleep otherwise. Last night was pretty spooky.''

It explained why she'd slept through my early morning arrival and the noisy thunderstorm. It occurred to me that it might also explain something else—where Mason Greenleaf had gotten the Seconals that killed him. I didn't say anything about it to her. If it was true, it was something she didn't need to know.

"I dreamed about Sully," she said, sinking back into the pillow. "His friend, Marlene Bateman, called again after you left. We talked about him for a while. You know, he never liked to drive at night." Cindy smiled sadly. "He never liked to do anything that put him out. He must've had a good reason to go riding around in a storm."

"He went to Columbus."

"How do you know that?" she said with surprise.

I told her about the speeding ticket.

"Unless he had a friend or relative up there that you know about, I'm guessing the trip had something to do with Paul Grandin."

She shook her head. "Sully's folks are dead. Marlene told me that. He really didn't have anybody, except for her and Mason."

Cindy put her hands over her eyes.

"Are you okay?"

She nodded. "It's just that I'd like this shit to end."

"I'm going to see to it," I said, putting my shirt on and slipping into my trousers. "Today."

While Cindy took a shower, I went into the living room and dialed Paul Grandin, Sr., at home. Grandin himself answered, sounding as if he was still half-asleep.

"Yeah? What?"

"Mr. Grandin, this is Harry Stoner. I talked to you the other day about your son."

"Paul?" he said.

"You were playing tennis with your daughter."

"I remember you," he said, suddenly pissed off.

"I don't know whether you know this, but your son is in trouble with the cops again. He was arrested several weeks ago for solicitation in a Mount Adams bar. From what I've been able to find out, he's been having a tough time of it since then.''

"I can't hear this," the man said with pain in his voice. "I can't look after him anymore. He's got to take the reins of reponsibility in his own hands.''

It was probably a lecture that Paul Grandin, Jr., had heard every day of his life—and ignored. The pathetic part was, it still sounded like the man was trying to convince himself—as if he had never quite given up on reforming his son, in spite of the public notice and the public humiliations. I knew his vanity was something I could use against him.

"I need to talk to him, Mr. Grandin. Several people are dead. If I don't talk to him, I'm going to have to go to the police.''

"Dead," the man said with horror. "Dead because of Paul?''

"I think so.''

"That cocksucker Greenleaf, for chrissake! Who the hell cares if he'd dead, after the shame he brought on us?''

It was hardly that simple, as the man well knew. But there was no point in going into it with him. I had to play to my strength—which was to make him fear for his wayward son and his own reputation.

"It's not just Greenleaf, Mr. Grandin. Another man, a lawyer named Ira Sullivan, is dead, too. And Paul was the last person he was seen with. Right now, all that's hanging over Paul's head is a solicitation charge. If I go to the police, it could be much worse.''

"I don't believe this," the man said—sounding like he believed every word of it. "Even Paul isn't this stupid and irresponsible.''

"I want to talk to you—and your daughter.''

"Nancy? Why Nancy?''

"Because she knows where Paul is staying, Mr. Grandin.''

The man exploded with rage. "You stay away from my daughter with your filthy lies. You stay away from her, or I swear I will kill you myself. She's not involved with any of Paul's problems.''

"Ask her yourself, Mr. Grandin.''

He slammed the receiver down. But I knew I'd made my point. I knew he'd ask her.

As I hung up the phone, I saw Cindy standing in the hall. I didn't have to ask how much of the conversation she'd heard.

"It's the only way, Cindy," I said, flushing. "I've got to get that girl to tell me where he is—or lead me to him. Otherwise, this thing will never come clear."

She nodded. "You had to."

But she was no more happy about it than I was.

We didn't say a lot to each other for the next half hour. Cindy puttered in the kitchen fixing breakfast. And I went through the rest of Greenleaf's mail. Bills and junk mail, mostly. But one of them turned out to be interesting.

"Who does Mason know in Indianapolis and Lexington?" I called out.

"He's got friends all over the place. Why?"

"His MasterCard statement. He booked a motel room in those cities on Friday the eleventh and Saturday the twelfth. On Sunday the thirteenth, he stayed in Columbus."

"You're kidding." She came out of the kitchen nook with a skillet in her hand.

"We know where he was, now, over that weekend. Traveling around."

The fact was, I could now account for all of his time from the Thursday meeting with Mulhane and Del Cavanaugh to the Monday rendezvous at Stacie's bar.

Cindy stared at me in bewilderment. "Why was he doing that?"

"Maybe he was looking for Grandin."

"But I thought you said Paul was in Cincinnati that weekend, staying with various friends."

"Perhaps Mason didn't know that."

She shook her head. "If Mason had wanted to find Paul, he could have. I mean, he did, didn't he? On Monday night?"

"Then I don't understand this. I mean, did he have special friends in these places? Friends he might have wanted to say good-bye to?"

She turned away, going back inside the kitchen. I'd upset her by implying that Greenleaf might have been planning to kill himself for days. After a moment I heard her say, "No. He didn't know anyone that well in any of those places."

I stared at the MasterCard charge slips. Indianapolis, Lexington, Columbus. The only things they had in common were that they were within a few hours' driving distance of each other, and they were major cities. He'd spent a day in each one. And whether or not he'd been looking for Grandin, he'd been looking for something he couldn't find in Cincinnati—something he couldn't confide to Cindy or Sullivan or any of his friends.

I didn't bring the subject up again. The way things had gone that morning, I didn't want to upset her any further.

We had breakfast at the trestle table. It was the first time I had breakfast there since I'd moved in. I think it was odder for me than it was for her.

"You'll have to get used to it," she said, smiling, "if you plan for me to keep coming over."

"I'll make the adjustment."

"I don't want to make you change too fast, Harry. You can take a few days off. Think about it. Get used to waking up to somebody in your bed."

"You know, when I got in last night," I said, "it was goddamn wonderful to find you in my bed."

She looked pleased. "Yeah?"

"I never liked being alone all that much, Cindy. The kind of work I do, the hours I keep—I got used to it. Of course, there's a lot of company in a fifth of Scotch."

She lowered her eyes. "I don't care if you drink."

"You might if you saw me drunk. I've been drinking pretty steadily since I got back from Viet Nam."

She didn't say anything.

"There are things you see, things you do . . ."

"I don't need to know," she said softly.

"Maybe you don't. But they've gotten in the way of my relationships in the past."

The phone rang suddenly, making her jump. I went into the living room and picked up the receiver. It was Nancy Grandin.

"Why did you tell my father about Paul?" she said with such anguish in her voice that I felt ashamed.

"Nancy, I had to. I have to talk to Paul."

"Dad's just crazy with thinking about it. He's so upset. I don't know what to do." She sobbed. "I don't know what to do."

"Meet me and let me explain. Then decide."

"You said you were going to go to the police."

"Not if I can talk to him first."

"I don't believe you. Everyone's against him, and he's got such terrible problems."

"I'm going to come to your house."

"No!" she cried. "Not here. I don't know what Dad would do if he saw you here."

"Then where?"

"I don't know. I don't know."

"Calm down," I said. "I just want to talk to him. I won't go to the police if I can talk to him. There's a Frisch's in Kenwood—near your house. You know what I'm talking about?"

"Yes."

I glanced at my watch. "I'll meet you there in the parking lot in half an hour. You let me explain. I won't make you do anything you don't want to do."

I said it. But it wasn't true. We both knew it.

≡26≡

BEFORE leaving the house, I told Cindy I'd call her when I had the chance.

"I'll probably go back to Finneytown," she said, as if the novelty of being in my house had worn off quickly. It didn't surprise me, as I had brought all the troubles she'd been trying to escape, and some new ones, home with me.

We kissed good-bye at the door.

"I didn't mean to cut you off before," she said, resting her head on my chest. "About your work."

"It's not for you," I said.

"You ought to be able to talk about it—to somebody."

"Maybe when we know each other better."

"You'll be careful, right?" she said, putting her hand on my cheek. "Because this is still scaring me. This kid's scaring me. People seem to die around him."

She wasn't wrong about that.

Because of the rain, it took me a little over a half an hour to drive out 71 to Kenwood Road. I wasn't sure Nancy Grandin was going to be there when I pulled into the restaurant parking lot, but she was there, sitting in the gold Mercedes, chewing on her knuckles and looking red-eyed and miserable. I parked beside her car and got out, walking over to her window.

"Let's go inside. I'll buy you coffee."

"I don't drink coffee," she said. "I'm just seventeen."

"Then I'll buy you a Coke."

She opened the car door and got out into the rain. She was dressed jauntily in jeans and a pearl silk blouse. But all frightened kids look alike. And she was terrified. I took her inside, back to a vinyl booth looking out through a picture window on the rainy lot. A waitress in taffeta brought her a Coke and me a coffee. Nancy Grandin stared at the drink as if it were poisoned.

"God, if Dad knew I was here."

"He still loves your brother, doesn't he?"

"Of course he does," she said, her eyes flashing.

"Then he wants what's best for him."

"He doesn't understand Paul. No one does."

She sounded exactly like her mother. Only, when her mother said the same words, they had a hollow, self-serving sound. I didn't have a doubt that Nancy Grandin meant them from the bottom of her heart.

"Mason Greenleaf tried to help him."

"Sure," she said with a snort. "Because he was guilty for what he did to him."

"Did Paul tell you that?"

"No. He's brainwashed. That man cast a spell on him."

I had the feeling it was the other way around, but I didn't want to argue with her.

"Paul loved him," she said grudgingly. "He doesn't realize how his life was ruined by him."

"How did he ruin his life, Nancy?"

"I can't tell you. But he did."

It was a little late in the day to be keeping Paul Grandin's homosexuality secret. But I could understand her reluctance to talk about it. And I didn't want to force her into a betrayal that would scare her off completely.

"He tried to help Paul," she conceded. "But it was too little, too late."

"Does Paul know that Mason is dead?"

The girl sucked in her breath. "He tried to kill himself when he read about it. It made the newspapers up there, too."

"You mean in Columbus."

"Oh, fuck," she said, angry at herself for giving it away.

"Look, I already know he's in Columbus."

"How do you know that?"

"Because a friend of Mason's went to look for him there."

The girl put a stubbornly blank look on her face. "I have no idea what you're talking about."

"Nancy, you do know what I'm talking about. Your brother was in a bar with Mason on the night he died, along with another man. They had an argument, and after that argument, Mason killed himself."

"You're wrong. Paul doesn't know anything about it."

"Then let me talk to him."

"He can't see people."

"Why not?"

"Because he can't." She glanced out the window and threw a hand to her mouth. "Oh, my God."

I looked through the plate glass and saw another Mercedes pull into the lot. Paul Grandin, Sr., was behind the wheel. He searched for Nancy's car and, when he spotted it, skidded to a stop.

"You gotta go," she said hysterically. "If he sees you here, he'll do something crazy. Please."

"You tell me how to get in touch with your brother, and I'll go."

"Please," she said desperately. "I'll call you. I promise."

She brushed around the side of the table and ran up the aisle toward the door. I watched through the window as she ran out into the lot. When he spotted her, her father got out of his car. She went up to him, and he grabbed her by the arms, shaking her. I could see him talking angrily to her and glancing, right and left, looking for me.

Maybe she told him I'd left. Maybe she told him some other

story. But after some more shaking and violent talk, he calmed down. I could almost see the flow of power reverse itself, as if it was draining out of him and into her. She kept talking to him, gently, reassuringly. It came to me that Nancy Grandin was the real emotional center of that family. After a while she led her father over to his car. She kissed him on the cheek as he got in. Then she got into her car.

Grandin drove out of the lot. Nancy stared after him through the windshield, then glanced quickly through the plate-glass window at me. I threw a couple of dollars down on the table and got up as she started the Mercedes. I made it to the front window in time to see her turn onto the expressway, heading north—away from her Indian Hill home.

=27=

I DIDN'T know whether Nancy Grandin eventually planned to call me or not. But I couldn't take the chance that she would try to warn her brother off before I'd talked to him. From the letter he'd written to Greenleaf, it didn't look as if he had ready access to a phone. Which meant that he would have to call her on some sort of prearranged schedule—or she would have to drive to him.

That, and the fact that she was a frightened child, was what I was counting on. She was no fool, but between me and her father, she'd been terrified enough to bolt to her brother in Columbus. Columbus was the general direction she'd been headed when she left the restaurant. And it was the direction I headed as soon as I got the Pinto started, following her onto north 71.

I wasn't sure I had her until I got to Wilmington—a good twenty minutes beyond Kenwood. Up until then, I was wondering how far I was willing to push it before going back. Nancy Grandin could have turned off at any number of exits without me knowing it. But as it happened, she hadn't turned off. I topped a rise and spotted her gold Mercedes in the distance—still running due north, running scared. After that, it was just a question of hanging back and waiting for her to get to wherever it was she was running to.

An hour and a half went by, full of flooded cornfields and solitary trees standing like gibbets in the hazy distance. A few miles south of Columbus, she turned off the expressway onto a state road. I almost missed the exit in the monotony of rain and flat, dripping fields. I managed to edge over to the ramp just as she turned west, crossing an overpass above me and heading into a short commercial strip. Golden arches and Pizza Huts and the usual skeletal plazas of gas stations and convenience stores. I lost her for a moment, then caught her again where the little stretch of Quonsets died off over a hump of railroad tracks into a pleasant, middle-class neighborhood: large frame houses, trim yards, an inviting look of prosperity even in the pouring rain. About a mile in front of me, I saw her turn left into a driveway. There was a sign posted on the side of the road where she turned off. I couldn't see it clearly until I was almost on top of it: EAST VIEW NURSING HOME.

When I got to the sign, I turned onto the short drive, following it down to a low brick building with a canopied entrance. I saw Nancy's Mercedes parked in a slot near the door. I found an empty slot of my own and parked.

I walked through the rain down the drive to the canopied entranceway. There was a reception counter inside the door, manned by a nurse. Hallways with numbered doors on them led away from the nurses' station to the right and left. The place looked spruce and clean on the surface, but the hallway smelled of incontinence, old age, and death.

"Can I help you?" the nurse said.

I didn't know how Paul Grandin had disguised himself, as an employee or a patient. I tried employee first, thinking it made the best sense. "I'm looking for a friend who works here—Paul Grandin, Jr."

The nurse gave me an odd look. "Paul doesn't work here. He's a patient."

"I'm sorry," I said. "I haven't seen him in a while, and when I found out he was at East View, I just assumed, because of his age, he was an employee."

The woman made a concerned face. "You obviously haven't seen Paul in a while, have you?"

I told her what she expected to hear. "No."

"Then you better prepare yourself for a bit of a shock. "He's
. . . not well.''

Her look and her tone of voice left no doubt that his condition
was serious. I began to have a very unsettled feeling about Paul
Grandin, Jr., And Mason Greenleaf.

"What room?" I asked.

"Down the hall to your right. Number one twelve. I believe his
sister is with him just now. I saw her come in a few moments ago.''

I went down the hall, past doors opening on empty rooms. Men
and women sitting in wheelchairs, staring vacantly at televisions, at
the rainy windows. Room 112 was around a corner, a little way
down another long dreary corridor. I could hear the girl talking as I
got closer to the door. She was talking about me.

"He said he'd go to the police."

"What difference does it make?" a man said in a listless tenor
voice. "I'm not going anywhere."

I came to the door and looked in. The sister was sitting with her
back to me. The young man sprawled on the bed in front of her was
wearing a blue hospital gown. His handsome face was drawn and
heavily circled under the eyes. He saw me in the doorway and
smiled.

"You're the one, aren't you?" he said.

The girl whirled around in the chair. When she saw me, she
flushed. Leaping to her feet, she whirled and came at me as if she
wanted to claw my face.

"Nancy, stop," the boy said to her.

"You tricked me!" she said to me between her teeth. "You have
no right! No right! Goddamn you!"

"Nancy," her brother said again in a calm voice. "Leave us
alone. I want to talk to him."

She turned her head, glancing at her brother, then pushed past
me, her head averted, out into the hall.

"Come closer," Paul Grandin, Jr., said. "I can't wear my con-
tacts anymore, so I don't see worth a damn."

I went over by the bed.

"You're the detective, aren't you?"

I nodded.

He pointed to the chair his sister had been sitting in. His wrists were bandaged with gauze and tape. When he saw me staring at them, he smiled, showing yellow teeth. "When I heard about Mason, I went a little . . . crazy."

"When did you hear about him?" I asked, sitting down on the chair.

Up close, he looked considerably worse than he had from the doorway. Haggard, sallow, sweaty, as if he were wasting with fever.

"A few days ago. I saw something in a newspaper." The kid took a deep, labored breath. "He shouldn't have done it."

"What?"

"Tried to help me. I didn't think he was going to. I didn't think anyone was. But he knew I was sick from last year—when we first came up here to have the bloodwork done."

"Last year?"

The boy nodded. "I hadn't been well for a while. I was getting a lot of colds. I half knew that it was the beginning of—what it is. I just wanted to let the thing run its course. But he made me come with him up to Presbyterian Memorial. So Tim wouldn't find out, so they wouldn't know at work. So I wouldn't lose my friends and the job."

"This would have been last summer?" I said, thinking about that first time that Mason Greenleaf had dropped out of Cindy's life. He'd said he'd gone home.

"Yeah, I guess. Summer or fall. After I found out, I moved out of Timmy's house. I couldn't keep being with him. After that I couldn't . . . be with anybody. So I bummed around from place to place. Freddy. That prick Rodner."

"You have HIV?" I said, saying what was obvious from one look at him.

"I got full-blown AIDS is what I got, mister." Paul Grandin, Jr., turned his head away, toward the gray window. Through it, you could see the backyard of a neighboring house, with a white swing-set dripping rain. "Can't keep it secret anymore."

It was why he'd left Tim Bristol, why he'd missed so much work.

Why he'd ended up getting fired by Steve Meisel, who thought he'd been goldbricking.

"Toward the end there, it was more trouble to fake being well than it was worth. I had to make a lot of excuses to a lot of people. It was lonely—not being able to make contact. It was almost a relief to get busted."

"Do the cops know that you have AIDS?"

"They know what they know—that I was a previous offender. The guy who busted me, he was the same one from before." The kid laughed. "Like I'm stupid enough to hit on the same cop twice."

I stared at the boy. "Are you saying you were set up?"

"I'm saying it doesn't make a difference anymore." He moved around in the bed, propping himself on the pillow as he stared out at the swings and the scattering of flowers and shrubs. "It's a gray day. It makes me think of the past."

Even though his life had led him to that hospital bed, even though he'd betrayed just about everyone he'd ever known, I started to feel sorry for Paul Grandin, Jr. He was just too young to be looking back.

"That night at the bar with Mason. What happened?"

He shook his head. "I don't know. Sully asked me about it last night."

"Sullivan came up here?"

"Del told him where I was. I guess Mason told Del where he'd taken me. Sully wanted to know if I knew why Mason had gone to the bar on the night he died. I told him I didn't know. I wasn't there."

I felt a chill run up my back. "You weren't in the bar?"

"How could I be in the bar? I was here that whole day. Mason drove me up and checked me in the morning after Charley kicked me out. I thought Mace had given up on me, too. But do you know what?" The kid looked at me with shining eyes. "He spent that entire weekend trying to find someplace that would take me in. He was all over the place. Here, in Indianapolis, Lexington. You know when you got what I got—sometimes they don't want to take you.

Plus, he had to find someplace private—where the cops wouldn't find me.

"He was the only one who looked after me. The others—" He laughed bitterly. "Oh, fuck, I deserved it. I deserve it all. I've done a lot of bad things. Caused a lot of people pain. People who loved me, tried to help me."

"Mason, too?"

The kid shut his eyes. "Especially him."

I got up from the chair. Not wanting to hear the details. Not much caring anymore.

"I haven't been out of here since Mason checked me in, except to use the phone in the hall to call Nancy," he said. "Last thing Mason said to me was that everything was going to be all right. That he'd call me in a couple of days. That's what I told Sully."

I didn't tell him about Sullivan. He already had enough pain to look back on.

"So," he said, folding his hands on his chest, "you gonna go to the cops, now?"

"No. You can stop worrying about them. I'll see to it."

He smiled his sickly yellow smile. "Why is it people always look after me? I've counted on it my whole life."

"You counted on it too much, Paul," I said. "You should've looked after yourself."

He laughed feebly. "Why? When so many people were willing to do it for me?"

=28=

THE girl was waiting just outside the door, her back against the wall, her face in her hands. As I came out, she dropped her hands and stared at me uncertainly, through wet eyes.

"Are you going to help him? Like you said?"

"I'm going to try."

She swallowed hard. "I'm sorry. I thought you came here to hurt him."

"It's my fault. I gave you that impression."

She put a hand back to her mouth and chewed nervously on a knuckle. "I don't know how Paul's going to pay for this—now that that man is dead."

"Have you talked to your father?"

She laughed forlornly.

"Talk to him," I said. "This is different, Maybe he'll listen."

But I could tell from her look that she had no confidence that she could sway her father.

"If that man hadn't killed himself," Nancy Grandin said, "we'd be all right. I just don't understand him. I don't understand why he did it." She looked over her shoulder at the door to her brother's room. "I don't understand why he did any of this. It's so twisted, really. To get Paul started on this way of living. Then try to rescue him when it's too late."

"Your brother told you it was Mason who had seduced him?"

"He never talks about it."

"Then maybe Greenleaf didn't do it, Nancy. Maybe he just wanted to make amends for other things in his life."

"But my father found those letters."

"From what your mother said, they didn't prove anything."

She shook her head. "Someone did this to him. Someone he trusted."

I didn't say it to the girl, but whether it was Cavanaugh or Greenleaf or some stranger in the dark, the kid had mostly done it to himself.

I drove back to town through the rainy cornfields. A tattered mist hung smokily in the distance, trailing from the branches of trees and crawling above the fields. Occasionally it drifted wraithlike across the road. At night, in the same hot drenching rain, the fog had probably cost Ira Sullivan his life.

He'd come up to Columbus looking for what I'd been looking for: an explanation of what had happened to Mason in Stacie's bar on the night that he died. But he'd known something that I hadn't known—he'd known that Paul Grandin wasn't at the bar with Mason. He'd known it because he'd already met one of the men who had actually been at Stacie's that night. Marlene Bateman had seen them together in the parking lot. He'd only gone to Paul Grandin, Jr., to find out *why* Mason had met with the other men. It was something I intended to find out, too.

Around one-thirty I got back to town. I took 71 all the way in, getting off at Dana and cutting over to Rose Hill—to Del Cavanaugh's stone fortress. I pulled up beyond the carriage circle, parked, and walked back to the front door pavilion. The garden to the side of the house, where Cavanaugh and I had sat and talked on Monday morning, was soaked with rain. I could hear it falling in the oak trees, see it dripping from the cast-iron patio furniture. In the rain the old stone house had a look of misery and abandonment.

I rang the bell and waited. After a time the mother answered. She scowled when she saw me.

"He's sleeping. He can't be disturbed."

"Mother?" I heard him call out.

The woman's face became vibrant with loathing. "I want you to go. I don't want you bothering him. My God, how much time does he have left?"

"Mother?" Cavanaugh said again.

I saw him appear in the dark wainscoted hall behind her. He was using a walker. He came into the gray light, dragging himself forward with an effort that seemed to me to be exactly commensurate to his mother's fierce determination to keep me out. It was what his life appeared to have come down to—a daily battle with his mother. For all I knew, that was what his life had always been like.

"Mr. Stoner," he said, breathing hard with the exertion, "do come in."

"I don't want him here," the mother said, addressing Cavanaugh. "Haven't you seen enough trouble?"

"Mr. Stoner is not here to start trouble, Mother. He's here to settle a kind of bet, a little wager I made with him about why our mutual friend did away with himself."

"Del, you are not responsible," the mother said icily.

The man raised his arm as if he were going to strike her. "Get out of the light!" he shouted. "Get out of my way!"

She shrank back into the hall, glaring at him. "There will come a time, my boy, when you will need things from me. Keep that in mind." She turned away and walked stiffly up the hall, directly up a wainscoted staircase—out of sight.

The man stared after her furiously. "She thinks I'm going to need her at the end," he said, half to himself. "She is quite mistaken. I have remedies of my own for that eventuality. She'll see."

Just from the sound of his voice, it seemed to me that he'd deteriorated in the few short days since we'd first spoken. He turned his skeletal face back to me, smiling gruesomely. "Do come in," he said, triumph burning like candles in his sunken eyes.

I followed him as he pulled himself down a hall, through an opening into a large living room with a stone mantel running half the length of the wall. The French windows on the other wall filled the huge space with diffuse, stormy light.

"This used to be a ballroom in my father's day," the man said with a touch of pride. "Many illustrious people played and danced in this room."

He pulled himself over to a tall leather chair, studded with brass, and sank down into it with a sigh. The soft, flattering light coming through the far windows fleshed out the decay of his face. For just an instant I caught sight of him as he'd once been—young and arrogant and cruelly handsome.

"Sit," he said, gesturing to another high-backed chair across from him.

I sat down, smelling the old soaped leather and the dust.

"So," he said, laying his hands one atop the other on his knee. "Was I right?"

"I suppose you were. But you didn't tell me the whole story, Del."

"What fun would that have been for a detective?" he said, grinning.

"Mason came back here again, didn't he?"

"Yes, I concede he did."

He wanted me to tease it out of him—just for the fun of watching me flail at the truth.

"He told you about another friend of yours, Paul Grandin, Jr."

"Poor Paul," the man said, without a drop of pity in his voice. "I understand he's experiencing some health problems. I warned him this could happen. I tried to instruct him in taking proper precautions. But you know young people won't listen."

I felt a wave of disgust well up in me like nausea. "You seduced him, didn't you, Del? Back when Mason was living with you?"

The man didn't say anything.

"That was why Mason left you, wasn't it? That's why Mason felt responsible for the boy—and took the solicitation rap for him."

"Mason's feeling of responsibility had nothing to do with me," the man said flatly. "He had his own cross to bear."

"You mean Ralph Cable."

"My, my. So many names from the past. Isn't it odd how infectious the past is? Yours, mine, Mrs. Dorn's. It all somehow becomes cross-pollinated and interwoven, so that we willy-nilly inherit parts of each other's history—and live them out as if they were our own story." The man stared at me with mild contempt. "Do you know what I would do, if I had it in my power? I would have the whole world wired to my heart. And when that heart stopped beating—why, the world itself would wink out."

"You're a piece of work, Del."

"Thank you," he said, grinning again.

"What did Mason tell you he was going to do, after he'd dropped Paul at that rest home?"

"Ira asked me that very same question, no more than a day ago. Do you know Ira Sullivan, Mason's lawyer?"

"I know he's dead."

The man flinched with his whole body, as if he'd been jolted with electricity. "What do you mean, he's dead?"

"He was killed on the interstate last night in a car wreck, coming back from Columbus—where you'd sent him, Del."

Cavanaugh's face trembled with an emotion so strong that he had to bite his own lip to keep from breaking down. I watched him battle his grief with a mixed feeling of pity and contempt. He'd literally willed himself to stop feeling anything for anyone but himself. But I'd taken him by surprise. With an effort that was almost as impressive as his march past Mom to the front door, he managed to keep from crying out.

"I did not know that," he said, fighting the tremor in his voice. "I confess I am sorry to hear it. Ira was a . . . friend."

"He died helping me try to solve this puzzle, Del."

"Then you must feel quite terribly responsible."

"I've had better days."

He nodded, as if the high jinks were finally over, as if the news about Sullivan had momentarily blasted him back into the human race.

"Mason came here on Monday evening. He told me what he'd

done with Paul. He told me he was going to meet with some people that night and try to settle things for Paul—and himself.''

''What did he mean by that?''

Cavanaugh took a deep breath. ''I assumed he was going to talk with the district attorney. Ira had the same impression. Ira had talked to a friend who knew Mason's problem, someone in the district attorney's office, and there had been . . . various allegations had been made.''

''What allegations?''

''I honestly don't know. I just know that he was going to try to resolve the problems that night. So that he and Paul could live out Paul's final days in peace.''

''He said that?''

''In so many words.''

But I didn't believe him anymore—not when it came to Mason Greenleaf's various loves. Cavanaugh's hatred for Cindy Dorn was so intense that he would have said anything to obliterate her memory of Mason.

When I told him I didn't believe him, the man stared at me contemptuously, as if I'd ceased to be a worthy adversary. He called out, ''Mother! Show Mr. Stoner to the door,'' as if he was calling a new opponent into the ring.

=29=

I WENT back to the office. As soon as I got upstairs, I searched my desk, looking for the little notepad on which I'd scratched the name and address of Ira Sullivan's last interview—his old friend from the DA's office. I found it under some loose papers: Connors.

I dialed the DA's office and got a general secretary who directed my call to Connors's secretary.

"I'm afraid he's not in today," she said, when I asked to speak to her boss. "A good friend of Larry's was killed in an automobile accident, and he decided not to come in this morning. He'll be back tomorrow, if you'd like to leave a message."

I told her there was no message.

The address that Cherie the Secretary had given me for Larry Connors was on Celestial, catercorner to Mason Greenleaf's condo on the hill side of the street—a rustic A-frame aerie fronted by large cantilevered wooden porch.

I parked on the street and stepped out onto the sidewalk, staring up the hill at the house. The only way in was through a gated fence, up a long flight of stairs that pierced the porch and ended at Larry Connors's front door. I went over to the gate, pressed the buzzer on an intercom, and waited.

A moment went by, and a man answered, "Who is it?"

"My name is Stoner, Mr. Connors. I'm a friend of Ira Sullivan's. He was helping me with a case I've been working on—Mason Greenleaf's suicide."

"Oh, yes, the detective," the man said and buzzed me through, as if I'd been expected.

I started climbing the stairs, glancing back halfway up at the row of houses on the opposite side of Celestial, colorless in the gray light. Beyond them, down the hill, I could see the rain falling in the river. By the time I got to the porch, I was breathing hard—it was that much of a climb. A middle-aged man was waiting for me at the door—tall, slim, with silver hair and a haggard, handsome face. He was dressed in a black turtleneck shirt and black pants—a kind of casual mourning. From the look of his eyes, he'd had a tough day.

He waved me through the door into a spacious white room with a cathedral ceiling and a second-story loft on its far wall, railed like a balcony. There wasn't much furniture in the room, adding to the sense of blank space. The few pieces he had, dark leather sofas and chairs, were tightly grouped in the center of the room—as if they had been gathered there while the painters worked.

"You want a drink, Stoner?" Connors said.

I could hear from his voice that he'd been drinking most of the afternoon. Scotch, judging from his breath.

"I'm okay."

He went over to a little bar below the loft and poured himself a Cutty in a tall glass, then carried it over to the sofa.

"I've been expecting you," he said, with a look of resignation. "Once I heard about Ira, I expected you."

"Why do you say that?" I asked him.

"Don't be coy. I know he talked to you."

"I never got a chance to talk to him, Mr. Connors. Not in detail."

The look of resignation on Connors's face changed abruptly. "He didn't mention me to you?"

"No."

"Then what brought you here?"

"Sullivan told me that he'd talked to a witness who had seen Mason before he died. You were the last person Ira talked to before he talked to me."

The man laughed. "How absurdly simple."

"There are other reasons I figured it might be you."

"Such as?"

"Such as you're with the DA, and Paul Grandin has problems with the police."

"What do you know about Paul Grandin's arrest?"

"Just that he was busted for solicitation a few weeks ago in a Mount Adams bar."

Connors took another pull of Scotch, chewing on it deliberately, as if he was considering what he was going to do about me. Before I'd told him the truth, he'd clearly assumed I had leverage on him —something Sullivan had confided to me that would compel him to cooperate. Without that leverage I had no way of forcing him to tell me what he knew. I had to hope that Sullivan's unexpected death would weigh in my favor. Connors clearly cared enough about the man to have stayed home from work—and gotten drunk—after hearing about the accident.

After a time he leaned back in the chair with a heavy sigh.

"Look, I don't have to say anything to you at all."

"I know that."

"But I promised Sully I'd . . . talk to you. Given what happened, I guess I ought to live up to the promise."

"You know something about Paul Grandin's arrest?"

"I know that there's some question whether he was actually soliciting anyone when he was busted," the man said, crossing his legs and resting the tumbler on his knee. "He claimed that he was being harassed by the police."

"How harassed?"

The man sighed. "How cops usually harass homosexuals—by roughing them up. One of the officers recognized Grandin from a previous arrest. He started giving Grandin a hard time outside the bar. Grandin ran back inside to escape him and was collared in the john of the bar."

"Who told you this?"

"Mason Greenleaf. I had a talk with him late one Wednesday night. At his house." He nodded toward the window, at Celestial Street. "The Grandin boy had come to Mason, looking for help earlier that week. Mason called me on Tuesday, asking me to look into it. After I nosed around, we talked it over on his porch the following night. I told him the truth: There was no way to prove the kid's story about the alleged harassment, not with the cop's partner backing him up all the way."

"Who was the cop?"

"A guy named Art Stiehl. He's a well-connected, well-liked veteran. Does a lot of undercover work. Got a spotless record, tough as nails, decorated for bravery, devout Catholic. Wife, two kids."

"Did you talk to Stiehl?"

The guy plucked the Scotch from off his knee and took a long drink. "No."

"Why not?"

He stared at me over the lip of the glass of booze. "Because I don't have the guts to get involved in this case. I still don't, even though Ira got himself killed on account of it. So don't bother to ask. My answer is no."

Given his close connection to Sullivan and Greenleaf, he didn't have to tell me why he feared involvement in a homosexual solicitation case. The callow son of a bitch flushed with self-disgust anyway.

"I can't expose myself in a matter like this," he said, leaning forward and dropping the glass like a gavel on the coffee table in front of him. "I told Ira that. Guys like Stiehl are untouchable. Everyone goes to bat for them. It's just the way it is."

I doubted that line of thinking had sat well with Ira Sullivan. He'd been a prig, but he'd had guts.

"What was Mason doing in Stacie's bar on the night he died?"

"I don't know for sure," Connors said. "I just know that Mason told me he was going to arrange a meeting with Stiehl."

"To do what?"

The man shrugged. "Try to talk him out of pressing charges. I don't know for sure."

"He did that for Grandin, huh?" I said, impressed with Mason Greenleaf's courage. Cops scared the hell out of him. And Stiehl, who had interrogated him in the Grandin case, must have been particularly frightening.

"That night on the porch, I asked him the same thing: Why bother? The kid had been nothing but trouble to Mason, stealing things from his house, lying to him, abusing his generosity. Why stick your nose out for him?"

"What did he say?"

"He didn't say anything. I told him to refer the kid to Ira, but he wouldn't do that, either. In fact he asked me to keep the conversation secret."

"Have any idea why?"

"I guess he just didn't want to explain Paul Grandin, Jr., to his friends. I mean, he was putting himself out for the kid he'd been accused of abusing. Ira, for one, would have had a hemorrhage. He did have a hemorrhage the other night, when I told him."

"You went back to Sullivan's apartment to talk?" I said.

"Yeah, why?"

"Someone saw you in the parking lot. A friend of Sullivan's."

"We talked at his office, then talked some more after supper. He was livid about the whole thing. You can imagine how the people at Nine Mile would have reacted. After all the protests that were made on Mason's behalf and all the friends who had gone to bat for him, it made him look guilty of something, you know?"

"Maybe he felt guilty," I said half to myself. Or maybe he just didn't know how to explain Paul Grandin, Jr., to Cindy Dorn. Losing her was the thing he most feared, according to Terry Mulhane. And whether Greenleaf was involved with the kid or not, the risks he was taking on the boy's behalf made it look like betrayal.

"Do you have any idea who Stiehl's partner was in the Grandin boy's bust?"

"Yeah. Ron Sabato. A cop in Vice."

After finishing with Connors, I drove straight down Celestial to the Parkway, getting off at Fifth and circling down below the distributor to the dell in which Stacie's was located. There were just a handful of cars in the lot at that hour of the afternoon. I parked near the door and walked up the flight of stairs to the bar floor.

The downstairs was virtually empty, save for a few self-starters sitting by themselves in dark corners of the room. I went up to the bar and crooked a finger at Max Carlson. He ambled up slowly, biting at the corner of his lip—as if he had an intuition that this was not going to be a fun visit. Maybe it was the look on my face: I wasn't disguising my anger.

"How long did you say you worked here, Max?" I asked him as he got close.

He shrugged his massive shoulders. "Fifteen years, maybe."

"So you pretty well know everybody, right? All the regulars? The old hands?"

He smiled uncertainly. "Yeah."

"How 'bout the cops, Max? Vice cops? They ever come in here?"

He took a step back, knocking against a stack of glasses on the ledge behind him, making them ring.

"Uh-huh," I said, nodding. "I know all about it, Max."

"I don't know what you're talking about."

"You better remember pretty quick. Or I'm going beat the shit out of you. Then I'm going to call Vice and tell them that you spilled the beans about Stiehl and Sabato."

The fat man's face went sheet-white. "Oh, Jesus, you wouldn't do that."

"Yeah, I would. Both parts."

He came up on tippy-toes, as if he didn't want to make a noise. "Could we—could we talk about this someplace else." His eyes darted nervously around the room, from drunk to drunk, as if each one was a potential betrayer.

"Sure, Max. We can talk about it with the district attorney."

"I can't fucking do that! Those cocksuckers would kill me." He snatched up a bar towel and scrubbed at the sweat that had popped up on his forehead. "You don't understand what Stiehl's like. He hates fags. I mean, he fucking hates 'em. We're not even human to him."

"Then your best bet is to put him behind bars."

The guy's face started to tremble—very close to tears.

"Please, Stoner. It don't work that way. He's connected, man. Jesus, they covered this thing up, didn't they?"

I stared at him. "You're saying Segal and Taylor knew that Stiehl and Sabato were the two men who'd met with Mason Greenleaf in the bar."

"Of course they did. They practically told me what to say and how to say it."

I wasn't sure I believed him—at least, I didn't want to. Because if Segal and Taylor had known, then there was a good chance that Jack McCain had known, too—and sat for it. "What really happened that night?"

He shook his head.

I hooked my hand through the shoulder strap of his apron and jerked his face close to mine. "What happened?"

"It was sort of like what you heard," he said, his face trembling with fear. "I mean, the two of them met with him—the old one and Stiehl. Except it was Stiehl who got all worked up and started shouting."

"What happened after that?"

"The guy left. Like I said."

"Drunk?"

"I don't know. Yeah, a little. I mean, he wasn't falling down."

"And then?"

He balked, and I practically jerked him over the bar. One of the waiters was watching us. He got alarmed and shouted, "Should I call the cops, Max?"

"Yeah," I said to him. "Call the cops."

"No!" Carlson shouted. "No, it's all right, Sam."

I let go of his apron and he straightened up, smiling at the waiter and the rest of the customers in the bar. "It's all right, everybody. It's fine. Just a little misunderstanding about some money."

The waiter snorted with disgust and went back to polishing one of the tables.

Swallowing hard, Max turned back to me. "Stiehl followed him out the door. Out into the lot. I don't know what happened outside. He come back in a few minutes later. The two of them had another round, then left."

"What about Greenleaf? Did he come back in?"

Carlson shook his head. "I never saw him again."

=30=

THE rain was falling again, thick and gray, as I walked up the Fifth Street hill, following Mason Greenleaf's track to the Washington Hotel. He'd had to drag himself up that damn hill, after Stiehl was finished. It had made him look drunk, the beating. Made him weave like a featherweight, according to the clerk.

The rain made a drumming sound on the hotel arcade that echoed down the hallway to the front desk. The old man, Pat, was sitting behind the caged-in counter, thumbing through a tattered *TV Guide*.

"You remember me?" I said to him.

He nodded. "He ain't here right now," he said, referring to the stout desk clerk. "Run out to get him a snack of dinner."

"You'll do, Pat."

He laughed. "What did you have in mind?"

I reached into my wallet and pulled out four twenties, laying them down one by one on the counter in front of him like I was dealing solitaire. The old man licked his lips.

"The guy that checked in and killed himself—what did he look like?"

"Drunk."

"Just drunk?"

"Beat up some."

"How beat up?"

"Had him a red forehead, a shiner, and a swollen jaw. You couldn't see it real good, till he turned into the light. But I seen it. He could hardly talk 'cause of it. Made him sound stupid."

"What did he say to you when he came in?"

The old man shrugged. "Wanted a room, up top. Said he was tired."

"Did he say anything about the beating?"

Pat shook his head. "Just that he was tired and didn't know if he could sleep. Asked me could I get him some booze to help him sleep. I told him in a place like this, you can get just about anything for the right price."

"You got him the bottle?"

He nodded. "Brought it up to his room."

"When was this?"

"Real late. Past two. I knocked on the door and he says, 'Come in.' I come in. He was lying on the bed, staring out the window. There was a tin of pills on the nightstand. I says, 'I wouldn't be taking no pills, if'n you plan to be drinking.' But he says not to worry. He'll be all right."

I didn't believe him—about the last part, the warning. But the rest of it sounded reasonable, if that was the word.

"Did you tell this to the cops?"

"Didn't talk to 'em. Lester did."

"He's the clerk?"

Pat nodded. "I tried to talk to them, but they wasn't much interested in me. Who's gonna listen to an old drunk like me?"

It was a point a defense attorney might make, too. I picked up the twenties and handed them to him. He folded the money up and stuck it in the pocket of his checked shirt.

I called Mulhane's office from a pay phone on Fifth. It was almost seven by then, and the office was closed. I got his home phone from information and dialed it. A woman answered. I told her who I was, and she called out: "Doctor, it's for you. One Harold Stoner."

"Hey, Stoner," Mulhane said, coming on a different line. I heard his wife hang up with a click. "I've been hoping you would call. In fact, I left a couple of messages on your machine. We've got to talk."

"About the autopsy report?"

"Yeah. Someone did a real slipshod job. I mean, it's almost criminal."

That was the correct word.

"If you got a few minutes, why don't you stop over, and I'll show you what I mean."

Mulhane's house was on Interview in the gaslight section of Clifton—a respectable red brick colonial in a neighborhood of proper red brick colonials. The rain was still falling as I pulled up out front. I parked in his driveway and dashed under a dripping elm tree, across the lawn to the stoop. He was waiting at the door with the autopsy report in his hand and a pair of reading glasses propped, like sunglasses, above his forehead.

"Come in out of the rain," he said cheerily.

Behind him, a pretty brunette woman smiled a quick hello, as she rounded a newel post and headed up to the second floor.

"That was my wife," Mulhane said, smiling after her. "Tactfully leaving us alone, I think."

I shook a little rain from my coat sleeve and stepped into the hall. Immediately on the left, a portal opened on a large study lined with bookshelves. There was a crowded desk on the far wall, a sunken conversation pit in the center of the room, and a baby grand piano near the door. Mulhane waved me through, then closed a pair of sliding doors behind us. He walked me over to the conversation pit. Sitting down on the couch, he reached out and directed a standing spot so that its beam was focused brightly on the pages of the report.

"Forensic medicine is an art unto itself," he said, paging through it until he found a color frontal photograph of Mason Greenleaf's corpse stretched out on a steel examination table. As I sat down beside him, he held the picture up in the beam of light. "If you take a look at this, you'll see Mason definitely died of asphyxia, probably due to the inhalation of vomitus—like the coroner's report says. The blue lips, the hemorrhaging of the eyes, those are classic indications."

Even in a photograph Mason Greenleaf's dead body was a gruesome sight.

"It's what the coroner didn't note that troubles me," Mulhane said.

Flipping down his reading glasses, he plucked a magnifying glass from an end table and held it over Mason Greenleaf's swollen face. "Take a look at the area around the left side of Mason's head. You see that large purplish contusion and swelling beginning at the corner of his mouth, extending up past the eye to the forehead?"

"Yeah."

"That's a goddamn blunt instrument blow, if I've ever seen one. And a helluva shot, too. I mean, they picked him up twelve hours after he died—you can see the lividity at the back of his arms. But the left half of his face is still puffed up and red. Which means there was considerable hemorrhaging in the soft tissue, maybe even a broken cheekbone. All this crap about him falling down or running into something is crap. I mean, it looks like somebody hit him with a baseball bat. That's the kind of force we're talking about."

He dropped the magnifying glass on the couch and leaned back against the cushions. "Somebody worked him over. I don't think there's any other reasonable conclusion."

"Are you willing to testify to that?"

Mulhane turned his head slowly toward me, peering over the tops of his reading glasses. "What do you mean?"

"I mean, I believe you. I believe Mason was worked over. I think I know who did it, too."

"Who?" Mulhane said breathlessly.

"A cop named Art Stiehl."

His face flushed with anger. "A cop did this?"

"That's what it looks like."

"Why? Why the hell would he beat up Mason? I mean, Mason was harmless, for chrissake. Mason never hurt anyone."

"I don't know why exactly. I just know this particular cop doesn't like gays."

"Son of a bitch," Mulhane said. "We've got to do something about this. We have to talk to the district attorney. I mean, I have friends—"

"We've got to make a case first. This man is well protected. In fact, certain cops may already be covering up for him."

Mulhane threw a hand to his head, passing it heavily through his hair as if he were trying to hold his top on. "Jesus, I've read things like this. Seen them on TV. Are you actually telling me that the cops are covering up a case of brutality?"

"It's possible. Maybe probable. Is there any way to tell how much bleeding would have resulted from Greenleaf's wounds?"

"Not really. There are some lacerations around the nostril, mouth, and the corner of the eye. But it looks like most of the bleeding was internal. Why?"

"I found some bloodstains the cops missed in the backseat of Mason's car. There wasn't a great deal of it, but enough to be sampled."

"They could possibly result from this kind of wound."

" 'Possibly' won't do it. This is important, doc. Are these photographs proof positive that Mason was deliberately mugged or beaten up?"

He sighed. "Proof, no. I mean, if they were proof positive, even the county coroner couldn't have missed the finding. What we got is a strong likelihood. And I will testify to that—and get colleagues to testify to it."

But likelihoods, even strong ones, weren't going to get a grand jury to indict a respected cop. Not in this town.

"What we need is a witness who will testify to the beating," I said, just saying it outright.

"But if the cops are covering up . . ."

"Maybe they're not all covering up." I glanced around the room. "Is there a phone in here?"

"On the desk."

I went over to the desk and dialed the CPD and asked to be transferred to Vice. "Ron Sabato," I said when a duty sergeant picked up.

There was a momentary pause, and then Sabato came on the line. "This is Sergeant Sabato."

"Ron, this is Harry Stoner."

"Yeah, Harry," he said in a friendly voice. "Did you get the autopsy report?"

"Picked it up last night."

"So what more can I do for you?"

"I'd like to buy you a drink, Ron. You're a Scotch man, aren't you?"

He laughed. "How the hell did you know that?"

"The bartender at Stacie's told me. You know, you put away a lot of Scotch that night when Mason Greenleaf killed himself."

There was a dead silence on the other end.

"I don't know what you're talking about," he said, sounding like a completely different man.

"Sure you do, Ron. You and Art. I'll be in Arnold's in about half an hour, you want to talk it over. You don't show up, I'm going to the DA and the FBI."

I hung up before he could answer.

Mulhane stared at me uneasily from where he was still sitting on the couch. "This is dangerous. Shouldn't we call the FBI?"

I glanced at my watch, which was showing a quarter of eight. "I'd like to make a case first. Unless I can find someone who will testify about the beating, this won't fly."

"What makes you think Sabato will talk to you?"

"I'm not sure that he will. But we've got to start somewhere."

= 31 =

I GOT to Arnold's bar a little past eight, found a booth in the back, and ordered a Scotch. It was a rainy weekday night, and I was almost alone in the tap room. Just me and a college-aged couple having their dinner.

Around eight-thirty, Ron Sabato came into the bar. He looked right and left, spotted me, and came over to the booth, slipping into the seat across from mine. He studied my face for a time, straightening the shirt cuffs beneath his sport jacket.

"You wearing a wire, Stoner?"

I shook my head.

"Open your shirt."

I unbuttoned my shirt, enough so that he could see there was nothing taped to my chest.

"Roll up your sleeves."

"I'm not wired, Ron."

A waitress came up, and he switched on a smile.

"Double Chiv, straight up, honey."

She went off to get his drink. Sabato looked back at me as I rebuttoned the shirt.

"It's on me," he said, pointing to my drink.

The girl brought him back his double. He pulled some bills out of his wallet and waved his hand across the table. "Take out for both," he said. "Run a tab with the change."

"That's generous of you, Ron."

He slicked his gray hair down, running his hands back from the corner of his hatchet face. "Yeah, well, I'm a generous guy." He cribbed the drink in his hands and stared into the shot glass. "This shit is going to kill me. I like it too much. You know?"

I nodded. "I've got the same thirst."

"That night we're talking about, for instance. Too much hooch. You stop thinking, reacting." He breathed out heavily through his nostrils, picking the shot glass up and taking a sip. "The stuff you see."

He took a long swallow, almost emptying it, then lowered the glass on the table and ran his right forefinger around its rim.

"Let me put you a hypothetical. Just—two cops talking shop in a bar. Okay?"

"Okay."

"Let's say you and your partner catch the night watch up on the Hill. You ever work night on the Hill?"

"No."

"Well, let me tell you, right away you're not crazy about the duty, 'cause of the queers and the hassle." He dug into his coat pocket and pulled out a wrinkled pack of Raleighs, shaking one out onto the table. Stowing the pack, he picked up the cigarette and stuck it in his mouth. "A lot of these guys have the virus nowadays, but they don't tell you they have it. You bust them, and they start to holler: Why me? Why me? You try to cuff them, and they go nuts because they've been down most of their lives and they've got nothing left to lose. I mean, they can throw screaming, clawing fits you wouldn't believe. Just lay a hand on them, and they spit at you, bite you, get blood on you. Try to give you their fucking life history. I mean, it happens all the time."

He plucked a book of matches from the ashtray, opened it, and struck a match, lighting the cigarette in a cloud of acrid smoke and tossing the matchbook back on the table. "So you and your partner are on a lousy shift," he said, wincing at the smoke. "It's late, toward the end of a long night. You're cruising St. Greg, and your partner spots a queer he busted for soliciting—years back. The kid's talking to another queer in an alley off a bar. There's some money showing. You figure drugs and pull over to roust them. The kid sees you, and right away he runs—I mean, he bolts like he's holding. He ducks into the side door of the bar, and when you run him down in the john, he's flushing shit down the toilet. Now you know he's a guilty son of a bitch. But you don't have a case, because he flushed the shit down the toilet. So what do you do?''

He held the cigarette between his thumb and forefinger, scribbling the air with it like it was a piece of chalk. ''You can't let him walk—not after you've seen him flush the shit away. And you can't rightly hold him for possession. So you bust him for whatever—for peddling his ass, which with this kid is a pretty sure bet. You go to cuff him, and the kid gets hysterical. I mean, like he's lost his parents at the fair. You try to talk to him. But he won't hold still and he won't listen. In a minute or so, there's going to be trouble from other fags in the bar. What're you supposed to do? Your partner, who maybe isn't as patient as you are, gets tired of this shit and gives the kid a hard shot in the belly—just to freeze him up so you can slip the cuffs on. You don't know it, but this kid is sick and the shot makes him throw up all over the fucking place. He bites his tongue. He pisses on himself. I mean, we got blood and shit all over us. And with this shit, you're not so sure it's gonna wash out—you know what I'm saying?

''Anyway, the aggravation puts your partner in a real bad mood about this kid. I mean, he's going to put him away. Period. End of case.''

''So a few weeks go by,'' he said, dashing the cigarette into the ashtray and gesturing with his other hand to the waitress. ''The kid makes bond. A trial date is set. You've talked to the DA and it's going to be a cakewalk. Then out of the blue you get a call from one of the kid's friends.''

The waitress came up again, and Sabato ordered another double. ''How 'bout you?'' he said to me.

I nodded. ''I'll take another.''

She went back to the bar to fill our orders.

"Anyway, the kid's friend asks you to meet him for a drink. Talk about the kid's case. You really don't want to bother, you know? But you look into it out of routine, and it turns out this friend has a record of his own—short eyes, you know? Plus, it's this very kid he queered the time he was busted. Kind of got the boy started on the road to ruin. And now the kid's got the virus and a world of trouble, and it doesn't sit so well with your partner that the friend didn't do time. That he wriggled out of it. It doesn't sit well at all. It never did."

The girl came back with the drinks and set them on the table, picking up the empties.

Sabato swallowed half of his booze before she'd turned to go.

"All right," he said, cribbing the glass again. "So you go to meet with this guy, wanting him to fuck up, half praying for it. And what does the guy do? He tries to shmooze you—like you're a fag, like you don't know the score: the kid is really all right, he's had a tough time, he's sick with the virus, couldn't we turn our backs just once? On and on, like this. Like he's this great humanitarian, and you're just a couple of pieces of shit who need a lecture on decency from a child molester. I mean, this is the same guy who queered the kid in the first place.

"You think it's funny because this guy doesn't really seem to know how out of line this is. But your partner doesn't think it's funny. He's a hard-nosed Catholic with a real strong sense of right and wrong—and an attitude about fags, especially fags who molest children—and he is definitely not amused. Plus, the way the guy is acting, you can't help thinking maybe he has something to hide in the way of a sex thing or a drug thing with the kid you busted—like maybe he's afraid that the kid's going to blow the whistle on him again, like he did the first time around. Anyway, after a few too many drinks, your partner goes ballistic."

Sabato picked up the glass and downed the other half of his drink. "Ballistic," he said again, putting the glass down. "He tells the poor son of a bitch that he's going to bust him for attempted bribery, for solicitation, for every goddamn thing he can think of.

He's gonna make him into a public spectacle, drag him into the papers and on TV, then put his ass away for the five to ten years he should have done in the first place. On the top of this, your partner, who's way past thinking clearly at this point, tells the poor bastard that he's going to drag the kid in again, too—because he thinks the kid's hiding something now, something about the guy himself. So he's going to get the bail rescinded and put the kid in the justice center until he tells him exactly what it is this guy is afraid he's going to tell us.

"Now the guy is like, beside himself. Can't believe he's brought this shit down on his own head and on his pal's head, just by trying to be a good guy. He's sort of dazed and gets up to leave, like he's in a dream, like he's hoping it'll all go away. And I'm thinking that maybe we should let it pass. But my partner doesn't see it that way. He follows the guy out into the lot. Fuck if I know what he does or says, but when he comes back, he's still pissed. Still talking about busting the guy's ass. You try to calm him down, talk him out of it. But he's serious. He *really* doesn't like this guy—from way back, from the first bust, which he squirmed out of. He's talking about getting a warrant for the son of a bitch and busting him where he lives—at the school where he teaches, in front of all the little kiddies. Bad shit."

He sighed a long sigh and gestured with his hand, as if that was the end of it.

"Did you get the warrant?" I asked.

Sabato ducked his head, tired of the make-believe, of the sound of his own voice. "Art didn't mention it the next day."

He stared at the empty glass on the table. "How the fuck did I know the son of a bitch was going to kill himself that night? I didn't know."

"The fact is that he did, though," I said. "Because of your partner."

"Look, I'm sorry it happened the way it happened. But the guy was wrong to come on to us like he did. Like we were for sale."

"The guy was a queer—isn't that more like it?"

Sabato sighed. "Maybe it was for Art. Maybe for me, too, a little."

I stared at him. "So what are you going to do about it?"

"What would you like me to do about it? Fucking burn my partner? He got carried away. It happens."

"I'm not going to let this drop, Ron."

"You do what you're going to do. But I'm telling you—Art is a fucking hard case. And he's got lots of friends. You take him on, you're going to get hurt."

"And you're going to let it happen."

"I'm not going to lose my pension over Greenleaf, Stoner."

He got up from the table, standing up pretty straight considering he'd had two doubles in the space of a half an hour.

"Shit happens," he said, as if that covered it.

Turning away, he walked out of the bar into the rain.

I sat in the booth for about ten minutes, nursing my drink and thinking about Greenleaf, about the way that the various lines of his life had been gathered up and cut in that bar where he shouldn't have been, with those two tough men he shouldn't have been with.

It was unlikely I could prove any of the terrible things that had happened to him—prove them to a grand jury's satisfaction. Nobody had been in that parking lot with Stiehl and Greenleaf, nobody had witnessed the blow—probably with the butt of Stiehl's gun. It would come down to the cops' word against my circumstantial evidence. The best I could hope for was to prove that there had been a cover-up, but even that wouldn't be easy to do if the cops stuck by their stories. Max Carlson wasn't about to put his neck on the line for Mason Greenleaf. And neither was Larry Connors. They had too much to lose, nothing to gain. I could go to the papers, maybe make Stiehl and Sabato's lives miserable for a few months, maybe even get them each a black mark on their records and in the public eye. But bringing them to justice—that wasn't likely.

So what was I going to do?

A man had died—a screwed-up man who, haunted by guilt and

AIDS, had tried to make amends for his real and imagined sins by trying to save one lost soul, whose corrupt life he felt, reasonably or unreasonably, responsible for. For years, he'd fed Paul Grandin, Jr., money and second chances. In the end he'd risked his own skin to save him. And when that risk had gone fearfully awry, he had made a desperate end in a desperate place—believing that he was going to lose his job, his friends, Cindy Dorn.

Mason Greenleaf. RIP.

Who knew whether he might not have made that same end sooner or later? People were dying around him daily. And in some peculiar toxic way, he blamed himself.

So what was I going to do?

I'd killed a man once, in cold blood, for torturing and terrorizing another man to death—a weak decent man, without any of the guts of Mason Greenleaf. I'd killed the thug who had killed Ira Lessing. And ever since then I'd carried the guilt around with me like Paul Grandin's virus. I'd tried to drink it away. I'd tried to talk it away, in bars and in bed. I tried to block it out of my system. But the truth was still there, somewhere in the river where I'd left it to rot. What right did I have to pass judgment on Art Stiehl and Ron Sabato, two cops who'd had a bad night on a hard job?

I signaled to the barmaid and ordered another Scotch. A double. With the rain plucking at the glazed window of Arnold's bar, I kept drinking until I was good and drunk.

≡32≡

AROUND one-thirty I left the bar, found the Pinto, and weaved my way out to Finneytown—to Cindy's house. As drunk as I was, I wasn't even sure why I went. I just knew I didn't want to go home. I parked cockeyed in her driveway and managed to stagger up to the door and bang on it. A light came on in the living room, and she opened up, dressed in that T-shirt, looking sleepy.

"Good Lord," she said, "what happened to you?"

"Got drunk."

"I can see that. Come on in."

She guided me by the arm through the door and over to the couch.

"Told you I drank," I said, settling heavily on the cushions.

"Yes, you did."

She bent down and unlaced my shoes, pulling them off. She came up on the couch and started unbuttoning my shirt.

"Sorry," I said, smelling her hair, her smell, as she undressed me.

"Why'd you get loaded?"

"You really want to know?"

She stopped fiddling with my shirt and sat back beside me on the couch, cocking her head on her hand and staring fondly into my face.

"Sure I want to know."

"It's not a nice story."

She passed her hand across my forehead, combing back my hair. "I want to hear it. No matter what it is."

"It's about Mason. I know what happened."

She tensed up, pulling her hand back from my face. "What happened?"

It dawned on me that that was why I'd gotten drunk. It was the only condition in which I could bring myself to tell Cindy the truth.

I told her about Paul Grandin, Jr. About where Mason had been those last five days of his life, searching for a facility that would take the kid in.

"Why didn't he tell me?" she said, breaking down in tears.

"He felt guilty about him," I said. "He didn't want you to think he'd been betraying you. Didn't want to explain to his friends. Maybe he didn't want to explain it to himself."

She threw her hands to her face and wept. I sat there beside her, stupid drunk, while she cried and cried.

"What happened to Paul Grandin?" she said, when she finally calmed down.

"He's in a rest home in Columbus."

"Where Sully went?"

I nodded. "He went to visit him."

"Why?"

"He wanted to ask him some questions about the night Mason was in the bar."

"What happened at the bar, Harry?"

I told her the truth—or most of it. The meeting with Stiehl and Sabato. The attempt to talk them out of pressing charges against Grandin. Stiehl's fury and threats. I didn't tell her about the beating in the parking lot—it was something she could live without knowing.

"It was the cops?" she said when I'd finished. Not really grasping it, yet. Not ready to.

"It was a lot of things, Cindy. The cops were just the last thing."

Her face went white. She bolted off the couch, up the half-stairs into the john. I heard her retching violently. The sound of the john flushing. It went on for a while.

When she came back down, her T-shirt was soaked with sweat, her face wet with it. She walked over to the couch and simply curled up beside me, hiding her head under my arms. I stroked her hair, her back.

"I could go to the DA," I said. "But it's going to be hard for a prosecutor to make a case. And this thing with Grandin will certainly come out. A good defense attorney could make it ugly for that kid—and for Mason's reputation, friends, family."

"What are they going to do about Grandin?" she said weakly.

"I don't know yet."

Most of the drunken high had gone away by then, and I just felt heavy-headed and weary and sorry for the girl.

"Have you talked to this one, this Stiehl?"

"No. I figure he'll come to me—after he talks to Sabato."

"Don't do it," she said sharply, lifting her head. "It's over. I don't want any more violence."

"We'll see."

"No, we won't see." She laid her head on my legs, and wrapped her arms around me. "We won't see. It's over now. It's already cost Sully's life. I will not have it cost you any further part of yours. You've done enough."

"We'll see," I told her.

I didn't sleep well, partly because of the liquor, partly because of Greenleaf. I did a good deal of tossing and turning, enough to wake Cindy up once in the middle of the stormy night. She pulled me to her and held me until I fell back asleep.

In the morning neither of us said very much, until I'd gotten dressed and was about to leave.

"You're not going to see that man, Harry," she said as we stood at the door. "You're working for me, and I'm telling you that the job is finished."

"What about Grandin?"

"I've thought about it, and if he meant that much to Mason, I'll talk to Mace's brother and see if he's willing to foot the bill for the rest home, like Mason was going to do."

"I doubt if he'll go for that."

"I won't give him a choice," she said quickly. "I'll make it clear to him that if he doesn't provide the funds, I will go to the papers about Mason's death. He'll cave in—I guarantee you."

I laughed. "He probably will."

"You'll call me?" she said, as I opened the door.

"In the afternoon."

"Promise?"

I promised.

She had it figured out fairly shrewdly, except for one thing. Paul Grandin was still under indictment for solicitation. Sick or not, he could still be brought to trial and locked down in a prison ward for the rest of his life, however short that might be. Even though the kid didn't really deserve much better, Greenleaf's death and Sullivan's after it made it seem important that that didn't happen. It was about the only thing that could be salvaged from the whole business: the last days of Paul Grandin, Jr.'s, miserable life.

So when I got to the office I started making the calls. The first one was to Ron Sabato at Vice. I told him what I proposed: my silence for Grandin's freedom. Like Mason Greenleaf redux.

"We don't make deals like that, Harry," he said, when I got through explaining it. "I thought I made that clear last night. We don't get bribed or threatened."

"You'll make this deal, Ron. Before the day's out. Or I'll call Art Spiegalman at the *Enquirer*. And then Dave Ratner at the FBI. They may not nail you and your pal, but they'll make life interesting for the next six to nine months—for the whole damn Vice division. You ever seen the FeeBees work an internal affairs investigation? They're pesky bastards."

"Harry, you're making a mistake. I'm telling you."

"Just do it, Ron. And that'll be the end of it."

After I got done with Sabato, I called Nate Segal at Six.

"You get the results of those blood tests yet, Nate?"

"Yeah," he said sourly. "It was Greenleaf's blood. So what?"

"It's interesting, that's all. Him bleeding all over the backseat of the car before he offed himself."

"He fell down and busted his nose."

"No, he didn't. He got slugged by Art Stiehl."

There was a silence on the line. Then Segal started to laugh a phony laugh. I really didn't want to go through the whole bit, so I cut him off before he could start.

"Let's skip the bullshit. I know it was Sabato and Stiehl in the bar. I know why they were there, and I know what happened. I also know you and Taylor covered it up."

"Now, just a second—"

"Don't insult my intelligence, okay? I don't much care why you did it. All I care about is getting the charges against Paul Grandin, Jr., dropped. You see to that, this thing stays quiet. You don't, and your name is going to be in the newspaper tomorrow morning."

"Hey, fuck you, Stoner. You don't threaten me."

"I am threatening you, Nate. You got two years to retirement, right? How'd you like to spend half of them answering questions for newspaper reporters and the FBI and lying through your teeth?"

"Nobody covered up anything," he said sullenly. "The cocksucker killed himself."

"He got pushed, Nate. Hard. You think it over. Talk to Taylor and your pals at Vice. I'll be in the office all day."

It occurred to me, as I hung up, that I was really asking for it. From guys who could deliver—and get away scot-free. It made some sense to talk to a lawyer. So I called Laurel Gould at her office and gave her the names of the principals and the details of the Greenleaf case. I also told her that if I ended up in a cell or dead in a ditch, she was to do her best to nail the bastards.

"That'll be a great solace to your survivors," she said acidly. "Why don't you let me handle this for you? I have friends in the DA's office."

"So do Art Stiehl and Ron Sabato. Tell me the DA in this town is going to do a pair of cops in a fag suicide without ironclad proof. Jesus Christ, this is Cincinnati.''

''You're crying over spilt milk, Harry. It's not like you.''

''I have my reasons.''

''You have a death wish, my boy,'' she said, hanging up.

What I had was a few deaths on my conscience.

As the morning wore on, I felt more and more as if I was doing the right thing. It gave me a short-lived feeling of decency. Which, when it died out, left me feeling in the right and afraid. I dug my Gold Cup out of the safe, where I'd left it for the last five years in an oiled rag. Field-stripped it. Cleaned and reoiled it. Found a clip, loaded eight rounds of hollow-point. Chambered a round. Stuck the thing in the desk drawer and waited.

Around noon, I called Cindy. She'd talked to Sam Greenleaf in Nashville. He'd agreed to the blackmail.

''I didn't tell him all of it. He didn't really want to know the details—like I figured.''

''You did good,'' I said. ''Phone Nancy Grandin and tell her. She's probably at her father's house in Indian Hill. On Camargo.''

''Why don't you call it a day, and we'll both tell her.''

''I have things to do.''

''Like what?''

''Things. I'll be home tonight. We'll talk.''

''You kind of like this domestic routine, don't you?'' she said with a laugh.

''It's good that I met you,'' I said. ''It's good that I feel like I feel again. I didn't think I could.''

''Come out here, won't you? I don't want to be alone.''

''You won't be alone. I'll finish up here soon.''

About an hour after I got done talking to Cindy, Stiehl and Ron Sabato showed up at my office door. It had begun to rain again. The sky was dark, and the thunder rattled the windows. They both came into the inner office and sat down on chairs across from my desk, like something from the street blown in by the storm.

I'd never seen Stiehl before. He was a big, muscular man in his early thirties, reddish blond, with a trim mustache that covered some of his upper lip. He had a flat, red, unsmiling face and cold blue eyes. Even if he hadn't been provoked, he looked like trouble. Sabato was nervous. He kept glancing from the door, to me, to his partner—all the time pumping his right leg like he had to pee.

Stiehl crossed his legs and stared at me. "One way or another, this is going to end right here, right now," he said with a mild vehemence.

"You can end it quick," I said. "Just drop the charges against Grandin."

He smiled coldly. "Just like that. 'Cause you said so?"

"It's the right thing to do."

" 'Cause you said so?" He stopped smiling. "Let me tell you where I'm coming from. I'd just as soon march you out of here right now. Take you downstairs to the alley, throw you in the trunk, drive you out to a place I know, and leave you there." He leaned forward menacingly. He was so worked up, he had begun to spit. "You threaten *me*! Without even knowing what the fuck you're talking about!"

"Art," Sabato said uneasily.

Under the desk, out of sight, I pulled the top drawer open slightly, enough to where I could see the Gold Cup, its oiled blue barrel gleaming in the stormy light.

Stiehl breathed hard for a few moments, staring at me, while I stared back at him—my hand just below the desk drawer. After a time he leaned back slowly in the chair.

"You want us to let that kid walk," he said with a dismissive laugh. " 'Cause you think you know what's going down. You don't know shit.

"There's a fucking fire burning in this country," he said, jerking at his coat sleeves, straightening himself up. "And the way I look at it, it's killing the right people—the people who started it. Don't expect me to feel sorry for them."

"What does that have to do with Grandin? He's dying of it."

"Let him die of it."

"What possible difference does it make to you whether he dies of it in prison or in a hospital bed?"

"He committed a crime. He goes to jail."

"What crime was that?"

"Stoner," he said, leaning forward to the desk, "I'm in the street every day. I know what I'm doing. I know what I see. This kid was holding drugs. He'd been busted for possession and possession for sale three times previous. I saw him flush the shit down the toilet. He lived a scumbag life and is dying a scumbag death. Now you tell me why I should forget what I saw?"

"Because of Greenleaf."

"I didn't kill him," Stiehl said.

"You helped. Look, I know the drill, too. Counting the army, I was a cop for seven years. I did some things I wasn't proud of. Every cop does. You can't second-guess yourself. I'm not saying you should. But when something's this wrong, it's got to be corrected. Last night in the bar, I was going to forget this whole thing because of something I did five years ago. Something I've been carrying around with me and never made right. Maybe that's why I'm doing this now—because somebody died because of me and I never made it right."

Stiehl stared at me. "You're saying somebody died?"

I nodded. "A man named Chard."

The two cops exchanged a look.

"What're you telling us this for?" Sabato asked.

"So we can get past this shit about who's got the upper hand and just do the fucking right thing."

"I don't get it," Stiehl said, shaking his head. "We're not priests. Confessing your sins isn't going to change a thing."

But it had changed something. I could see it in his face. I'd given him some leverage. It was what a guy like him mostly understood: the physics of dominance.

He glanced over at Sabato. "Go on out in the hall, Ron. I got something to talk about with this one you don't have to hear."

Sabato got to his feet. "I don't want any shit in here, Art."

"We're past that," Stiehl said.

Sabato grunted, went over to the door and out into the anteroom, closing the door behind him. Stiehl stared at me.

"Look, I don't apologize except in the confessional. I do what I think is right and live with it. That night at the bar is no different. This guy, this Greenleaf, was acting like we could be bought— bought by the likes of him. I put him straight on that. And when I went after him in the lot, I'll admit I was going to work him over." He paused for a moment and said, "But I didn't work him over."

I gave him a look. "You're saying you didn't beat him up?"

"I didn't have to," Stiehl said. "I followed him over to his car, calling him every fucking name I could think of. Telling him I was going to bust his ass in the morning. Laying it on thick about how he was going down and going away. I'm dead serious, Stoner. And this guy knows it. Each word, he bends over a little more with the weight. Anyway, he gets to the car, turns around, and smiles. Weird fucking smile. I tell him to wipe the fucking smile off. And then the crazy son of a bitch does something like I've never seen before. He raises his head, still smiling, and bashes it into the roof of his car. Just . . . bashes it into the car—face first, right down on the car. Two, three times. Until he knocks himself silly and falls down on the pavement."

Stiehl shook his head disbelievingly. "I never saw anything like that in my life. And I've seen a lot of guys do a lot of shit. I stood there with my jaw hanging open. He's scrambling around on the ground, groaning, crying. I was so fucking shocked, I give him a hand into the backseat of his car. Told him he was a fucking idiot. Then turned around and went back into the bar. I never hit him, Stoner. That's the truth."

I sat there, thinking about the raw terror and self-disgust of Mason Greenleaf's last hour on earth. "What difference does it make if you hit him or you didn't, Art?"

"Not much," he conceded. "But I didn't."

Neither one of us said anything.

"If I go along with this, it's not like I'm admitting I did the wrong thing," Stiehl said after a time. "As far as I can tell, Greenleaf deserved what he got. He queered that kid, and then when the boy ended up with AIDS, he tried to pull the kid's ass out of the fire and cover his own. What kind of friend is that?"

"If it makes a difference, I don't think he did a thing to that kid, except show him charity. He felt guilty about his own life and wanted to find a way to make up for it."

"Then he should have gone to a priest. He shouldn't have come to me." He glanced at the door and called his partner back in.

"You done?" Sabato said, edging nervously into the room, looking relieved to see I was still in one piece.

"We're done," Stiehl said to him. "So what do you say? Do we pull the plug on Grandin?"

Ron shrugged. "What's it cost us to go uptown? We didn't really catch him with the goods. He's dying anyway."

Stiehl thought about it for a moment, then got to his feet. Sabato stood up, too.

"You're a lucky man, you know that?" Stiehl said to me. "I was pretty close to killing you when I came in."

"I know you were."

He held out his hand, and we shook.

They walked out the door. When I was sure they were gone, I opened the desk drawer fully and took out the Gold Cup, unloaded it, and wrapped it back up in its oilcloth in the safe.

= 33 =

I DROVE straight out to Cindy's house, drove like a kid out of the army going home. And when I got there and found her there, I hung on to her for a long time. I never did tell her what Stiehl told me about Mason's last half hour in Stacie's lot. And she seemed content not to hear it, as if she knew it would be terrible, as if she'd turned a corner in our relationship that had taken her away from the violence of Mason Greenleaf's death, as if we both had.

Terrible it had been. In some fashion, that fire Stiehl talked about had consumed Mason Greenleaf, too, while he was trying all alone to put it out. He'd simply gone to the wrong person for help. Maybe there hadn't been a right person. Maybe those last five days had been a circuit that merely took him back, through Cavanaugh and Paul Grandin and Ralph Cable, to a guilt and regret he'd never been able to shake. In the end the retribution that Mulhane had said he was waiting on had been waiting on him. I'll admit it haunted me a little, even though I'd managed to get that kid off the hook for him.

Later that same week, Stiehl and Sabato did what they'd said they'd do. The charges were dropped, and Paul Grandin got to spend his last few months out of court and out of jail. He died in the winter of the year, alone, staring out the rest home window at the snow.

Throughout the winter Cindy made a slow adjustment to life

with a PI. I made my adjustments to life with her. I don't drink as much as I used to, or as often. We spend as much time as we can together and toy with the idea of getting married—maybe after I retire. The only time she talks about Mason Greenleaf is sometimes at night, when he comes back to her in dreams.